Gordon Linton grew up in the North Midlands, and is now a student at the University of Sussex. He has worked as a canteen assistant, a hospital porter, and a postman. This is his first novel.

He can be reached at heurism@onetel.co.uk

The Sacrifice

GORDON LINTON

First published 2002 by GMP (Gay Men's Press),
PO Box 3220, Brighton BN2 5AU

GMP is an imprint of Millivres Prowler Limited,
part of the Millivres Prowler Group,
Worldwide House, 116-134 Bayham Street, London NW1 0BA

www.gaymenspress.co.uk

World Copyright © 2002 Gordon Linton

Gordon Linton has asserted his right to be identified as the author of
this work in accordance with the Copyright, Designs and Patents Act 1988

A CIP catalogue record for this book is available from the British Library

ISBN 1-902852-39-7

Printed and bound in Finland by WS Bookwell

Distributed in the UK and Europe by Airlift Book Company,
8 The Arena, Mollison Avenue,
Enfield, Middlesex EN3 7NJ
Telephone: 020 8804 0400
Distributed in North America by Consortium,
1045 Westgate Drive, St Paul, MN 55114-1065
Telephone: 1 800 283 3572
Distributed in Australia by Bulldog Books,
PO Box 300, Beaconsfield, NSW 2014

PART ONE

One

It's crazy. I've just finished the last of my finals, but instead of dropping charlie or chugging back the brown stuff, like a normal person, I'm sitting in my room, staring out at an afternoon sky pregnant with rain. The weather, and my mood, operate against the desire to celebrate because for me, it's not over. It *can't* be, until I commit it all to paper. I have to write it down, chronicle the weird events – *connected* events – that have occurred over the past eight years. I need to capture them, shuffle through them, sort them into some kind of cohesive order and then, perhaps, the larger pattern may appear. But where should I start? I've been wondering about that. At first I thought I should start with Kit because, after all, he was the catalyst for everything that happened later. But now I realise I have to go back further than that, because I didn't just *meet* Kit – I encountered him under very specific circumstances. Kit was... is...

The room darkens as ranks of low clouds disgorge their cargo. May 20th, and it's too dark to see by daylight. Oxford in the summer... I snap on my angle-poise lamp and the electric bulb fights weakly for supremacy as a thin syrup of light falls on my desk, highlighting my waiting hands. As I stare down at my fingers, I notice there's something odd about the quality of light – half natural, half man-made – that makes them appear illuminated from within. Like millstone grit in sunlight.

And suddenly, as a pugnacious rain clatters gustily against my windows, I know where I must begin.

In 1993, when I was twelve, my family moved from London to the village of Horton-in-the-Moors. Although I found it dull after twelve years in a large city, life there had its good points. There was countryside all around. The boundary of the Peak National Park was only three and a quarter miles away, which meant that I could escape when I needed to. Other positive attributes (I search so hard for them now, through the halls of memory) were the profound silence and absolute darkness on a winter's night – excellent for star gazing; the quaint, if too-perfect, architecture; the rough-hewn medieval well, which, according to local legend, was the site of at least one murderous drowning; and an ancient alms house, owned by a big-shot barrister in Newcastle – Under-Lyme, that is, not Upon-Tyne. It's a hyphenated part of the country, The Potteries. The nearest major shops are in Stoke-on-Trent. In short, Horton was – and still is – the kind of place that history teachers enthuse over, and is often mentioned in those slim but shiny guide books so beloved of the terminally middle-aged. Needless to say, my parents loved Horton – especially my mother. And it seemed that Horton loved her back.

My mother worked from home a lot at that time, and inveigled her way into village life with astonishing alacrity. She's the sort of person that everyone likes. Even those villagers who generally hated commuters moving in from 'outside' loved my mum – although, ironically, it was my dad who'd spent part of his child-hood in the area. Mum's niceness was a bit overpowering at times, but it meant that, as a family, we were accepted into the bosom of the village right away – me, my two sisters, and my father. Like my mother, my sisters were perfect village fodder. They liked to go to church and sing in the choir – which I did too, but not for pious reasons – and they helped around the parish and went off for tea with the various Horton-in-the-Moors' luminaries at every opportunity. I realise that I've described this existence as something of an idyll – if you can call somewhere as boring and claustrophobic as Horton idyllic. But then, an idyll is necessarily boring, isn't it, if it's stagnant, static? The trick is to find the balance, the dividing line, and exist there. Pleasure can turn so easily into pain, and what at first sight seemed difficult, or actually inappropriate, often turns out to have been the better choice... But I'm leaping ahead of myself. After all I've been through, I begin to see allegory in everything, but when I was twelve, all I knew was that life ought to be more exciting than it was.

Another important reason why we were so well accepted in the village, apart from my mother being so pleasant, was that we hadn't moved out to the country for the usual upwardly mobile reasons, or to become absentee landlords. We'd moved because of mum's lungs. She needed fresh air. We demonstrably did not have an executive house or an executive car. Instead, we lived in a cramped three bedroomed millstone grit house with a lean-to at the back, which I slept in. It was not a proper bedroom, as such, and neither was it a conservatory, regardless of what the estate agent might have said of it. But it was a private space, and I loved it. Having shared a room for most of my life, it was extraordinary to have completely inviolable territory at last. Somehow it freed my thoughts. There are some mental processes, deeply personal ones, that are simply impossible except when utterly alone. That's why the easy access to the open moors was so important to me. But having a room, a physically marked space that was all my own, was much better. Private space and public space, however solitary, are two quite different dimensions of experience.

Nevertheless, despite the excitement of having my own bedroom, and my nascent adolescence, it is fair to say that life in Horton was uneventful. I mean, as I mentioned earlier, *nothing happened.* Nothing pleasant or stimulating, anyway. Horton sat there, architecturally unspoiled, saved from development partly because it was so near the small sewage works that sat, scab-like, a few hundred metres downstream, and partly by the fact that the sides of the small valley in which it rested were scooped, scallop-like, by old quarries, thus making other places logistically more appealing for architects and planners. By odd coincidence, however, the day my parents exchanged contracts on the house, the sewage works were closed down. Within a year the site was flattened and redeveloped. Also, by that time, the quarries had been disused for so long that they were at last generating their own mini eco-systems and had started to look attractive with their craggy edges and dark, slatey pools. The result of all this was that the value of our house tripled in three years. (As I write this, I am conscious that I just described this process as a coincidence, and must now qualify my assertion by saying that I have become extremely wary of that word since then.)

Then, when I was thirteen, everything changed, and for someone who'd thought that moving house was the most profound change that a boy could undergo, it came as a big surprise: I fell foul of Neil Braithwaite. Neil was a village boy, a little more than a year older than me. He wasn't unintelligent, but delinquency and petty criminal behaviour was as ingrained in him as the soot that still blackened our house almost a generation after the last smuts fell on it. I had learned about him on the village gossip grapevine, garnered in sweet shops and bus stops, almost as soon as I had arrived in Horton, and thus had made a strenuous effort to avoid him. So, although I hardly ever saw him, and never spoke to him, I knew more about him than I could easily explain, and he became a part of the backdrop of my life. My parents thought him rather wonderful, and weirdly approved of him, as though boisterousness and physical energy were things that would propel a person onwards and upwards through life without

6

the need of further effort. In a way that disturbed me, I could see their point. Neil represented another world altogether. He wasn't anodyne, or safe. He belonged to the mysterious world of crime, of lawlessness; a world where one habitually broke the rules. It was a world that was at once dreadful and strangely attractive. Of course, this attractiveness only existed when I conceptualised him in his absence – it faded as soon as I encountered him in the street. The reality of Neil was far less inspiring than in my imagination, where he wasn't just a petty thug – he belonged to the forbidden world that contained not just crime, but passion, scandalous behaviour, a certain kind of drunkenness and dark desire… All the things that people say are wrong, yet which you inevitably hanker after when life is too wholesome; the behaviours that those people one truly admires – folk heroes, pop stars, artists, and disreputable writers – have indulged in, or over-indulged in. And why? Why is bad behaviour so attractive? It's the Idyll Trap, the obverse of that sensible American homily my father was so fond of: "if it ain't broke don't fix it." But just as it's hard to stop prodding the sensitive crater of an extracted tooth with the tongue, I always found it hard to leave well alone for long.

Of course, my mother had more basic reasons for liking Neil. She was flattered by the way he flirted so outrageously with her.

"He's a fifteen year old boy, it's obscene," she would say, trying to turn her thrilled smile into a frown.

Neil was aware that I was gay, in the way that people are. As far as I know, I display none of the stereotypical gay traits, but somehow people always manage to guess anyway, don't they? And I knew that he was the sort of person who wouldn't approve. I also knew that, although I was strong and self-confident in many areas of my life, if I tried to stand up to Neil I would not come out the winner. So it was a matter of self-preservation to avoid being alone with him, which, as I've already said, I managed to do for two years – a real feat in a village the size of Horton.

There was a narrow alleyway leading from the bus stop down to my house and although I avoided it after dark, during the day it was generally safe. On the day that I am thinking of, however, when I wandered down it, it was not safe. Halfway along, on the almost horizontal stump of a beech tree that had been felled by a gale at some point before my arrival in Horton, Neil Braithwaite sat – probably not waiting for me particularly, but certainly waiting for someone. I didn't notice him until I was quite close, and even then I didn't think to be worried, because I had done extremely well in a school test that day and Mrs Hodson, my English teacher, had made me stay behind in order to confer on me her special praise. It may well be true – I can admit this with the benefit of hindsight – that, as a result of this and other praise I'd received, I was conceited to the point of deserving a reality check. But then again, if someone told you that you were the best pupil they'd ever had, how conceited would you be?

So, that day, I'd just said goodbye to my friend Richard Murray and was walking down the sunless alley thinking – not to put too fine a point on it – that I was utterly brilliant. The moss-covered, drystone walls and the bare branches of the elder and beech trees that bristled beside me were still damp with the morning's dew, even at the end of the afternoon. I smiled to myself. Would I become a writer, or should I be a journalist? And then I was confronted by Neil, sitting on the stump with a nonchalant expression on his face, his dark hair tousled, his brown eyes watchful. My mind was elsewhere, unconcerned by thoughts of harm from Neil, so I was shocked and surprised when he leaned out and grabbed the sleeve of my jacket.

"Greg Chaley," he said. Coming from him the words sounded ominous, threatening and unpleasantly intimate all at the same time. "How ya doin'?"

"Fine, thanks, Neil," I said and tried to continue on past him.

"Hey, Greg," he said. "Don't you want to stop for a bit of conversation? Why are you in such a hurry?"

"I'm not," I said.

"Well, then," he said. "That's alright."

He retained a vice-like grip on my jacket, so I stopped and waited for him to say something. He looked up at the winter sky, at the cloudless, pearlescent near-dusk.

"I hear you're a budding genius at school, Greg, my man."

I was still feeling brash and confident at this stage, so I smiled knowingly and said nothing.

"Well," he said, "are you?"

"It's not for me to say."

He pulled me towards him.

"Budding genius? Budding queer, if you ask me. What have you ever done except pansy about? So what if you're doing well at school? I bet you don't lie in bed at night doing equations. I bet you lie there, desperate for some straight lad like me to come and shag the arse off you."

I looked away from him and didn't answer. He tugged at my jacket.

"*Well?*"

I considered pulling away and running for it, but realised how pointless that would be. I tried to calm my breathing, and think.

"Well, what?" I asked.

"Well, what have you ever done in your life that's not pathetic and queer?"

"I've done lots of things," I told him.

"Like what?"

I hesitated, blank. Neil pulled a packet of cigarettes out of his pocket, calmly took one out and put it in his mouth in a slow, rehearsed movement. He lit it with an extremely flashy lighter, which he then held up to me.

"Cool, huh? You know where I got it?"

"No."

"I stole it."

"Oh."

He smiled.

"The Murrays, here," he said, pointing over the wall, "got burgled last week. Did you know?"

"I heard," I said. "Richard Murray is in my class at school and he told me about it. Why, did you do it?"

Neil laughed.

"Wish I had. What a cool job. No one saw anything. No one heard. They may not have got away with much, but they were real professionals. One day, I'll be able to do as slick a job as that."

He laughed and took a drag on his cigarette, then held it out to me as though we were friends. I shook my head.

"So," he said, "you haven't answered my question. What have you ever done that isn't fairy?"

There was a short, ominous silence.

"When we were on holiday in the summer," I said, "dad gave me driving lessons."

"Oh yeah? You're only thirteen. Don't talk shit."

"He did," I said. "He *did*."

I was particularly proud of the fact that I had managed to manoeuvre the car through the dunes that flank the northerly shores of Morecambe Bay and it was infuriating that the first person I'd ever tried to impress with the information refused to believe me.

"Anyway," Neil sneered, "that's not what I meant. *I've* been joyriding. That's better than pissing around in a car with your dad."

"You went joyriding, and you were driving?"

There was the slightest hesitation, as he breathed in.

"Yeah," he said. "Yeah, as a matter of fact, I *was* driving."

"Now you're the one who's talking shit," I told him.

Neil released my jacket, but caught the collar of my shirt. He half lifted me from the ground and banged me against the wall. I could feel the gritty stone pressing against the back of my neck.

"Calling me a liar?"

His face was inches from mine and I could see that he was calmer than he sounded. Calmer, and crueller. He wanted to draw this encounter out. To torture me for as long as possible.

"Calling me a liar?" he repeated, his cigarette dangling. "Let's go down to the main road and we'll steal a car and I'll *show* you."

"No," I said. "It's okay, I believe you."

"Dead fucking right," he said, letting me slip down the wall until I was on firm ground once more. "You're just a pansy wimp," he said, "and you deserve what's coming to you."

He breathed in, towered over me, and I thought, *This is it. He's going to beat seven kinds of shit out of me.* He was far too strong for me. I'd never get away from him. And there was nowhere for me to run, in any case.

And then it seemed to come from nowhere. I heard my voice as though it was someone else's:

"I did it," I said.

"What?" he asked, surprised that I'd said anything.

"I did it," I said. "I burgled the Murrays' house."

Neil looked at me carefully, and then laughed.

"Don't talk shite," he said.

"You know Richard had a Swiss Army Knife? Look, here it is." I pulled my own from my pocket and handed it to him. "And you know he had a CD Walkman with a microphone? Look, here it is." I pulled my own Walkman from my other pocket and handed that to him, too.

"Jesus," he said. "You didn't, did you?"

I was about to reply, when he laughed derisively.

"You nearly had me there, but you would never be able to do something like that. You haven't got the nerve."

"It wasn't just me," I said. "I did it with my cousin, Andy, the one from down South. I showed him how to get in at the back, and then he took over after that. I was just his accomplice, really. I kept a look out, then helped him carry stuff."

"No shit?" Neil said. "You're not shitting me?"

"No," I said. "Honestly."

He let go of me.

"Wow," he murmured. "Wow!"

I smiled inwardly.

"How *did* you get in at the back?"

"Richard showed me one day," I said truthfully. It didn't matter saying now – both the door and the lock had already been changed. "The lock on the back door was faulty. All you needed was a bit of wire. It was easy."

Neil nodded.

"So what did you do with the stuff you stole?"

"Oh," I said, warming up to my story. "Andy's got his own car now, so we took it down to Hanley and sold it to a bloke who's got a workshop near the station. We split the proceeds fifty-fifty."

Neil took a long, thoughtful drag on his cigarette.

"Hmm, I'd like to meet this cousin of yours."

"He doesn't come up very often," I said quickly. "He won't be back before the summer."

"Call me over when he does," Neil said.

"Okay," I agreed. "Now, I'd better get home."

I reached out to take my Walkman back. As I did so, Neil pulled away from me and held the Walkman and the knife to his chest.

"Here," I said, still holding my hand out, "they're mine."

"No they're not," said Neil. "They're Richard Murray's."

"They're mine now."

"They're stolen property," said Neil, "and I'm going to keep them. What are you going to do about it?"

I hesitated, trying to think of what to do or say next. Neil, with a flick of his wrist, hit me in the face with the Walkman.

The corner of it caught me just above my right eye and I heard a cracking sound before I felt the pain.

"Well?" Neil demanded as I felt the slickness of blood prickling through the hairs of my eyebrow, "what are you going to do about it?"

What could I do? What could I say? The Walkman crashed against my cheek.

"Well?"

"Nothing," I mumbled.

"Pardon?"

"Nothing," I said, more loudly.

"Good." He smiled. "Now fuck off."

I backed away a few paces before turning and running down towards the house.

"And thanks for these!" Neil shouted from behind me.

That afternoon was the first time I ever entered my room without going in through the front door of the house. Dad had partitioned off the end of the lean-to so that people didn't need to go through my room to get to the garden, and it meant that I could slip in without being seen.

The first thing I did was look out a handkerchief to wipe away the blood on my face. It had dribbled down and smeared over my eyelid, then trickled in a single line down my cheek to the corner of my mouth. In fact, it looked pretty cool. If I'd been going to a fancy dress party, I would have left it as it was.

There was a distinct lump on my eyebrow and another one on my cheek, but it wasn't the pain that made me so breathlessly agitated, it was the *link* with Neil. I had lied to him, and it had cost me my Swiss Army Knife and my Walkman. The knife wasn't so important – I'd largely outgrown it and wouldn't miss it. But the Walkman had been my Christmas present only a month ago. It was one of those presents that mum had argued with dad about, saying that I was too young to have such an expensive toy, and dad had said, "He'll be fine with it, Claire." And mum had said, "You look after it, Greg. You know what you're like. I don't want you dropping it, bashing it, or leaving it on the bus..."

"Oh God," I said aloud to the ceiling.

Why were parents so awkward? If there was any justice in the world, I'd have been able to go up to them and say that Neil had taken it, and leave it at that. But no, they'd insist that I get it back. They'd go and 'talk' to Neil's parents. Neil would deny everything, I wouldn't get my Walkman back, and then I'd get the crap beaten out of me. Parents don't understand that kind of thing, do they? Which is weird, considering they were once young themselves.

I lay back on the bed and stared at the sloping ceiling in an attempt to calm myself down. The room was freezing because one wall was all window and had little or no insulation. (In summer, of course, it got unbelievably hot for the same reason.) Now, as I lay there, on the verge of shivering, I could see my breath misting in front of my eyes. At the far end of the room was the partition that dad had built, with a narrow bookshelf that I'd built on either side of the door. I was particularly proud of these shelves. Dad had found some huge, old, damaged oak bookshelves and I'd cannibalised them to make these smaller ones. Dad was a builder and carpenter by trade, and he was teaching me some of his skills. I liked working with wood, because it can be used for so many things, and looks stylish if you make a good job of it. Also, it teaches patience, something that I have always had a tendency to lack. And to get the most out of wood, especially such beautiful wood as oak, takes time and effort. You have to remove layers and layers of dark stain to rediscover the real, fine colour beneath. It's almost like archaeology. Building those shelves seemed to confirm a principle that I, at that naive age, still believed: that you derive from any task – be it an essay, job, assignment, friendship, or even life itself – exactly as much as you put into it. That you get what you deserve. How simple. And how wrong. Even in esoteric and occult terms this is a gross simplification. Why on earth are we inculcated with the reductive non-truth that *life is fair*?

But I digress. Suffice to say that I was working on my room and intended it to be an impressive monument to my new and increasing expertise in carpentry. Aside from the shelves, I was in the process of building a custom-made desk that would have niches for my computer and relevant electronic paraphernalia. At that time, in 1994, I only had an obsolete first generation 286, but for my birthday dad had promised me a 486 with Internet access. I'd be able to log on, play games like Doom and Lemmings... and squeeze in an occasional piece of homework, too. I'd be independent. Autonomous. I was even going to be paying for half of it myself. Dad gave me money for helping him when he had work over the weekend. He paid me one third in cash, and the remaining two thirds went into the computer fund.

I had conflicted feelings about this. On one hand, I felt that it was an unacceptably capitalist exploitation of cheap child labour – dad could get work out of me that made him more money than he paid out, whilst neatly absolving him of the need to give me any other form of pocket money. But on the other hand, I enjoyed the work, and it generated more income for me than bog standard pocket money would have done. And besides, I knew we were hard up. Although mum was earning a small part-time wage, it wasn't that much. She was the Postal Action Campaign Manager for a small animal rights charity, which meant working from home, writing letters and that kind of thing. On top of the income problem, the main worry was mum's poor health, which was a constant financial drain – a never-ending litany of costly private treatments, special diets, supplements, and consultations – because the NHS only go so far in helping with allergy-based conditions, and then it's up to you. They will hospitalise you when you get bad enough to need it, pump you full of pharmaceuticals – that kind of thing. Crisis intervention. As a back up it can save your life, so

I suppose we should all be grateful for that, however woefully inadequate it is by other standards. But as far as coping with daily life goes, they aren't interested.

So, money was tight. And that's why it was such a big deal when Neil grabbed my Walkman.

I decided to try and forget about it for a while and went through to the kitchen to get myself a biscuit. My mother was in there, sitting at the kitchen table working through a pile of correspondence whilst minding some kind of stew that was on the stove. She jumped up when I saw her.

"Greg!" she yelped. "You gave me a fright! I didn't know you were home."

She held her hand to her chest and breathed in deeply to calm herself.

"You should learn to meditate, mum," I told her. "That kind of tension is bad for you."

"What's happened to your face?" she asked as I pulled the top off the biscuit barrel and rummaged around in the digestives for a coconut cream.

"I ran into the pole during basketball," I said.

"You haven't been fighting?"

"No."

She nodded. Of course, she believed me. I never got into fights.

"Let me look at you." She came around to where I was standing. She dismissed the bruise on my cheek and ran her fingers over the cut in my eyebrow.

"Not too bad," she said.

"Mum?" I asked as she went out to get a flannel from the bathroom.

"Mmm," she said from the stairs.

"Can I have a key for the back door?"

"Why?" she asked, coming back in and running hot water over the flannel.

"So I can get in round the back."

"What's wrong with the front door?"

"Um," I said. Good question. "Lack of privacy?"

Mum stopped, the flannel poised only inches from my face, and smiled a cooing sort of smile, then laughed.

"Really," she said, "I can see it now. You'll be wanting to smuggle lovers in before too long."

I noticed the lack of gender specifics. She hadn't said 'girlfriends', she'd said 'lovers'. It was another one of those moments in which my mother tacitly acknowledged the fact that I might be growing up gay. I felt myself blushing, which, of course, she noticed immediately.

"Fine," she laughed, "fine. Enough said. I'll get one cut for you at the weekend. Now let me have a go at that eyebrow of yours."

As she dabbed, she murmured "*Adolescence*" to herself. Then, more loudly, she told me, "Of course, I was extremely jealous of my privacy at your age."

Two

It was inevitable that Neil would be waiting for me when I got off the bus the following afternoon. I was with Richard Murray, as usual, and Richard looked surprised when Neil beckoned me over with a jerk of his head. He looked even more surprised when I said, "See you tomorrow, then, Richard," and followed Neil down to the cobbled area between the Post Office and the river.

Neil sat on the edge of the well and looked at me.

"We've got some unfinished business," he said.

"Oh?" I said, my heart sinking.

"Yeah. That was Richard Murray on the bus with you wasn't it?"

"Yes."

"What do you think he'd say if I told him that you were the one who burgled his house?"

"Oh, that," I said, looking around. There were a number of people about in the village, and the pub was on the other side of the road. I could attract attention here without any problem and so I felt more secure than I would have done in the alley.

"I was only joking about that," I told him. "I didn't steal anything from Richard's house. I made it up."

"Oh *did* you?" said Neil. "But what about the Walkman and the knife? How've you got hold of them, unless you stole them?"

"We had the same kind of Walkman and the same kind of knife," I said. "We both asked our parents for the same presents. We went out looking for Walkmans together in November…"

"Yeah, yeah," Neil said, as though bored. "Do you think the police will believe that? And what about when I tell them that Richard had already *shown* you how to break in? You'd be in a lot of trouble then."

He paused, to see if I would say anything. I remained silent. What a fool I'd made of myself. The police probably *would* be suspicious of me, under the circumstances. Why had I said that Richard had shown me how to break into his house? Why had I boasted? And to Neil of all people.

"I suppose you know that the Murrays are offering a reward of £200 to anyone who can give them information that leads to a prosecution?" Neil said. "It's on the parish notice board over there."

I nodded.

"So, I could make myself £200 by going to the police and telling them about you."

"But you wouldn't do that."

"I can't afford to pass up £200," he said. "I've got *expenses* these days. Girls to impress. That kind of thing. Now, I need the money, so it would be stupid of me to give up this chance, wouldn't it. Unless…"

"Unless?"

"Unless you gave it to me. That would be easiest. I'd get my £200, and you'd get no trouble from the police, or from Mr and Mrs Murray. They'd be so disappointed, wouldn't they? You're their son's best friend."

"But," I said, "I haven't got £200."

"You could get it if you wanted to. Your dad's a professional man. He's probably got it lying about the house."

"Of course he hasn't."

"Look," Neil spat, grabbing my shirt front, "I don't give a shit how you get the money. I'm going to get £200, either from you or from Mr Murray. It's your choice."

He pushed me back so that I stumbled and nearly fell.

"I'll give you a week."

That evening we went to choir practice. Not in Horton, but in an old chapel on the outskirts of Hanley. It was a more serious affair than the village choir in Horton, which basically consisted of our family plus a few sundry lesser voices. The Bucknall Choir, on the other hand, took itself rather more seriously than that and had sung all over the Midlands. It was rumoured that if we did exceptionally well this year, we might even get invited over to Holland at the end of the summer to sing in a choral festival there.

One of the 'initiation stories' which seems to hold an almost mythical place in gay folklore is that of the virgin chorister being sodomised by his choirmaster. Even I held this fantasy for a while – in a strictly abstract sort of way. But our choirmaster, Mr Griggs, was clearly straight and was not the sort of person anyone would want to be touched by – let alone sodomised. He had virulent halitosis, and skin that looked like a membrane over candle wax. That evening, however, thoughts of sodomy couldn't be further from my mind. I was realising, for the first time in my life, the fragile nature of equilibrium. I was being blackmailed by Neil Braithwaite. If I didn't come up with £200, I was going to get a criminal record. Why had I lied like that? Why had I lied!

We were singing a cantata by Taverner, difficult early music often considered too tricky for amateurs. The boy soprano part is more usually sung by women these days, but I seemed able to cope with it – not because my voice was particularly fine (I was no Paul Phoenix, I knew that), but because I had tremendous range. One of the things that was both a joy and a burden to me at that time, was having one of the star voices in the choir. I had a clear soprano which Mr Griggs wanted to use as much as possible whilst it was still around. I was thirteen-and-a-half and, although I was small for my age, it was clearly not going to be all that long before my voice changed. Some people's voices break at almost the first sign of adolescence, but not mine. Whilst I already had a reasonable thatch of dark hair sprouting round my dick, and a distinct growth of it in my armpits, I also retained the voice and face of an angelic twelve year old. Part of me wanted my voice to break there and then, and part of me knew that if that happened I would be relegated to choral obscurity. Could my ego take it – being only one competent voice amongst many? Maybe I'd be asked to leave the choir completely? Maybe I'd want to leave? Anyway, the fact that I, and the rest of the choir, could manage these haunting chants, all in Latin, commanded a great deal of respect from other choirs, both local and not so local. Hence our tentative international debut. So in a sense, I was central to the choir. Once my boy soprano vanished, there would be no more Taverner, which would mean less kudos for the Bucknall Choir.

I glanced around me miserably as the practice proceeded. Even the soaring notes, as my line danced above the medieval mesh of voices beneath mine, failed to elevate me. Then I noticed my sisters, standing with the altos off to my right. They followed their sheet music with flat expressions, totally unaware of my anguish, and I became furious. I had always regarded their lives as twee beyond belief: anodyne, stultifyingly dull. Now I found to my surprise that I envied them. They would never have got into my kind of trouble, because they would never have lied in the first place. If only I could get out of this, I thought, I would be happy to be ordinary and dull. I would be happy to live a life in which I didn't have the threat of criminal proceedings, personal humiliation, and the potential for a severe beating from Neil if I breathed a word to anyone. If only I believed in God, I thought, I might pray to Him for help. But I didn't.

I had fallen right into the Idyll Trap.

So consumed was I by these new and disturbing feelings of envy for my sisters, that my concentration wandered and my timing deserted me, throwing off the whole choir. Quite legitimately, Mr Griggs lost his temper in front of everyone, something he'd never done before, and which only served to increase my sense of failure, shame and misery. It was Neil's fault. Neil had managed to infiltrate the one area of my life in which I'd believed myself immune to him. My parents noticed that something was wrong and asked me about it in the car on the way home, but I said nothing and stared out at the frozen winter streets, and remained sulky until I had a chance to get off to bed.

In my room there was a highly polished walnut money box, which I'd made by myself, in which I kept all my earnings. I took it out and counted my cash.

£94.50.

I had a building society account that I'd opened when I was thirteen and first did a little work for dad, but there was only a few pounds in it. I preferred to be able to see my money, to touch it. £94.50. It had seemed something of a fortune to me the previous week. I'd been considering spending it on clothes, music, or perhaps some software for when I got my new computer. But in relation to the £200 that Neil was demanding, it was hopelessly inadequate. What would I say to him the following week? There was no other money I could get my hands on.

The next six days were a nightmare. I didn't see Neil in that time, which was something. But the day of reckoning was approaching and, on the seventh day, I felt physically sick as I returned home from school on the bus. Richard saw this and asked me what was wrong. I told him that lunch had made me feel pukey, which he was ready enough to believe. When we got off the bus, I wandered off without even saying goodbye. I could see that he was concerned – we'd been getting some ideas together for a possible website, anticipating the arrival of my new computer, and he couldn't understand why I had turned silent and sullen.

I deliberately didn't walk down the back alley that day, but Neil had guessed that I wouldn't and met me at the top of Leek Lane. Although it wasn't as private as the alley, there was no one else about. To one side there was the side wall of the alms house, and to the other, an open field, with the hills beyond looking bluish grey in the late afternoon sun.

"Okay," said Neil. "Have you got the money?"

I was prepared. I handed over £51.75 (I thought it would look better if it was an odd amount).

"This is all I've got," I told him. "Everything."

He counted it quickly and then handed it back to me.

"I don't want it," he said. "It's an insult. I'll go and get the £200 from the Murrays. They'll be happy to pay up straight away."

"Look," I said quickly, "I can probably get you some more by next week."

Neil looked at me with disdain, then, as though he was doing me a great favour, relented with shrug, taking the money and stuffing it in his pocket.

"Okay," he said with a grunt. "I suppose I don't mind instalments. So long as I get what I'm owed." With that he sauntered off, his gait a waddle rather than the film-star swagger he imagined. Under other circumstances, it might have made me laugh.

And so began the reign of terror.

I kept up the instalments at first. Sometimes I managed to get away with offering five or ten pounds, and sometimes such a small payment would be greeted with casual violence that left me dazed – not just physically, but right to the very heart of my being. Neil never punched me; or at least not hard, and not in the face. He had far more sophisticated forms of torture than that, most often entailing the twisting of my arms and legs, pulling my hair, making me sit on agonisingly sharp stones for long periods, or putting my feet into the icy water of the stream until they burned with cold. None of it sounds particularly extreme now that I write it down, but I suffered in many ways. It wasn't simply the physical pain, although there was plenty of that. It was the fear, too – a dread of my weekly assignation so great that it brought on night sweats – and the humiliation of disempowerment. Everyone noticed my change in mood, especially Richard Murray. But he was the last person I could confide in. I just kept my mouth shut, and suffered. My school work suffered, too. And worse still, my singing went off the boil. I don't know why. Maybe it was my breath control. Singing has to be executed from a point of rest, and I was never even close to that mental state. Whatever its cause, Mr Griggs was furious and thought it was mere petulance on my part, symptomatic of that dreaded adolescent 'difficult phase'. Whilst he never showed it openly, I sensed a building animosity in him. His dreams of storming Holland with a concert of Early Music were evaporating before his eyes, and I was to blame. Which may have been partly true. And if it was, it was a result of my living in constant terror.

And in all that time, nobody did anything to help.

Perhaps they imagined they *were* helping, in a leave-him-alone-and-he'll-get-over-it sort of way.

But I didn't get over it.

The first day that I didn't bring him any money at all, Neil didn't react – and I wasn't at all relieved. I knew I would be punished for turning up empty handed, and I wanted to get it over with. His silent, thoughtful stare was much more worrying than the abuse I had come to expect.

"Okay," he said eventually, blowing out his cheeks and drumming his fingers against his thigh. "I've got to do something tonight and I need an alibi. Don't worry, I'm not going to ask you to come with me. You'd probably fuck it up anyway, with your fairy ways. You just need to cover me for twenty minutes or so."

"Why, what are you going to do?"

"Don't sweat, it's not *that* bad," he said.

He leaned in and looked at me closely, his large features seeming too big for his face.

"I've seen that you sometimes go in and out of your house round the side."

"My room is at the back."

"Good," he smiled. "This is what we'll do. I'll come over to your place today at around eight. You can tell your parents that you're going to show me something in your room. We'll go off and then I'll climb out of your window. I'll go over the side wall and twenty minutes later I'll come back and you can take me through to say hello to your mum and dad."

With a sinking feeling that things were sliding way out of control, I nodded my agreement, and left for home. When I mentioned that Neil was coming round later, mum laughed.

"He's the last person I'd have expected you to get friendly with," she said.

"It's good to have a wide range of friends," said my father.

"Absolutely," she agreed.

No, no, no, I thought. *He's a monster. Who'd want to be friends with him?*

When Neil arrived, at eight as he said he would, he was charming to my parents. He asked about my father's work, expressed an interest in interior decorating (!) and had my mother cooing over him in the most revolting manner. I had no idea why she thought he was so sweet and handsome – a phrase she inexplicably employed later that evening. Once in my room, Neil flicked through my CDs dismissively, then smiled and pulled out The Charlatans' *Some Friendly* and put it on at full volume, which isn't saying much, given the little ghetto blaster I had at that time. He lay back on my bed and lit a cigarette.

"You keep away," he said. "I don't want to be molested. It's bad enough being in a queer's bedroom, but to be in it with the queer himself is *not* cool."

"Don't worry, I won't touch you," I replied with ill humour. He was not difficult to resist. Why did straight people always assume that gay people would have sex with anyone?

After a few minutes, Neil clambered out of the window as he said he would, and disappeared into the darkness. I sat on the bed, nervously awaiting his return. In a way, I wanted my parents to come in, to ask me where Neil was, so that I could confess everything to them, to receive their punishment, followed by their forgiveness and a welcome back into the warm safety of the family. But they didn't. Neil came back, breathlessly, after a quarter of an hour, and after a further minute or two we went through to where everyone was watching television. My sisters were wary of Neil, but mum made him coffee, and dad just laughed when he said, "I'd rather have a beer." He stayed for nearly an hour, every second of which was anguish. And when he finally did go, mum said, "Nice lad. Tell him he can come round whenever he wants."

"He won't," I said. "We don't really have anything in common."

"Why did you invite him round tonight, then?" dad asked.

"I was trying to explain something to him about carpentry earlier on, but I needed to show him."

"You should have more friends like him," mum said. "Richard's fine, but he's not so lively is he? Someone like Neil would pull you out of this terrible mood you've been in for the last month or two."

And that was that.

The next day, of course, when I heard that there had been a failed break-in at the Post Office, I knew who'd done it. There had been no more than a ruined lock and a broken window, but I felt as bad as if I'd done it myself.

The following week I earned seven pounds and, for the first time, I stole fifteen from my mother's purse – which was bulging because dad had accepted a cash-in-hand payment the day before – to make up an instalment for Neil.

"Twenty two pounds," Neil said when I saw him. "Not bad, not bad." He clapped me on the back. "Let's go out and get a beer. There's a bloke up Horse's Hill who sells it to me if I give him a bit extra."

'Going out for a beer' was one of those dark, adult things that I'd always looked forward to being old enough to do. I'd always imagined that I would go to the pub with a group of select friends when we were maybe sixteen, if we could get away with it. I had never envisaged doing it with someone like Neil.

"No thanks," I said, "I've got to get home."

He shrugged.

"Okay. Next week, then. Tell your mum I'll be round again. I'll bring a bag of beers to drink in your room, and then I can sneak out again like last week. It worked brilliantly, didn't it? Well, the alibi, if not the crime."

He laughed.

"You know, your mum's a bit of alright? Your sisters look like they've got pokers shoved up their arses, but your mum's okay. And she likes me, too, doesn't she? Do you think she'd be nice to me if I bunked off school one day and went round when your dad was out?"

This couldn't go on. Being an accessory was one thing, but now he was being lewd about my mother...

"Look, Neil, I can't see you next week," I said. "I've given you enough money. At least £200. Why can't we leave things at that?"

"Because you're in too deep now," Neil said with a nasty grin. "What would the police say if I told them about you abetting me in my crimes? If anyone discovered that it was me who tried to do over the Post Office last week, I could prove that you were the one who gave me a false alibi. You'd be in deep shit then, Greg, wouldn't you? No, you're in it with me up to the hilt. But all you have to do is carry on with our little weekly adventures and everything will be fine."

"No, Neil. Find someone else for your adventures. Someone who *wants* to join in with them."

At that, he grabbed me, and although I struggled, it was no use. Within seconds he had me on my front on the roadside, his knee in the small of my back, my face pressed onto the tarmac. That was the price of a forceful response to Neil's 'suggestion'.

"I think you need to understand," he said, calmly, "that you have to do as I say. You have no choice. Understand?"

I tried to say something, but choked on my own spit instead. Neil grabbed my hair, lifted my head and bashed my face into the gritty road.

"Understand?"

"Yes, yes," I managed.

"Alright, then," he said, releasing me. "No more argument, then?"

"No."

"I'll see you next week?"

"Yes."

I got up and turned away. Neil patted me on the back.

"It'll be fun," he told me.

I'd hoped that going home would offer me a feeling of sanctuary, but it didn't. Precisely the opposite, in fact. I found that the homeliness, the *niceness* that had so infuriated me in the past – the insistence on watching dull-but-educational and unchallenging television, the idle conversation – now excluded me. Before, however boring life had been, I'd always felt a part of it. But not any more. A few months previously I would have laughed if someone had asked me whether I'd be upset about the loss of it. But now, I would have done almost anything to regain that warmth, that emotional safety.

I went to my room, lay on the bed and stared at the ceiling. My life seemed to be already mapped out for me. I was destined to join Neil in a life of petty crime. I would become a criminal accomplice and probably an under-age drunk; and then at some point we would inevitably get caught. I'd get a criminal record, would never get a job, and my family would disown me... My life was more or less finished before it had even begun. It sounds melodramatic, I know, but that was how it felt. I was only thirteen. The future then seemed dark, unpleasant and ineluctable. I was disconsolate.

Three

And then I met Kit, at school, a few days later.

The school squatted at the edge of Burslem, one of the five towns of The Potteries that make up Stoke-on-Trent, and it was sort of urban yet hokey at the same time. The school buildings reflected this conflict, too. What had clearly once been a modest sized local school, had been repeatedly added to – largely during the 1970s, to judge by the unforgiving concrete architecture – until it had become a Frankenstein's monster complex, full of strange outcroppings and excrescences. There's almost nothing to say about it. It was a modern school. Brash, noisy, ugly.

It was the lunch break and I was outside, sitting on a low wall at the edge of the basketball court. It was a place of relative privacy, as Northern lads prefer to kick a football than to shoot for hoops, so the majority of them were scuffling untidily on the playing fields behind me, with blazers for improvised goal posts. Their dreams were of Gazza, not Magic Johnson.

It was quiet where I was, which was good, because I was in need of some solitary thinking space. That morning, I'd been bollocked by Mrs Hodson during my English lesson, for the first time ever, for not paying attention. I was mortified. It seemed that my whole life was going to be ruined by what was happening with Neil. It was appalling. Even my parents had become short-tempered.

They'd sat me down for a long 'talking-to' the previous night. They'd tried to get me to tell them what was the matter, but I couldn't. Perhaps I should have simply thrown myself down the well back home and allowed my problems to float gently away.

Even though the March sun was shining and there was a touch of warmth to the air, my spirits were as low as they'd ever been. Considerably lower, in fact. So at first I was too busy wallowing in self-pity to notice the approach of one of the older boys, and then, when I did notice, I looked up angrily – annoyed to be disturbed.

I'd seen Kit Stephens about. He was one of those odd types who looked as though he should have plenty of friends when in fact he didn't. He was bright, good at sport, clearly self-confident. In fact, he had everything you'd need to be popular. But there was something slightly strange about him, too. I hadn't heard anything specific, but I knew there were rumours.

He was good-looking in a way that people didn't particularly admire. I hadn't come across the word 'androgynous' at that point, but that's what he was. I felt a little sorry for him, really. In another place or at another time, he would have been considered devastatingly beautiful, like Rupert Brooke. Ten years earlier, during the New Romantic and Gender Bending era, he could have passed for a pop star. But male beauty was frowned on in the early nineties. You could be rugged, or laddish – but not beautiful. Especially in the North.

Although I had dreamed of summoning the courage to go up and talk to him on a number of occasions in the past, I was annoyed that he'd disturbed me and I stood up to wander off elsewhere. But he stopped me with a gesture, a sort of half-wave.

"Don't go," he said. "I've come over to talk to you."

"Oh," I said, surprised. He was two years above me and older boys never talked to those in the first year, except to bully or tease them, so I was wary.

"Do you mind if I sit here?" he said. He ran sensitive fingers through his blondish, floppy hair, brushing it back behind his ears.

I shrugged. He sat beside me without saying anything and looked out across the urban landscape, at the long lines of roofs marching off into the distance. Beyond these, just at the edge of visibility, it was possible to see the green of the countryside, and the undulations that were the very first hills of the Pennines.

"Beautiful," he said. "Do you live in town, or out there?"

He pointed out over the roof tops.

"Out there," I told him. "More or less. On the edge of out there."

"Great," he said. "Do you have a bicycle?"

"Yes."

"I bet you get out into the hills whenever you can."

I looked into the distance.

"I've kind of outgrown my bike," I said. "It's far too small and I need a new one, but it was either that or a computer this year."

"And you're getting a computer?"

"Yes."

"Pity."

He looked down at his hands for a moment and then back up at me.

"Where do you live?"

"Horton-in-the-Moors."

"Oh," he said, "not far from me."

He looked back out towards the fuzz of green at the edge of visibility.

"I love this area," he told me, "it's so good for biking. I've just got a new downhill racer. If you could somehow get over to my place, I could lend you my old one. It would be about the right size for you. We could go for a ride together, if you like. Are you free this Saturday?"

I was confused. Nobody ever offered unconditional friendship to another person like this, out of the blue. It was weird. But then, wasn't Kit supposed to be a bit weird?

"It's okay," he laughed, "you don't have to say yes. It was just a thought. There's no need to be frightened of me. I know I'm going about this in an odd way, but I saw that you were lonely and thought I'd come and talk to you. Forget about the bike thing. It's not important."

I didn't know what to say to this, so I didn't say anything.

"Look," he said, "maybe the easiest thing would be for me to tell you why I decided to come over to talk to you."

"Okay," I said.

"Let me start by saying that I noticed you as soon as you started here in September. You had a look about you. I don't mean that I was attracted to you. At least, not physically. It was something else. That isn't important at the moment. We'll talk about it at another time if you want to. The important thing is that I noticed you, and I've been watching you, on and off, ever since."

"Oh," I said, genuinely surprised.

"Yes, and I've noticed several things recently. The first is that something has happened to make you unhappy." He gave an empty laugh. "That's so obvious it hardly needs stating."

I shrugged, non-committal.

"As soon as I noticed this, I began to watch you more closely, and to wonder *why* you'd become unhappy. You were so different from that when you first arrived. At first I wondered if the problem was here at school, but there was nothing that I could see. Then I wondered if it was to do with life at home, but that didn't seem right either. Problems at home don't usually happen overnight, do they? They slowly creep up on you over a period of time, unless there's an accident or something. But you didn't look as though that kind of thing had happened. So I decided that something had happened to you personally, some influence that was outside school and outside your home. Am I right?"

I wasn't sure whether I wanted to share this with another person, especially an older boy that I didn't know. But I was intrigued that he had taken so much interest in me, so I nodded.

"Good," he said, "I thought so. Now here's the interesting bit. I have an ability – when I bend my will to it, and when the conditions are right – to do something quite close to mind-reading. And I propose to do that now."

He looked at me with an intensity that I'd never seen in anyone before, which stopped me from laughing or walking away, both of which I had felt inclined to do a moment before. As I looked at him, his light hazel eyes glinted in the sunlight. I could see the iridescent edges to his pupils, and his nostrils flared slightly as he breathed. Weird. I looked away, at the distant hills, and felt extremely self-conscious.

"Mmm," he said. "I can see that you have a major conflict. You feel trapped. And you're in a situation in which you're acting like a coward. But you're not a coward. That's interesting. And I presume there's someone else involved..."

I opened my mouth to speak.

"No," he said, "don't say anything. Let me see what I can find out."

Kit stared at me intently and I let my eyes slide off towards the slated roofs beyond us once more.

"There's someone else involved, and he's bullying you," Kit announced at last. "But we all get bullied from time to time," he mused. He shook his head. "No. That's not all. There's something else. But what?"

He paused and looked down at the ground, frowning with concentration, then looked up with a smile.

"Blackmail. This boy is blackmailing you. For money... and more."

He closed his eyes tightly for a moment.

"He's making you be his accomplice in some way, and you

don't want to be one, but you can't see how you can get out of it. Isn't that right?"

I was amazed.

"How did you guess that?"

"I'd like to say that it was magic," he said, opening his hands as if to reveal a secret device of some sort, "but it isn't. Or at least not in the way that you would define magic. Come on, let's walk for a bit. I'm getting cold sitting here."

We began to wander round the perimeter of the basketball court.

"When a person is in distress, they spray out their distress in all directions," he told me. "It's just a question of interpreting what is being sprayed out."

"You make it sound so simple and ordinary," I gasped, "but I've never seen anyone do anything like that before. It's incredible. You should be on tv."

"You think it was some kind of trick?"

I shrugged.

"I was right, though, wasn't I? About the blackmail."

"Yes."

"Okay, good," he said. "That was the first bit. The second part of the exercise is to decide what we're going to do about it."

We.

"I'm not sure I understand."

"It's simple," he said. "When you've got a problem, it grows and grows until it seems insurmountable. You need to share it with someone, someone who can give you a fresh perspective on it. Which helps, even if they don't do anything more than that." He sat down again on the wall at the far end of the court. "So... Tell me about it."

It was odd. Maybe it was because he'd guessed the basics any-way, but I found it easy to tell him my story. In the telling, it all seemed rather pathetic and undramatic, but there was no getting round the fact that Neil was capable of making me suffer in a number of nasty ways if he wanted to. It was just that that kind of petty tyranny – and it *was* tyranny – sounds so mundane. Kit seemed aware of this. He nodded every now and then as I talked and was about to speak, but the bell went for afternoon lessons.

"Look," he said as he stood up to leave, "meet me at the front gates after school finishes and we'll continue this. Okay?"

"Okay."

But during lessons, I had second thoughts. I began to realise how weird Kit's show of mind-reading had been. When I thought it through, I decided he had somehow cleverly read my mood, watched my reactions to the things he'd said, and then put two and two together. It wasn't mind-reading at all. It was a slick psychological trick. But what a trick. And he had been so accurate. If he was that perceptive, I wasn't sure I wanted to let him delve any further. It wasn't what I thought of as friendship. It felt more like therapy.

At the end of the afternoon, I told Richard that I had to go and talk to Mrs Hodson and that I'd make my own way home on a later bus. Then I waited for a few minutes. After a decent interval, I made my way out of one of the two side gates instead of leaving by the front, as I'd arranged with Kit. But as I emerged, there he was, standing on the pavement, waiting for me.

"I thought I'd see you here," he said, laughing at my consternation. "It was obvious that you wouldn't meet me at the front. I could see that you were freaked-out, and I guessed that you would try to avoid me."

Spot on.

"But I could have gone to the *other* side entrance. What made you think I'd come out of this one?"

"Hunch. If you like," he said, then smiled a warm smile and fell into step beside me. "Let's stop off for a coffee," he added after a moment. "How about that place on the way to Hanley? Have you got time? I'll pay."

The place was actually a restaurant, with waiter service, in a converted bank. It was more up-market than I felt comfortable with, but at least we could be sure that no one from school would disturb us. Kit ordered a cafetière of Blue Mountain blend, for two, and sat by the tall, imposing window staring out into the street. I sat with my back to the light, looking out over the dark, curved wooden counter (beautifully crafted, I noticed) with its bottles of spirits up-ended into their optics, and art deco style lamps spring-ing up from the bar like mushrooms.

"I've been thinking," Kit said as he plunged the plunger on the cafetière, "about this blackmailer of yours. You've got to find a way to get rid of him."

"But how?" I said.

"You could always kill him."

I laughed, but nervously. I couldn't be certain that he wasn't serious.

"No," he said, "maybe not. That sort of action tends to have major consequences. Though, in many ways, it would be the easi-est solution all round, wouldn't it? I'd better check him out. Perhaps I could have a word with him."

"He wouldn't listen," I said. "And you'd only get the shit kicked out of you."

"Maybe so," said Kit, tilting his head to one side. "But I want you to point him out to me. Today, I mean."

"Oh." I blinked. "Well, he's usually hanging around in the vil-lage somewhere."

"Okay. I'll come back with you on the bus."

"What? Now?"

"Why not?"

So after we finished our coffee, that's what we did. It was odd, sitting with Kit on the bus home. He talked a little about how he'd moved to the area from elsewhere, like me, although he didn't say where from. I wasn't surprised by this news. He had the air of an outsider to me – a certain something that set him apart. This was partly because he spoke with no discernible accent, but there was something else, too, that I couldn't quite pin down.

He treated me as though he'd known me for a long time, falling into a casual familiarity that I'd previously only experienced with Richard, and which seemed false, almost, or at least disconcerting, coming from someone that I'd only spoken to for the first time during the lunch period that day.

When we got off the bus, we were immediately in luck. Neil was standing talking to another couple of lads by the river. I pointed him out to Kit, who smiled and said, "Okay, you can go home now. I'll see you tomorrow. Or soon, anyway."

"What are you going to do?" I asked, now alarmed that he might be about to make things worse; to warn Neil not to bully me – which would have just the opposite effect.

"Don't worry," he said. "I'm only going to have a look. I certainly won't talk to him whilst he's got company."

With that, I left Kit standing there in an attitude of passive nonchalance, his hands deep in his pockets. I wasn't sure whether to feel relieved or not. Of course, it had been wonderful to confess to someone about the trouble I was in, and even more wonderful not to be ridiculed for it. But what was going to happen now? As I let myself into the house, via the back door, I realised that a great deal of my life was characterised by feelings of dread, and I couldn't help including this new situation with Kit in that.

Lying in bed that night, I wondered why he had decided to show an interest in me. Perhaps he was gay himself and had recognised that in me? If so, he must have known from the moment I'd started at school last September, because that was when he said he'd first 'noticed' me. Or was it something else? And if so, what? It was all a bit scary and mysterious. And exciting too.

But I still dreaded meeting Neil the next afternoon.

Four

That day was the worst school day of my life, characterised by an agonizing tension which sapped all my energy. My body felt as if it weighed tons, and I felt achy and weak, as if I was developing a nasty dose of flu. All day I kept vacillating between different plans: I'd tell my parents all about Neil. I'd go to the police and confess to giving him an alibi. I wouldn't go home at all at the end of the day... But it was fruitless. I knew that, whatever I did, and however much trouble I got Neil into, he would always be able to corner me when I came home from school and make my life hell. But, then again, I couldn't go on like this or I would snap.

I took the bus home with Richard, as usual. He was happy that he'd done well that day in French, and chattered on beside me as though unaware of my withdrawn state. I know he was worried about me, and I appreciated that he was making an effort to lift my mood, and I liked him for doing so. But nothing could help. I brooded moodily, staring out of the window as houses and fields and cars slipped past, and remained inviolate and unreachable in my misery.

When we arrived in Horton, Richard went straight off with a perfunctory "See ya." He didn't wait to see if I'd invite him back for a cup of tea, and I felt incredibly sad, as I watched him go, that our friendship had suffered because of all this. I slung my rucksack over my shoulder and set off to walk the long way round to the house – I'd avoided the alleyway for many weeks now as it was too enclosed and secluded. I realised that I was holding my breath as I walked. It kept coming out in gasps every now and then.

But there was no sign of Neil.

When I got home, everything was horribly normal, which was unbearable and somehow made me panic even more. I knew that Neil would turn up and bang on the door at eight o'clock, and my stomach knotted at the thought of it. Yet there was mum, happily singing in the kitchen; dad laughing with my sisters about something or other in the sitting room; and me, quietly hyperventilating in the corner, pretending to watch tv.

I could hardly eat my dinner, and when dad made an irritated remark, mum laughed and said, "He's alright. He looks a bit lovesick to me," and she winked and no-one said anything further, and I thought *If only*.

But Neil didn't turn up later. For the first time since the whole nightmare had begun, he didn't show up. Of course, it made me wonder if Kit had had anything to do with it. But what could he have done? Killed him? In some odd way I could almost believe that he might have murdered him. I remembered the calm way he'd referred to just such a solution in the café.

With a shudder, I looked at the shelving unit that I was making for my computer, and realised that I hadn't done any work on it since I'd been commandeered by Neil. It was my birthday next month, and I'd have to get a move on if it was going to be ready. I fell asleep wondering what was going on.

By the morning, the pall of dread had reached epic proportions. Or perhaps it was no longer dread. Now I had become convinced that something major – and bad – was about to happen. I walked to the bus stop with Richard, who had joined me as I passed his door, and we wandered along together. It was a lightly overcast day, though mild, and daffodils were much in evidence in the gardens we passed, not that I took much interest in them in the state I was in. Then, as we turned onto the crossroads by the Post Office and pub, I saw Neil coming towards us. He saw me immediately and stopped. I thought, *Oh no, this is it* and felt my body become instantly rigid. But he didn't come up to us. He stared at me with an odd expression, as if he was gagging, and then the expression changed, briefly, to one of fear. And then he turned around and walked down Leek Lane, away from the bus stop.

Richard and I stared at one another in surprise and astonishment.

"What was *that*?" Richard asked. "Why did he look at you like that?"

I shrugged.

"I don't know," I said, truthfully.

"Weird," Richard murmured, "that was *so* weird."

At school, lunch time couldn't come quickly enough. As soon as I could get away, I rushed down to the basketball court to wait for Kit, and sure enough, a few minutes later, he followed me down there.

"What did you do?" I asked him.

"Why, what happened?"

I explained that Neil hadn't come round the previous night, and then told him about the odd look on Neil's face that morning when he saw me. Kit smiled, pleased.

"I did have a word with him, in the end," he said. "Those boys we saw him with went off soon after you left. It was the perfect opportunity for me to have a chat."

"But what did you *say*?" I couldn't think of anything that someone like Kit might say that would be so spectacularly effective.

"Oh," Kit said, "I made it clear that it wouldn't be a good idea for him to persecute you any more. I was quite... *persuasive.* And he definitely got my point."

That was all Kit would say. I pestered him for ages about it, but he would say no more except, "You wished for him to be gone, and I helped you put that wish into practice. That's all."

At the end of the lunch break, as we were about to go back to lessons, Kit said, quite casually, "Oh, one more thing."

I glanced at him, expectantly.

"Don't think you can go back to how you were before."

"How do you mean?"

He sighed and looked up at the overcast sky.

"I shouldn't have said that," he said. "I'm sorry. Forget it. I shouldn't try to direct you in any way. It's just that I have a theory about you and... it's easy for me to want to make it happen."

That was more or less the end of the Neil Braithwaite episode. Only a week or so later, his family left the village, quite suddenly. Richard Murray heard a rumour that Neil had had some kind of breakdown, but we never found out for sure. One's son having a nervous breakdown is no reason to move home, I'd have thought. But who knows...

It was incredible. My life suddenly blossomed again. Home felt like home. In a cathartic moment, when dad asked me why he hadn't seen me with my Walkman for a while, I confessed to everything. It was wonderful. He called mum in and I gave them all the details of the bullying and the handing over of cash. I even confessed to stealing fifteen pounds from mum's purse. They were wonderful.

"So *that's* what it was all about," mum said. "We were so worried. We even had a call from school. Mrs Hodson thought there might be something wrong at home and they phoned up to ask about it."

I was forgiven. Mum said suitably awful things about Neil and what she would have done if he were still living in Horton, and life settled down. Of course, I didn't mention Kit. Anyway, what could

I have said? I started making an effort at school, and especially at choir practice, and found, once more, that I was in everyone's good books. Mr Griggs started to sing my praises, if you'll pardon the pun, and I began to fantasise about becoming a professional singer after leaving school. I even stopped ignoring my sisters. One day dad came across some sheets of walnut veneer in an old workshop he was clearing out and brought them back for me, for my desk. I put in an hour or two every evening and, by the time my desk was finished, it was my birthday and my new computer had somewhere to sit. And I got a new CD Walkman, too. Richard started coming round again, and we did some more work on learning how to construct a website.

I had been re-assimilated by the Idyll.

Or, almost. Behind all of this lurked a tiny, vague shadow which crouched, spider-like, at the back of my mind. I wasn't even aware of it at first, though when I eventually did notice it, I realised that it had been there all the time. It was an emotional *residue* from the whole Neil business. I had felt so alienated from my family during the period in which I'd been so unhappy that when I reconnected with them, as it were, a certain element of my inner self *remained* separate. It was that element of me that couldn't mention Kit and the part I knew he must have played in getting rid of Neil. It was the part of me that realised there was a way of living in that other world, a world that was stranger, more attractive and more *dangerous* than the kind of life that I was living right now. Kit was part of that other darkly alluring life, and Richard and my family weren't. The Trap was still waiting...

Things might have been so different if I'd listened more carefully to what Kit had said to me. Now I know that not a word of his was ever wasted. In retrospect, I can see that he was implicating me in the disappearance of Neil, and if I had learned that lesson the easy way, the way he wanted, things might not have got so out of control later on. I am also ashamed at how little gratitude I showed Kit for the help he gave me. But I was young, and I was too relieved at having my old, easy life back to think very much about anything else. I remember that I did go out cycling with him a couple of times. The first time we went out, I cycled my old bike over to his place to meet him, my knees barely clearing the too-small handle-bars. He lived in an old, dark detached house which stood in a courtyard surrounded by great glowering pine trees that reared up over what must have once been a stable but had now been converted into a double garage. At the time I thought the place huge, though I now doubt it was any bigger than an average town house. It was the walled garden, and the house's isolation amongst the fields, that gave it scale. I asked what the house used to be, thinking it must have been a grand old rectory, but Kit said that it had been built for the unmarried sister of a minor industrialist who had refined the process of firing glaze onto porcelain, and when I asked to be shown round he shrugged it off with an evasive, "Another time." But he did give me his old bike, which was yet another act of generosity on his part for which I wasn't sufficiently grateful. The next time we went cycling, he arranged to meet me half way between our houses, so I never did get to be shown round his home.

At first, my parents wouldn't let me accept the bike as a gift, and mum phoned his parents to talk about the possibility of borrowing it for a while. She got Kit instead, and ended up talking to him for nearly half-an-hour.

"What a nice young man," she said when she'd finished. "So grown up. I assumed he was the father at first."

She didn't mention not accepting the bike after that.

Of course, I saw Kit at school, and we'd talk a little, but there was something so vague about him, so odd, so disconcerting, that I actually began to avoid him in the end.

That's not to say I didn't think about him. You can't witness something like the expression that I saw on Neil's face, for which I held Kit responsible, without being intrigued. Yes, Kit clearly had a kind of power. Was it a strange physical technique whereby he could overcome a stronger boy by using an arcane martial art? Or was it more bizarre than that, along the lines of hypnosis? Whatever it was, it fascinated me. But not enough for me to put the effort into continuing our friendship. To be fair to myself, it wasn't only a case of *me* withdrawing from *him*. Kit seemed to be, not exactly evading me, but maybe giving me my own space. I can't describe it any better than that. Nevertheless, I had an unshakable sense that he was watching over me, that he was still concerned about my welfare.

My mother once asked me, "What happened to that Kit boy who gave you his old bicycle? Do you see him any more?" I said I saw him around, but that was all. The summer, and the school holiday, was approaching, and – it seems incredible to me now – I didn't think any more about him.

Except occasionally at night, when I sometimes imagined Kit as a dark, erotic power. I imagined him as having a mesmeric ability that was seductive, ardent. Electrifying. But the Kit of my dreams was different from Kit the schoolboy – bigger, darker, older, physically stronger. More masculine. Although inspired by Kit, in some ways, this fantasy person was not someone that I connected with his counterpart in real life. He was merely a nocturnal image, resulting in stained sheets and wide eyes. Once or twice I wondered if, perhaps, I would have fallen in love with Kit if we'd continued our friendship. But it was an unanswerable question and so I put it aside. Instead, I spent a lot of time with Richard, who was the perfect antidote to the confusion engendered by Kit. Richard was obviously growing up straight. His ideas and aspirations were clear, simple and focussed. I felt no confusion when I was with him, no uncertainty about the reason for our friendship, and no erotic pull.

I now think that I was simply too young for what happened with Kit. A couple of years later, I would have been far more interested in hustling for an explanation of his apparent mind-reading ability, and of what he'd said or done to Neil to make him stop bullying me. But as it was, I had found it all so disturbing that I wanted to forget about the whole thing and get back to normal as quickly as possible.

Over the course of that summer my sexual fantasies took on a more blurred, generic form. I spent a lot of time out and about on the bike that Kit had given me, taking photos with a new camera I'd been given by dad, listening to music, or working on the computer with Richard. For the record, I must say that we came up with a crackingly dull website. But then, *of course* it would be dull. We were two schoolboys who'd had no life experience, who had never done anything and who had nothing to say. We indicated who we were, showed a map of where we lived, listed our interests and hobbies. I uploaded some of my photos, and Richard added some silly captions and a few jokes. This lead to a number of email correspondences with other school kids that petered out after a while, once we'd established that we had nothing to say to each other. But then, as dad rightly said, it wasn't a waste of time because it was a good skill to learn, proof of which being that I helped mum put some ideas together when she had to give input into the construction of a website for her charity.

Then, quite suddenly, my voice began to break. I left the choir with instructions to take things easy for a while, until it settled down, after which Mr Griggs would give me another voice test. Oddly, whilst I had known this would happen at some point, I was surprised at how excluded it made me feel. My parents and my sisters still went off once a week to choir practice, and I stayed behind. Of course, the Dutch choir festival never happened – and the choir's repertoire changed, replacing the now-unsingable Taverner with something easier – but the choir still went off to

Manchester and Birmingham, and I missed these outings.

I now see that this exclusion from family activity was beautifully symbolic. It represented the dissolving of a link, the first of many that would gradually break along with my voice. Even though I never consciously remembered those words of Kit's, *Don't think you can go back to how you were before,* the sense of them certainly lurked on beneath the surface of my thoughts.

Five

If this was a film from the 1950s, there would be a montage at this point: leaves flying from a soft focus calendar to represent the ano-dyne passage of a year. Two. During that period, Richard's family moved from Horton to Newcastle, so, although I continued to see him at school, we didn't travel together on the bus any more, and we gradually stopped hanging around together. I got on with my studies as GCSEs approached, school remained hum-drum, and nothing happened at home.

But things changed when I began singing again.

The school were putting on a varied choral programme of reli-gious music for their Easter concert, and I was recruited as a light tenor. My voice, once broken, had a husky quality to it that I quite liked, but it made me realise once and for all that it wasn't particularly special. It was perfectly good for a serious amateur, but unimpressive at a higher level than that. The first time I realised it, I smiled at the recollection that this had been my Worst Case Scenario when I was the boy soprano star of the Bucknall Choir. Sure enough, after my voice broke, I'd simply become one of a number of male singers with a highly compe-tent voice. My father, I now realised, had a better voice than I did, and so I abandoned the idea of cosseting it and nurturing it. To give myself credit, it is a testament to how minor my fantasies about becoming a professional singer really were, that I didn't particularly mind. It had simply been a useful thing to say when asked the "what do you want to do when you grow up?" question by my grandparents. And now, I could always point to my interest in woodwork instead.

Rehearsals were held in the assembly hall, and as I entered the room, who should I see but Kit, standing there looking calm and assured. I was surprised to see him because I didn't know that he could sing. As it turned out, he had a clearer voice than mine, but with nothing like my range or power. He was a light tenor, too, and we were put next to each other. It was the spring term, and Kit was in the thick of mock 'A' levels, gearing up for the exams in the summer. I asked him how they were going.

"Okay," he said with his bright, casual smile. "I don't know why so many people get into such a state about them. They're not *that* important. I mean, good 'A' levels help, but to hear people talk about them you'd think that to get a grade less than you'd hoped for is equivalent to having a limb chopped off – crippling you for life. It's ridiculous."

He looked down at the sheet of music that he'd been handed, then back at me.

"How about you? How are your GCSEs going?"

"More or less the same, by the sound of it," I said, "only without so much hysteria, because there's less at stake."

It was a strange meeting. Although I'd seen Kit around for two-and-a-half years at this point, it was, oddly, the first time I'd really had a chance to examine him close up without it being obvious. There were twenty-five of us altogether in the choir – eleven boys and fourteen girls – and we all stood there facing Mr Evans, the music teacher, and I could cast sidelong glances at Kit, standing only a foot or two away from me. He had filled out somewhat in the two years since the Neil episode, though he still retained that androgynous quality that set him so apart. His face had firmed up, though, and his full lips now had a strength about them where before they had been more child-like. In fact, that was the difference – he looked completely adult now. If I'd never seen him before and he walked into a classroom I would have taken him for one of the teachers rather than a pupil. It's difficult to describe, but there was definitely something ageless about him. From some angles he could have passed for thirty, or more. It was weird. But then, that was his thing wasn't it – being weird?

After the rehearsal was over, Anne Grehan, a lively girl from my year, made straight for me and dragged me off to a corner, as if her life depended on it. There was an endearing breathlessness about Anne, and the baggy rap-style clothes she favoured seemed almost to be inflated by her own perpetual excitement.

"Greg," she announced, "I've been wondering for ages if you were gay – but now I know. God, you couldn't keep your eyes off Kit Stephens. I mean, I know he's dreamy, but... well, don't let some of the boys see you going gooey like that, or you'll be in trouble."

I was completely taken aback.

"I wasn't aware that I was being so obvious," I said.

"Your eyes were out *on stalks*," she laughed. "If Brian Hogarty saw you, he'd make your life hell."

Brian Hogarty was the boy in our class who was thoughtlessly opinionated, and vociferously so. Every class has one. I despised him, but had managed to avoid any trouble from him because I was on friendly terms with a couple of his mates. It didn't stop him sneering occasional abuse at me, but he only did it in a half-hearted way.

"I'd be careful about Kit if I were you," Anne went on. "Apart from anything else, he might be gay as well."

I thought about that for a moment.

"And that would be a *problem*?" I smiled.

"Look, Greg, it's all very well having the hots for someone, but when you're talking about a person like Kit Stephens, then you want to do it from a distance. You know, like having a photo of a film star on your wall. The idea of actually becoming *involved* with him... well, he's queer in more ways than one, if you know what I mean."

"No, I don't know what you mean," I said stubbornly.

"You must have heard some of the stories," she said.

I shrugged.

"None of the specifics." That much, at least, was true.

She looked at her watch and her untidy fringe fell across her face.

"Do you need to dash off anywhere?" she asked.

"No."

"Have you got any money?"

"Some," I said, digging in my pocket and feeling about for change.

"Alright then," she grinned, "buy me a pint and I'll tell you everything."

And so I 'went out for a beer' with *Anne*. It was not how I'd imagined my first foray into a bar, but it could have been a lot worse. Anne knew a pub in Tunstall, The Bishop, that didn't ask for ID.

"You look eighteen, easily," she told me. "You'd be okay in any bar."

I laughed. My sixteenth birthday had been the previous week.

"You'll be fine," she assured me.

And I was. I felt thrillingly adult, ordering us both a pint – and *getting* it.

"Right," I told her as we sat down on a corner seat at one end of the bar. "This is my half of the bargain. Now you can keep yours."

"First," she said, "you've got to tell me if you're gay."

"Of course I'm gay," I said, and she laughed.

"It's okay," she told me. "My brother's gay too. It's cool. He's six years older than I am and one of the nicest people I know."

She held up her pint and we clinked glasses.

"Okay. Sex therapy's over," I told her. "Now I want the gossip on Kit Stephens."

She dipped her head and looked round the bar, as though there might be people that we knew who could overhear us.

"I actually saw the first thing I'm going to tell you with my own eyes, so I know it's not apocryphal," she said. "It happened at the end of last year. I was in the library doing some reading, and Kit was doing the same at the table next to me. He was kind of distracting – you know, looking so gorgeous." Anne blushed. "I was sitting there thinking I should go somewhere else if I wanted to get any work done, when Dave Carlisle came in looking furious."

Dave Carlisle was one of the boys from Kit's year. Troublesome is the word that springs to mind when I think of him, although arsehole is another that seems rather more apposite.

"That's when it got weird," said Anne, looking up at me. "I was sitting there, and Dave came over to me and hissed, 'Have you seen Kit Stephens?' But there *was* Kit – sitting ramrod straight and completely still – less than four feet away from us. I was going to say something sarcastic like 'He's right in front of you, you cretin', but something stopped me. It was the look on Kit's face. Well, the absence of a look, really. He was completely blank. Almost alien. I was totally freaked out…"

Anne shook her head and took a sip of her beer. She was frowning now.

"And then Dave walked out of the room, and Kit gradually came back to life. He turned round to look at the door, and when he turned back he had this odd, smug look on his face. I might have thought the whole thing was some bizarre oversight on Dave's part if it hadn't been for that look. But… now I don't know what to think. It was just weird."

She took another gulp of her beer before going on.

"After that, as well as keeping an eye on Kit, I also kept an ear out for gossip about him. I was talking to one of the girls from the upper sixth last term, and she'd been freaked out by Kit, too, during an English lesson. They were doing Forster's *A Passage to India*. Have you read it? It's dull as hell. Anyway, this girl says that Kit was looking out of the window, or doing something else that made it clear he wasn't paying attention, and Mr Blandford noticed and came over to him. You know some of the teachers hate Kit, because he's so dismissive of them? Well, Mr Blanford dislikes him more than most, so he was keen to pounce on Kit. He rushed over to Kit's desk in that ex-army I'm-going-to-get-you way of his, and Kit only noticed him at the last moment. He looked up at Mr Blandford, surprised out of his dream, and said, 'They're important because they represent the ephemeral nature of relationships, sir.' And Mr Blandford's jaw dropped open – I can just imagine it – and he said, 'How did you know I was going to ask you a question about the Marabar caves?' And Kit sat there, calm as anything, and said, 'Oh, I thought you had, sir'."

She paused for effect and looked at me.

"Now," she said, "how's *that* for weird?"

"Pretty weird," I said, thinking back to the occasion two years before, when he had demonstrated his mind-reading abilities to me with such great effect.

"But it's not the weirdest thing," she went on. "Something even odder happened a couple of weeks ago. You know Diane Holt's mother's been very sick?"

"Yes. Leukaemia or something."

"*I* thought that, but apparently it's some other kind of complicated blood disorder. She was rushed to hospital and given a week to live – right in the middle of Diane's mock 'A' levels. Obviously, she was really, really upset, and broke down in the sixth form corridor. A couple of the girls were trying to calm her down when she got hysterical and said the stress of it all was too much for her to bear. And then Kit, who was passing, said to her, 'Don't worry, all your problems will be over by Friday afternoon'. Well, her last exam was on Friday and she thought he was referring to that. She went ballistic and screamed that she had a dying mother, and then the other girls joined in and called him a callous bastard, to his face. Well heavy. Anyway, he apologised for upsetting her, but reiterated what he had said about her troubles being over, and went away."

Anne's eyes were wide with wonder as she reached the climax of her story.

"The thing is," she told me, "that on Friday afternoon, Mrs Holt suddenly started to get better. When Diane went to the hospital after her exam, the doctors called her in and said that the blood work had come back and that, contrary to all precedent, her mother was recovering. The doctors were completely baffled. Of course it'll be weeks before she's back home, if not months, but that Friday was the day she started to get better."

Anne took a deep breath, put her elbows on the table and leaned her face against her hands.

"So," she said. "How did Kit know that? How did he know that Diane's mother was going to get better?"

"Maybe he didn't. Maybe he *was* just being callous."

Anne snorted.

"Of course he wasn't. He may be weird and distant, but he's not deliberately cruel."

I pondered for a while before speaking.

"So," I asked at last, "what do *you* think of the things you've told me? Do you really believe that he somehow made himself invisible in the library, that he read Mr Blandford's mind, and that he cured Mrs Holt?"

"I don't know what to think," Anne said. "That's the thing."

I wondered if I should tell her about my own experiences with

Kit. But I didn't. On one hand, it was all so long ago, and on the other it was a private memory, somehow, and precious because of that.

At our second choir rehearsal, Kit wandered straight over to me. I was one of those people who was on fairly affable terms with most people, but it struck me, then, how isolated he was. Or even more than that. Anne was clearly not the only one who had heard the rumours about him, and there was a palpable undercurrent around him. Frankly, people were avoiding him, which he either didn't notice or didn't mind. But what *I* noticed was that, when I spoke to him, I became locked into his isolation with him. No one came up to talk to me, either. Strange.

"Do you still go out on your bike?" he asked.

"Not really," I said. "I've grown out of that one, too. I should go out and buy another one—"

"I've got a spare one," said Kit.

"Oh, I've got the money to buy another one," I said, a little defensively. "I just haven't got round to it. I spend so much of my time working with dad at the moment."

"Doing your woodwork?"

"Yes. I'm learning some of the skills of the trade. Dad wants me to work with him eventually, and I don't see why I shouldn't. In fact, I think I like the idea. He's had a couple of big jobs back to back, so for the last couple of months he's been working seven days a week, and I've been putting in as much time as I can. I get good money now that I'm up to a proper professional standard for basic joinery, but the problem is, I don't have time to spend what I earn."

"We should get out into the countryside again," he said. "There are some brilliant places in the National Park up towards Buxton. Now that I've passed my test, we could chuck a couple of bikes in the car and head off out there one weekend."

"Mmm," I nodded, not really taking the invitation seriously. Anyway, I had several weekends of carpentry already booked up.

The rehearsal got underway. In the absence of the orchestra, Mr Evans played everything on the piano. I can't remember anything about it except that at one point Kit and I were sitting things out at the side, when Mr Evans started talking about the betrayal of Jesus in the garden of Gethsemane. Kit didn't say anything, but he jerked his head up as Mr Evans spoke, and I could see his nose twitch, rabbit-like, as though he'd encountered a bad smell. We were being exhorted to put all that passion into our singing – the great, tragic melancholia of impending loss, of great things brought down by individual acts of betrayal. Because of Kit's intense interest, I listened closely to what was being said, but it was the same old bible story everyone knows, even though Mr Evans, as a devout Christian himself, did manage to imbue the story with a sense of contemporary human emotion.

After the rehearsal was over, I turned to Kit and said, with a casualness that I didn't feel, "Do you fancy going for a drink after this?"

He looked surprised at this query, then consulted his watch. It was 6.30.

"You mean a *drink* drink?"

"Yes. There's this place in Tunstall that doesn't ask for ID. You'd be okay anywhere, of course. You're eighteen."

Kit nodded to himself, then smiled.

"Okay," he said. "But aren't your parents expecting you back home?"

"I'll phone them on the way over."

And so I ended up in The Bishop again, buying a round of drinks for Kit and myself. When we were ensconced with our pints and a couple of packets of dry roast peanuts, Kit raised his glass.

"Did you hear Mr Evans talking about Judas earlier?" he asked me.

"Yes. I saw you looking all interested, but there didn't seem anything unusual about the story as far as I could see."

"But it was all wrong," said Kit. "Every last bit of it. The whole thing."

"Of course it's all wrong," I said. "At least, in as much as it's all a fiction, it's wrong."

"But I don't think it *is* fiction," Kit said earnestly. "I think we've badly misinterpreted what happened, that's all."

I thought about that for a moment.

"Okay," I said, "so what *did* happen?"

Kit held up his glass and looked into his beer for a moment, as if in its clarity he would find what he was looking for. Then he took a long, appreciative gulp.

"Alright. The fundamental point of the Christian faith is that Christ died for our sins. Yes?"

"Yes."

"And it's fair to say that without the crucifixion, we would have nothing more than the teachings of yet another talented but unremarkable Jewish mystic."

I nodded my agreement.

"Well, it was Judas who set the whole thing off – who started the ball rolling that would lead to the one of the greatest martyrdoms in history."

"So?"

Kit looked at me.

"I'm saying that without Judas, there would be no Christianity. He's the vital force."

"But if Judas hadn't betrayed Jesus, the authorities would have found another way to get him. It would have happened with or without Judas."

"That's by no means certain, and it's not the point," he told me. "The point is that, through human frailty, Jesus was arrested and sent for trial. Judas represents not betrayal, but intrinsic *human frailty. Anyone* could have been Judas – everyone *is* Judas at some point in their lives, in however minor a capacity. We shouldn't blame Judas for what he did. Jesus said 'He who is without sin among you, let him first cast a stone'. Well, how many people have never let another person down, hmm? How many? I'll tell you. None. If our petty betrayals don't lead to cataclysmic results, it's simply because of the time and place in which we do them. Judas had the bad luck – if you want to call it that – to be there at one of those points when the world is in a fine balance; when it can be tipped one way or another. And because of what Judas did it was tipped against Jesus, thus enabling him to make the ultimate, the all-important sacrifice. *Judas* did that. He facilitated the birth of Christianity. It's Judas who should be held up alongside Christ, not John the Baptist. Nathaniel Hawthorne talked of Adam's 'fortunate fall' – the idea being that unless we fall we cannot be redeemed. Well, that's how we should think of Judas's role with Jesus. Jesus may well have died for men's sins, but so did Judas – because Judas's 'sin' is a universal sin that is in all of us. Because of it, he committed suicide and died an outcast, and has remained an outcast *throughout history*. And it's the ultimate hypocrisy to forget that sacrifice. That's the problem with all dualistic religious constructs – you know, like cowboys and Indians. Black hats and white hats. God and the Devil. Jesus and Judas. They always have to reduce it to the Good Guys and the Bad Guys. It's pathetic."

"You mean you think Judas was a 'good' man?"

Kit looked at me warily, as though not sure if he'd gone too far. Then, after a pause, he went on.

"No," he said, looking at me intensely, "I mean Judas was a human being like the rest of us, and we should respect that about him, and envy him his central place in the history of Christianity, not despise him."

"How can you praise someone for betraying another person, no matter how human that betrayal may be?"

"I'm not saying that you should praise Judas's actions. I'm saying that you shouldn't condemn him for them. The point is that it's all a matter of statistics in the end. We all make mistakes and, by the laws of averages, just as someone somewhere will win the lottery at a chance of fourteen million to one against, someone somewhere will also make a blunder that is hugely more significant than his or her action warrants. That's why we should forgive Judas and, in forgiving him, forgive ourselves. Isn't *that* the key tenet of Christianity?"

"Well, it's certainly something to ponder," I said, thinking that this conversation was way too heavy to conduct whilst 'out for a pint'.

"You should never take the world as it appears at face value," Kit told me. "Never. You often have to invert it to see it properly."

"You mean, what's good is bad and vice versa?"

"No. I mean, people often have a dry moral perspective on things. I'm not saying that you should listen to what people say is right and then do the opposite. I'm saying that you should listen to what people say is right, or what people say you should do, and then look at that thing obliquely, to look at what's *behind* it. That's what I mean. And if you do that, then people will often accuse you of turning good into bad. But you're not; you're just stripping the original concept of its moral hypocrisy. Removing the built-in invisible agenda."

Six

That conversation had a profound effect on me. As I mulled over what Kit had said, I realised that I *had* taken the world very much for granted until then; had taken it at face value. What Kit said about Judas may not have been true, but it was an important lesson for me, demonstrating that *any* moment in history is open to multiple interpretations. And not just history. All action could be reinterpreted, misinterpreted, twisted and resubmitted with an agenda that may not be common knowledge... It was an exciting thought, yet ultimately depressing because it meant that the world was a darker place than I'd imagined, that 'knowledge' and 'facts' were merely relative terms, and therefore open to abuse.

These thoughts piqued my curiosity to learn more about the so-called facts handed down from the bible. I knew my sister had one, written in modern English, and so I asked to borrow it – which raised an eyebrow – and read the story of Judas. I could see that both Mr Evans' and Kit's interpretations were there to be read into the text, depending on one's attitude when approaching it. And I found that the four Gospels had wildly disparate views on certain key teachings – the so-called 'true' parts of the story. And what about the Apocrapha? All those gospels and testaments that hadn't quite fitted the political climate at various times during Christianity's chequered history, and had been unceremoniously excised, so as not to contradict the version that certain individuals wanted to promote. Agenda. And how many other interpretations could you extract, I wondered. It all depended on what you wanted to prove.

Large as these new thoughts were, they were driven to the back of my mind when Kit asked me to go out cycling with him that Saturday. I happily agreed, then felt guilty, because it meant that I wouldn't be able to work with dad. When I broached the subject he was annoyed about it, but fortunately mum rallied to my defence.

"Greg hasn't had much of a social life lately," she told him. "We should encourage him to take as many days off at the weekend as he wants, and only to work with you when he's not busy with something else."

Dad grunted.

"And besides," mum added, "I think it's about time *you* took some more time off yourself."

Armed with my compact camera, which fitted neatly in my back pocket, I cycled over to Kit's place, in the middle of nowhere on the road to Biddulph Moor. Although sunny, it was cold, and I cycled hard to keep myself warm. I felt leggy and ungainly as I pedalled because the bike was too small for me, but the countryside was exhilarating, and the first tentative hints of the new year's greenery lifted my spirits. Somehow the spring sunlight made the tumbled-down dry-stone walls and the rotting gate-posts look pleasantly rural, where in the winter they'd merely seemed derelict and depressing.

Kit's house had been repainted and restored since I'd last seen it; not that it had been in bad condition before. But, despite the face-lift, it remained essentially unchanged – bulky, dark, shaded. I cycled up to the front door, and saw that there was a Volkswagen estate parked in the cobbled courtyard with two bicycles stacked carefully in the back. Kit came out, wearing full cycling gear, before I had a chance to ring the bell.

"Are you cold?" he asked.

"Only my hands," I told him.

"Wait here, I've got another pair of mitts." He disappeared for a moment and then came back out with a pair of thin black gloves made from something synthetic. "Here. And you can ride the Marin," he told me, indicating a well-ridden dark green bike. "It's easier to ride because I've put some road slicks on it. Where do you want to go? I thought we could start off at Cleulow Cross and take the back road round to Shutlingsloe."

"The hill?"

"Yes."

I nodded my approval. Dad had driven us all out that way one weekend ages ago and I relished the idea of seeing it again. My sisters weren't interested in getting out into the countryside and my parents always seemed to have other things to do.

Kit got into the driver's seat and, as I walked round to get in the other side, I looked up at the house. Its dark walls were secretive; the freshly painted windows looked almost too clean. The word immaculate came to mind as I noticed the fresh guttering and newly painted external drains. I wondered about Kit's parents – whom I'd never met and who Kit never spoke of; wondered if they might perhaps be looking out at me from the shadowy upstairs windows, or through the huge arched window of the stairwell. I couldn't see into the house at all. It was impenetrable. Perhaps his parents were invalids, or dead, and this was the home of some mad uncle...

"It's a well maintained house," I said as I got in.

"You would know," Kit laughed, "being the son of a builder. I should have asked you to come over and lend a hand. There were workmen in here for months. I expect there was plenty that you could have done. And you'd probably have got more money than from your dad. And," he added more quietly, "I'd have seen more of you."

With that, he started the engine and the car rumbled out over the cobbles of the front courtyard. We turned right, under the stretching branches of a couple of beech trees whose branches were clustered with the palest green shoots.

"Even copper beech leaves start off green," Kit said, looking up.

It was the strangest feeling, being driven by Kit. It was a breath of adult freedom.

"Were your parents at home when I arrived?" I asked. "I've never even seen them."

Kit looked across at me and smiled a secretive, private smile absolutely devoid of humour.

"We're out to have fun, not to discuss my parents," he said, gently. "Is it okay if we leave it at that?"

"Okay," I said. "Fine."

I watched him as he drove. I could see the sinews in his forearms as he held and turned the steering wheel; the slight frown of concentration as he braked and cornered on the narrow roads. I remembered my conversation with Anne Grehan of ten days before. It didn't seem possible that this person beside me could have strange powers. He looked too vibrantly fixed in the physical world to have any hidden dimension. And yet... and yet, I remembered what he'd said to me about Judas's betrayal of Christ, and I knew there was far more to him than I'd ever had a chance to experience, even if I put the Neil Braithwaite business into the equation. I suddenly yearned to know more about him, to understand him better.

"Do you go cycling a lot?" I asked. "You've certainly got all the gear."

I looked down at my old jeans and trainers, and felt suddenly self conscious and underdressed in comparison to Kit's state-of-the-art ensemble.

"Mmm," he nodded. "I go running as well, but with running you inevitably do the same circuits over and over again. Whereas with a bike you can go much further afield."

"You look great," I said, "I should get some gear for myself."

"Don't," said Kit. "At least not at first. You can cycle perfectly well in what you're wearing. Only buy some proper kit once you've decided you want to get serious about cycling. Otherwise you'll spend a lot of money on things that you'll never wear."

"Okay," I said, privately thinking that I didn't want the gear for the activity of cycling so much as to look cool whilst doing it.

We stopped at Cleulow and got the bikes out. The route that Kit chose went steeply uphill from the start. Of course, there was nowhere in that part of the world that didn't involve going uphill, but that first ascent was a killer. Still, when Kit stopped at the summit, the triumphant view made my petulant complaint die on my lips. I looked out over magnificently flowering gorse to a great, wild swathe of countryside. To one side was the higher, conical hill of Shutlingsloe, and to the other the flatness of the Cheshire plain. The broken cloud dappled the countryside with patches of light and shade. I took out my camera and looked through the viewfinder. At one remove, like this, the landscape still retained its wild beauty, and I took several shots, two including Kit – the first of him poised on his bike like a *Tour de France* competitor at the starting line, and the second, a close up of him turned slightly away, his eyes half closed, which I thought captured his mysterious beauty extremely well.

The whole afternoon had a magical quality to it. Despite the fact that I wasn't nearly as fit as Kit and found myself flagging several times, I had an odd sense of revelation that came back again and again – that cycling was *my* sport. It hadn't felt this way when I'd come out with Kit two years before, but this time the feeling of synergy between my body and the bicycle I was riding was extraordinary. The way in which I could power on through a landscape, or idle along looking around me, was wonderful. Kit's own enthusiasm was infectious, too, and his laughter touched something in me that responded with a curious exhilaration.

When we arrived back at Cleulow, dusk was falling. Kit put the bikes in the back of the car, but instead of getting in, he said, "Here, I want to show you something. It's not far."

We walked along the main road for a couple of hundred metres, then climbed over a fence and up a short incline. There was a knoll covered with mature beech trees through which we climbed, our way hampered by the twisted roots of the trees, dusted with the husks of last year's beech nuts. It was darker under the trees, even though their branches were almost bare, and as we neared the top I could see – absolutely black in silhouette against the sky – a roughly hewn standing stone set on a step-like plinth.

"It's marked as a cross on the map," said Kit, "but it's not, is it?"

I went up to it and placed my hand on the cold, uneven surface.

"No. I wonder how old it is, and who put it here – and for what purpose."

Kit came up beside me.

"It doesn't matter who put it here," he whispered, "or why. Our purpose is to look for the manifestation of the other-worldly. To look at it and feel... stillness."

I shivered at his words and was about to ask what he meant by 'other-worldly', but he turned away and began to make his way downwards through the gathering darkness.

In the car, I decided that I had to say something about the fact that I was gay. I felt I had to clear it up. Not so that I could confess my attraction towards him – or at least not only or primarily for that reason – but because I didn't see how we could continue our friendship without him knowing. Also, I needed to know if he was gay, too. Normally, I could tell these things, but Kit's strange sensuality wasn't obviously one thing or another.

"Look," I said as we set off, "there's something I've got to tell you."

Kit looked at me with an amused glance.

"Yes. Yes, I know," he said, but not dismissively. "You're gay. And you want to know if I am, too."

He laughed at my surprise, and patted my knee.

"I know you'll say I'm mind-reading again, but I'd hardly call it that this time. You'd have to be totally insensitive not to realise that those questions were in the air."

I was embarrassed, but pleased that I didn't have to explain further.

"And are you?" I asked.

"I suppose in some ways you might say that I am."

It was my turn to laugh this time.

"Whatever *that* means." I turned to look at him. "I knew you wouldn't give a straight answer to a direct question. It's not your style, is it?"

He shrugged and smiled his secretive smile, and continued to drive.

I tried to work out what he'd meant, but in the end it didn't matter. The important thing was that he wasn't 100% straight. However obliquely he might like to refer to his sexuality, that was all I needed to know.

"Have you ever been to a gay bar?" I asked.

"Yes. Have you?"

"No."

"Would you like to?"

I smiled.

"Do you think I'd get into one without ID?"

He switched on the internal light and inspected me carefully. I felt a flush of embarrassment creeping up my neck, and the stirrings of an erection.

"You'd be fine," he said, clicking off the light and looking back at the road. The beams of the headlights seemed to cocoon us, somehow, in the confined interior of the car. "Look," he continued, "I've got to go into Manchester in a couple of weeks' time. Why don't you come in with me and we could have a wander through the gay village?"

"Are you sure?"

"Of course."

"Wow! I mean, that's great."

"Okay, then. It's a deal. I'll be leaving after lunch, so it won't be an early start.

We lapsed into silence for a while and I thought, *It really is beginning. My life really is beginning.* Kit hummed something that I couldn't quite catch, and the timbre of his voice reminded me of choir practice.

"Anne Grehan says that a lot of the teachers don't like you," I said at last, to break the warm silence. "Particularly Mr Evans, who thinks you don't respect authority."

"Mr Evans doesn't like the fact that I don't respect *him*," Kit answered. "But teachers are human beings like anyone else, and therefore have to earn respect rather than assume it. It's not a divine right. Take Mrs Hodson, for example. Now, there's a teacher I thoroughly respect. When she was teaching us GCSE English, she was so *enthusiastic* about her subject. She worked hard to make it interesting to everyone, and she never gave up on people; she took time to praise people and time to help anyone who was struggling. Mr Evans, on the other hand, lacks patience and resorts to sarcasm as a means of humiliation. Why *should* I respect him?"

The next day I bought myself a bicycle. Dad drove me into Hanley, and I rode it back. I bought the bike itself, and he bought me the mud-guards, D-lock and lights. Despite being stiff and saddle-sore from the previous day, it was fantastic to be out on the road again.

It was a sunny morning and I felt light-hearted as I rode, although I could hardly walk by the time I got home.

I didn't see Kit for several days after that, which was a shame because I was keen to talk about my bike and to arrange to go out for a ride with him again. Still, I had Manchester to look forward to, and I was going to see him at the rehearsal on Thursday.

But he didn't turn up.

When she arrived, Anne came over to me and patted my shoulder.

"You look positively lovelorn," she said. "But you'll have to get used to it. Kit's dropped out of the choir."

"Oh," I said. "How do you know?"

"I heard Mr Evans mentioning it. He was visibly pleased."

And that was that. I felt supremely disappointed. Even throwing myself into the singing didn't help. *At least he could have told me,* I thought. I didn't know when was I next going to see him. We hadn't made definite arrangements for Manchester, and it felt as though it was all slipping from my grasp.

As I listened to Mr Evans talking us through the pieces, I kept thinking of what Kit had said the previous week about Judas, and about how there are other ways of looking at things than the standard interpretation. Well, there were certainly other ways of looking at Mr Evans. I hadn't previously thought much about his way of doing things, but now I focussed on him, I realised that Kit was right. He did get pleasure out of humiliating those who weren't particularly talented. I had avoided his withering remarks and petty jibes because my voice was good. But singing was supposed to be a pleasure, and it annoyed me to think that he had turned it into something that one could fail at.

As if to prove my point, a few minutes later he stopped the rehearsal.

"Alright, alright!" he yelled, "Stop there. This piece is supposed to be about *passion*, the passion of Our Lord. We're not singing the telephone directory, Jonathan, so do *try* to put some feeling into it, if you're capable of such a thing. I assume you *are* capable of passion?" He shook his head dismissively. "No, well, perhaps not. Just imagine something intense but basic, then, like hunger. At least that has an emotional undercurrent to it. Even you should be capable of that, hmm?"

He harassed various other people for a while, and I drifted off into a reverie of my own. When I next tuned in to him, I realised that he was talking about Judas.

"Betrayal is one of the worst things a person can do to another person. And Judas didn't betray just any old person, he did it to the Son of God. He paid the price, of course. Man's conscience is a God-given leveller. When Judas thought about what he'd done, he passed sentence on himself and condemned himself to death – a fitting penalty for an action of such enormity. Think for a moment about how Jesus must have felt at that moment. At the moment of betrayal. There was still so much work to be done, and suddenly, to have it snatched away..."

"But," I said, "Judas *enabled* Jesus to make the ultimate sacrifice. Without the betrayal, trial and crucifixion, there's no centrepiece to Christianity, is there? No focus. Judas gave Jesus the chance to do what he knew he had to do."

"Shut up, Greg," he said. "I don't expect to hear you spouting that kind of garbage. If you start on the 'If good comes from bad, then the bad must be good too' argument, you're just playing into the hands of the Devil."

"All I meant was that it's not as black and white as you're making out."

"It *is*," he said, pausing to take a breath. "Okay, Judas was a human being and what he did was human, but it was also evil, and evil grew from it, and he was fully responsible for *that*."

Mr Evans' devout religious zeal was sparked, and I could see an evangelical fire flickering in his eyes.

"But Jesus *prophesied* Judas's betrayal, just as he *knew* that Peter would deny him three times," I said. "Jesus knew. It was all pre-ordained. He knew that he was in danger of arrest, but he still went to the Garden of Gethsemane and deliberately put himself into danger. He allowed himself to be arrested without resistance – even Pontius Pilate gave him a get-out, which he refused to take. This means that Jesus walked into his martyrdom with his eyes open. He *made* it happen. He *needed* Judas to betray him, so therefore Judas was serving a divine purpose, for which he should be respected."

"Now *that*," Mr Evans said with disdain, "is something I would have expected to hear from a troublemaker like Kit Stephens, rather than you, Greg. You haven't been associating with him have you? I noticed that you two looked very... friendly, last week. I'd advise against it. He's full of wilfully non-conformist ideas – disagreeing for the sake of disagreement rather than from a genuine desire for knowledge. It's extremely unhealthy in a boy of his age." He paused. "And of course, there are certain other things about him that are unhealthy, too." There was general smirking laughter from various quarters in the room. "Whilst I see that some of his ideas may have rubbed off on you," he went on, "I hope that none of the other comes with it. We don't want you gaining any sordid little habits."

"That's it. I'm not going back," I said to Anne, as we sat drinking a pint in The Bishop. "He can do without me."

"Oh, don't take it so personally, Greg," she said. "Mr Evans is just one of those older generation homophobes. Those ideas are one hundred percent disposable, and everyone knows it – like when the headmaster says that smoking grass is as bad as taking heroin. You know it's rubbish and you ignore it."

"If only everyone *did* think it was rubbish. I mean, you your-self said that I shouldn't let people know that I fancy Kit. If there wasn't homophobia amongst pupils, it wouldn't matter, would it?"

"It *doesn't* matter," she said. "Most people suspect you're gay, anyway. But you get away with it because you're not obvious about it. Whereas Kit wanders round looking so fey and superior. *That's* what gets people's backs up. So long as you stay low-key—"

"Oh, great," I said. "You mean it's fine, so long as I'm not open about it."

She shrugged.

"That's like saying it's okay to be black, so long as you don't speak with a West Indian accent."

"I still think it's no big deal," she said. "I mean, sure you'd get a bit of hassle if you came out. But everyone gets hassled for standing out from the crowd. You'd get the piss taken out of you if you suddenly put on two stone. It's the same thing. It's petty, mean-minded and ignorant, but it's not worth losing sleep over."

"That's easy for you to say," I told her. "You've never been the brunt for that kind of piss-taking."

"And neither have you."

"No."

"If you were ten or twelve, Greg, I wouldn't say what I've just said. But we're young adults now. We know that the world is full of people who are stupid and prejudiced. We're old enough to go on being ourselves in spite of that. Mockery and bullying in childhood can be disastrous, but to be shunned by ignorant people – well, it's a plus in a way. If they avoid you, then you don't have to bother avoiding them."

"That's true," I said.

She clinked glasses with me and laughed. I looked around the bar. There were perhaps a dozen other people in the room and the buzz of conversation was comforting; homely.

"I think I'm falling in love with him," I said.

"I know," she said. "But be careful. I think he's gorgeous, but if he were to ask me for a date, I'd say no. I'd be thinking of all those stories about him. You could never have an ordinary relationship with someone like Kit, could you?"

"I suppose not."

I pondered this for a while.

"But then," I added, "maybe I wouldn't *want* an ordinary relationship. With anyone."

Seven

The following day I delivered a note to Mr Evans saying that, due to the pressure of exam revision, I'd decided to give the choir a miss. He, in turn, sent me a message demanding that I see him at lunch time on Monday.

"I don't know why you took our little *contretemps* on Thursday to heart, Greg," he said as we stood in the dingy corridor outside the staff room. "There's no point in sulking. It's childish."

"I've got a lot of revision," I told him.

"No you haven't," he said. "In Kit's case, his 'A' levels are coming up, and whilst I don't believe for a moment that's the reason why he left, at least it's a vaguely plausible excuse. But as for you... I've asked around, and it's clear that you're going to do effortlessly well in your GCSEs. So don't try to use revision as an excuse, especially this early on."

I shrugged and looked down.

"Okay," he said, "I want either a proper explanation of why you don't want to continue in the choir, or I want you to be there for our next rehearsal on Thursday."

I looked at him, irritated by his headstrong 'I always get what I want' expression, and a profound antipathy towards him welled up inside me.

"It's not the Judas thing," I told him. "It's something else."

"What?"

I held his glance for a moment, but he looked away almost immediately.

"And please don't give me an 'I'd rather not say'," he sneered, "or I really will accuse you of being childish."

I was dithering in a 'shall I say it, or shan't I?' limbo. On one hand, I did love singing, and dropping out of the choir could be seen as an expensive gesture. But then I thought of Kit and what he would have done, and I knew that he would have stuck absolutely to his principles.

"I've decided to drop out," I said, "because I found your homophobic remarks offensive."

"I'm sorry?" he said, surprised. "*Homophobic?* We were discussing Judas, Greg, not homosexuality."

"You said that there was something unhealthy about Kit Stevens – clearly referring to the rumours that he's gay – and you warned me to be careful not to develop any 'sordid little habits'. I found that offensive."

"Oh, for goodness sake, Greg, that was a joke. You do know what a joke is?"

"Yes," I said, "a joke is meant to be funny. Not derision intended to arouse hatred."

Mr Evans snorted in irritation. "Is that what you think? That I want people to hate you and Kit, just because there are rumours that you're both gay?"

"Yes. That, and the fact that you dislike Kit personally."

"Really, Greg, I can hardly believe I'm hearing this. It doesn't bother me whether either or both of you are gay."

"Well, I *am* gay," I said, "and I resent teachers who spout homophobic rubbish. We're here to be educated, not to be exposed to hatred and intolerance."

I was amazed, and also a little scared, by my nerve. Insubordination on this scale could have serious repercussions, but I couldn't stop myself. The conversation had gone out of control. Mr Evans had begun to look explosively furious, his face mottled and clammy, but he responded in an uncannily calm voice.

"Look, Greg, this conversation is pointless," he said. "Your homosexuality makes no difference. Alright, so I dislike homosexuality. I've never made a secret of that. I think homosexual acts are a sin. I also think sex outside marriage is a sin. But this is because I believe in the fundamental truths of Christianity and it's a part of my faith. Nevertheless, I accept that these things happen amongst the pupils and that it's not my place to interfere or to try and stop it. You would all do what you wanted whatever I said, anyway, wouldn't you?"

He sighed with exasperation.

"The point here," he said, "is not whether you're gay, but that we need you for the choir. You and Kit have the best tenor voices in the school. Losing Kit was bad enough, but if you go, too..."

He paused to contemplate this for a moment.

"Look, let's make a deal. You continue with rehearsals, and I promise I won't say anything homophobic – about you, Kit, or anyone else. Alright? Don't leave simply out of adolescent pique. If you don't want to sing for me, then sing for yourself. Sing for the school. Sing because your voice makes a real difference. Sing because it will bring pleasure to others."

It wasn't much of a victory, but it was something. I was pleased to see him back down, to whatever small extent, and having faced his own homophobia, perhaps he would think a bit more carefully about his prejudices in future.

"Alright," I said. "I'll be there on Thursday."

"Good," he said.

On Thursday, mum packed me some extra sandwiches, as I was staying on late, and I sat on my own to eat them in the late afternoon sun. Afterwards, I made my way to the hall, and at once noticed the excited buzz all around me. This was to be our first rehearsal with the orchestra, and everywhere were the sounds of instruments being tuned and warmed up, which gave me a surge of adrenaline. Anne came up to me as soon as I walked through the door.

"I thought you'd dropped out?" she said.

"I did, but Mr Evans persuaded me to stay. He came as near to giving an apology as he's capable."

"Good, I'm glad," she said. "I was beginning to regard our after-choir pint as a regular thing. There's no one else here I'd want to go pubbing with."

"That's the only reason you wanted me to stay?"

"Of course," she laughed.

Mr Evans came in, and the obligatory hush fell on the room. We grouped ourselves around the orchestra and he sat down at the piano. After some preliminary directions to the musicians, he looked down at the keys beneath his hands for a moment and then stood up again. He walked to the centre of the room with his arms folded, and all eyes were upon him.

"Before we start," he said, "I'd like to make an announcement."

Anne glanced at me questioningly and I shrugged back at her.

"There has been a suggestion made to me that I am homophobic," he said. "I would like to say something about that, to you all, so that we can be clear where I stand on this. Yes, I dislike homosexuality; yes, the thought of it makes my skin crawl, and yes, I would rather it didn't exist. But it does exist and there is nothing I can do about it. However – and I want to make this absolutely clear – if a pupil at this school is homosexual, I absolutely defend their right to be here and to continue with their education. They are human beings like every one else, and should be respected as such, no matter what we privately think of their morality. The fact that Greg Chaley is homosexual is a great disappointment to me, because I fear that his life will be blighted by it, but that doesn't mean that I would ever condone any kind of persecution of him. If I ever see this happen, or hear of it happening, I will make sure that it is dealt with severely. Do you understand?"

There was utter silence in the room. He looked at me directly for the first time.

"It is for God to pass judgement on Greg, and not anyone in this room... Now, let's get on with the rehearsal."

Throughout Mr Evans' speech, I had felt paralysed with shock. Now that he turned away from me, my breath came out in a gasp of anger. Anne leaned over and grabbed my arm to reassure me. But I couldn't stay in a room with someone who professed acceptance, whilst actually encouraging precisely the kind of hatred that he was pretending to disapprove of, by so blatantly outing me. I stood up, still speechless. Mr Evans was flicking through his music and pretended not to notice as I left the room. As I closed the door behind me, I heard a sudden explosion of astonished conversation, followed swiftly by Mr Evans' raised voice trying to quieten things down.

When I got home, I made my excuses to mum, then jumped on my bike and cycled over to Kit's house. I was seething to such an extent that I couldn't remain still, and pumping away at the pedals was a relief after the dreadful physical agitation of sitting on the bus. What a bastard. What he'd done was clever, of course – pretending to forbid homophobic attacks on me, whilst actually using the occasion to both out me and to condemn homosexuality. Clever. And hateful.

Kit answered the door when I rang the bell and said, "Let's go up to my room, where we can talk privately."

The long, dark hall had shiny wooden flooring strewn with red and black rugs. The stairs were shallow and the banister was wide and well-polished. Kit's bedroom was long and relatively narrow, with a bed at one end, and a desk and bookshelves making up a kind of enclave at the other. There was an office chair at the desk, which

Kit sat on, and an arm chair by the window which he indicated for me. I dropped into it and explained to him what had happened.

Kit contemplated what I'd told him for some time before saying anything.

"Don't hate him for this," Kit told me. "Hate is such a destructive emotion. Hate is reflected back deep into the psyche of the person who hates. It rebounds on itself. Also, it can..." He paused, as though thinking better of what he was about to say.

"Also what?"

"No, it's okay."

"Come on, Kit, don't do this to me."

He looked at me for a long time, searchingly.

"What I was going to say," he said slowly, "is don't... project any of your hate onto him. Don't release any of your destructive energy in his direction. Don't wish him harm."

"But I *do* wish him harm," I said vehemently. "I hope he breaks his fucking fingers. I can't help it."

"You *can* help it," he said. "And besides, being outed to the rest of the school isn't that bad. It's hardly going to be a surprise. There have already been enough rumours, haven't there? What difference will it make if people actually know?"

"Don't be naive," I said. "People are much less likely to react to a rumour than to a fact."

"That's not necessarily true," Kit said.

"And there are boys in my year who will feel *obliged* to react to it, now. Which Mr Evans knows as well as anyone else."

"That may be true," Kit admitted with a small nod. He looked at me carefully. "Then you're going to have to learn to protect yourself, aren't you?"

"What, take up karate or kung-fu?"

"No."

Kit stood up and moved behind my armchair. He rested a hand on my shoulder.

"I think," he said, "it's time I told you one or two things."

I felt a shiver race up my spine as he said this. He let go of my shoulder and went back to sit at his desk. He was clearly wondering how to start.

"Do you know anything about meditation?" he asked eventually.

"A little," I said. "I mean, I know roughly what it is, though I've never tried it."

"One of the basics of meditation is that you empty your mind of the restricting preoccupations of everyday life," he said. "That, obviously, is an over simplification, but in essence it's true."

"And you practice meditation?"

"Yes. But I also practice something else which is like meditation, but different. It's a way of focusing the mind on things, to make them happen. It's a kind of distraction, in a way, from the real purpose of meditation and so I don't use it that often, but it can be very helpful under certain circumstances."

"Such as?"

"Such as protecting yourself from bullying."

"I'm not sure I understand."

"What I can do," he said, "is give you a few simple breathing exercises to help empty your mind, and then a protective visualisation."

I smiled.

"You're going to teach me one of your secret powers!"

"This isn't a joke," he said, "I'm deadly serious."

I tried to calm my thumping heart. I thought back to the mind-reading episode of two years before, and the stories that Anne had told me, and felt suddenly breathless.

"I know it isn't a joke," I said. "I'm sorry."

"Now," Kit went on, "the first thing to impress on you is the need for absolute secrecy. It's not a question of being part of a secret sect, or of trying to encourage the formation of an elite. It's just that some people have this ability and some people don't."

"And you think I have this... ability?"

"I *know* you have it," he said quietly. "That's why I came and talked to you that day when you were being bullied, back in Horton."

I found this difficult to take in.

"What kind of *ability* are you talking about?" I asked.

"I don't want to go into that right now," he said, "there isn't time. What I want to do is teach you a useful visualisation."

The breathing technique was straightforward as far as the mechanics went (though the act of calming the mind was easier said than done). The visualisation was simple, too. It had two parts: firstly, I had to visualise a cool, blue light coming down and encircling me, forming a protective barrier between me and anything I might feel threatened by; and secondly, if there was an individual who was potentially going to be troublesome, I had to close my eyes and visualise that person standing alone, facing me, on a great, flat plane that was empty apart from a long staircase that ascended straight up into the heart of the sun. Then I had to smile at them, wish them well, and make them turn around and walk slowly up the staircase and into the sun.

"You protect yourself by giving a gift of love," Kit told me. "Hatred works too, but it will hurt you at least as much as the person you are trying to protect yourself from."

It felt strange, cycling home in the dark. I navigated almost by memory and rode slowly, as the frail beam from my light was hardly of any use at all. The visualisation that Kit had made me practice had the curious effect of making me feel that the only light was the imagined sunlight in my head. I didn't know what to make of what he'd told me – that I had some sort of unspecified *ability*. It was a strangely thrilling concept, though part of me wanted to just laugh and disparage it as ridiculous.

By the time I got home, I found that my agitation had ceased and, when I went to bed, I fell asleep immediately.

The following day, Anne came up to me after assembly.

"Greg," she said, "I couldn't *believe* what Mr Evans said to you last night. I was furious. And not just me, several of the other girls were, too. We've decided to get a petition together to take to the headmaster, demanding a public apology from Mr Evans, and a statement about the school's attitude towards homosexuality."

"Well," I smiled, "I'm impressed."

"When I got home last night," she said, "I kept remembering the shit my brother went through when he was here."

Anne was joined by a couple of other girls who said they'd already signed Anne's petition. It was heartening, but I still practiced Kit's exercise, in which I visualised Brian Hogarty walking up a staircase into the sun. Of all the boys who were in a position to make my life hell, he was the one I suspected would be the worst.

As I came into my class, a hush fell on the room. I ignored it and went to my desk. After a few moments, Brian Hogarty broke away from the group of boys that he was talking to and walked over to me.

"Hey, Greg," he said and sat on the corner of my desk.

"Hello Brian."

"So, Anne's got this petition, then?"

"As far as I know."

"About Mr Evans calling you queer last night."

"Well..."

"And are you?"

I looked him straight in the eyes.

"Yes."

He shrugged.

"Anne, hand me your piece of paper. I'll sign it. Richard Murray and the lads think you're okay, Greg, and personally, I'd like to see Mr Evans get whatever's coming to him. I hate the bastard."

He took the petition from Anne and signed it, then handed it on to one of the other boys.

"Just remember one thing, Greg," he said. "Leave *my* arse alone, okay?"

There were a few sniggers.

"I don't mind what you get up to with Kit Stephens, but please, do it behind closed doors so that none of us have to even *think* about it."

Brian wandered back to his desk and sat down. In his way, of course, he was just as bad as Mr Evans – signing the petition in an act of apparent liberalism, just because he'd succumbed to peer pressure, whilst actually sneering at my homosexuality. But it was better than being beaten up by him.

I expect Kit would have said that this signing of the petition was a result of the visualisation I'd done. All I could say was that it was the one outcome I would *never* have predicted.

At lunch time, Anne came over to say that everyone in my class had signed the petition, but that substantially less than 50% of the other pupils she'd asked had done so. A lot had said they would think about it, which we both knew amounted to a guilty 'no'. When I sat down to eat my lunch, I noticed an odd buzz of interested conversation. I began to realise that it was centred around me, and that people were glancing over to me as they spoke. I began to feel more and more self conscious, and wondered if this was how life was going to be from now on. I was surprised when Kit came over.

"Greg, can we talk? Outside," he said, his voice strangely tense.

I got up and followed him out, and a strange feeling of emptiness crept into my stomach. There were a few whistles and one or two murmurs of 'fucking queers', but mostly there was an odd, almost sinister silence.

"What was that? Everyone was acting so weird." I said once we were outside.

"You haven't heard about Mr Evans?"

"No." I felt suspended in mid-air.

Kit began to walk over towards the basketball court.

"He was in a car accident on his way home from rehearsals last night. He's in hospital with head injuries and a smashed arm."

I stopped dead and stared at Kit, my mind in turmoil.

"Arm?"

"Yes. Apparently his right arm was broken in two places and his fingers have been crushed so badly that a couple of them might have to be amputated."

"Oh, no," I said, the horror dawning on me. "That's what I *wished* on him last night. I wished that he'd break his fingers…"

I sat down on the low wall beside us and stared down at my feet. There was a sense of complete unreality about what Kit had just told me. But behind the unreality, there was a sense of my own culpability.

"I did it," I said to Kit. "I did it, didn't I?"

Kit didn't answer.

"That's what you were telling me last night, wasn't it, when you told me not to release any of my destructive energy? You knew that something like this might happen if I focused my anger on Mr Evans."

Kit sat beside me and looked out into the distance.

"You can't blame yourself for this, Greg," he said. "If anyone's to blame, it's me, for not realising how strongly you could direct your… energy."

"But you do think there's a connection between me wishing that Mr Evans would break his fingers and him actually breaking his fingers?"

"Yes. Don't you?"

Although my thoughts seemed chaotic and irrational, some curiously detached part of me was adding and collating information and concluding that this was the case. It was the part of me that had been alerted at the time of the Neil Braithwaite episode, the part that had realised some kind of power was involved. My rational self was still far from able to accept anything as outlandish as the fact that I could wish harm on people, but my irrational self realised that it was simply – though in a way that I had yet to understand – an extension of my connection with Kit.

Kit sighed.

"Let's say," I said, "let's say I *did* do this... then it's unforgivable, isn't it? I mean, absolutely unforgivable. If I went up to someone and maliciously caused them head injuries, and broke their arm and fingers in a fight, I'd be thrown out of school, and probably get prosecuted by the police. And rightly so. It's appalling behaviour. Even someone like Brian Hogarty would never be as violent as that."

I buried my face in my hands at the horror of what had happened.

"No, no," Kit said, "you've got it wrong. Lots of people wish harm on others; it happens all the time. What about the people who called us fucking queers when we left the dining hall a moment ago? The thing is that people do it without ever thinking that anything will happen as a result of those thoughts. Would you have wished for Mr Evans to have an accident if you had thought it might actually happen?"

"No, of course not."

"Exactly. So you can't blame yourself. It happened because you have certain... energies... that you haven't yet learned to control. Now that you know there's this possibility, you'll never do it again."

"But it's never happened before," I said. "Why should it suddenly happen now?"

"It's never happened *as far as you know*," said Kit, "although actually, I agree. I think it's unlikely to have happened before. If you're going to have these powers, they generally appear during or just after adolescence."

I took a deep breath and tried to steady my thoughts. I felt absolutely cursed, and was seized by an awful panic.

"Okay. Okay," I said, "so, if you're right, what does this mean for the future? Do I have to spend my time trying not to think anything bad, just in case it happens?"

"No," Kit said with a smile. "This was a kind of anomaly born of inexperience. Once you've learned to control your emotions, particularly your negative ones, then you'll be fine."

"I don't want this," I said. "If this is the kind of difference that you've got, then I don't want it."

"I'm afraid you have no choice."

I turned away from him, angry, humiliated. It was difficult enough to try and sort out what I thought about everyone knowing I was gay. But this? And, anyway, maybe Kit was wrong. Or maybe he had an agenda of his own? Hadn't he told me not to take things at face value? Coincidences happen; they happen all the time. There was no reason why I should have had *anything* to do with Mr Evans' accident.

But in my heart, I knew I had, just as I had known that Brian Hogarty's behaviour in class had been influenced by my visualisation. I had performed some kind of magic. I shuddered. What had previously seemed awesome in Kit, now seemed terrible in me.

"Listen," Kit said, putting his arm round my shoulder. "I felt like this, too. I felt as though I'd been cursed. But it's not a curse, Greg, it's a blessing. When I realised what I was—"

"But I *don't* know what I am," I said, turning angrily back to him. "None of it makes sense to me at all."

"It will," he assured me.

A bell warbled in the distance, signalling the end of the lunch break.

"Sod it, we've got to get back," Kit said. "Look, don't dwell on these things too much. You'll feel calmer in a few days' time."

With that he strode off, but turned back after a few paces.

"And don't forget Manchester tomorrow."

I watched him recede, walking with such assurance, and felt more confused than I had ever felt before. Our planned trip to

Manchester – which had loomed so large a few days earlier – seemed futile, insignificant, now.

Back in the classroom, Anne looked as though she never wanted to talk to me again, but she came over, hesitantly.

"Under the circumstances," she said, "we've decided to abandon the petition. I think Mr Evans has suffered enough."

"Quite."

She turned and was about to return to her desk, but she stopped herself and came back to me. Leaning over, she spoke in a whisper.

"You're like Kit, aren't you? It's not just that you're gay. It's something else as well."

She sighed, and looked down at her nails, her hair swishing forward as she did so.

"I *told* you to be careful of Kit, didn't I? There's something wrong in all this. Terribly wrong. And I'm worried that you'll get caught up in it and chewed up by it. You haven't got the same kind of strength as Kit. That arrogance. You'll end up getting hurt, like Mr Evans. Or worse."

I thought about that on the way home. *Did* I believe that there were strange forces that I could key into? How could I know for sure? But suppose, *suppose* there were... Then Kit was my only hope. He was the one who'd told me not to direct anger at people, but to give out love instead. That didn't seem bad. If I had some kind of *energy*, then surely he was the person who could teach me the right way to deal with it? If I ignored it, and gave up on Kit, what would happen then? Would I inadvertently spray out harm from time to time, whenever I was annoyed with someone?

Eight

That night I didn't sleep. I had cyclic thoughts about Mr Evans, imagining him lying there in his hospital bed, his head bound up with bandages, mummy-like, and I felt dreadful. I wanted to apologise to him, somehow, but knew that I never could because it would mean saying something like 'I have a power', and outside the parameters of what I knew, it sounded utterly ridiculous. Instead, I made up a visualisation and, like the blue-glow of protection that Kit had described to me the day before, I visualised a golden glow of healing. I visualised Mr Evans on a great, pale plane, with soft sunlight above, and a long staircase leading up into a silver light, like the light above an operating table – a clear, bright, angular, surgically clean light – and I visualised him, suffused by the golden sunlight, walking slowly up the stairs and into the prismatic light that would reconstruct him. Whether or not this would help, I didn't know. But it was worth a try. If there was energy to destroy, then there must also be energy to rebuild. There must be. But remorse, and a desire to put things right, didn't seem to have the same lightning-bolt intensity that comes with flashes of hatred like the one I'd had the evening before.

I kept it up for a while, but soon my mind felt sapped of energy and I no longer had the ability to conjure the imagery I wanted. I fell back to thinking about Kit. Although on one hand I could see him in a positive role, inasmuch as I genuinely believed that he wanted to help me, on the other hand, I had a deep and growing conviction that none of this would have happened if I'd never met him in the first place. He had somehow pulled this power in me up to the surface, like a magnet, simply by being in my presence. If he hadn't come over to me that day when I was so upset about the mess I'd got into with Neil Braithwaite, then none of this would have happened. And what *had* he done to Neil Braithwaite, anyway? I suddenly felt cold inside as I recalled the rumour of nervous breakdown. Had Kit focussed ill will on Neil and made him detonate mentally? The thought was deeply disturbing. But, there again, Kit had saved me from a situation that was leading towards a crisis. It would be ungrateful to forget what a relief it had been to be free of Neil's unwanted attention.

And then, on a different level, there was the fact that I fancied him; wondered whether I was falling in love with him. But how could I proceed if I was also growing scared of him?

It was all far too complicated.

Part of me decided not to go to Manchester with Kit, to keep my distance from him; and part of me realised that I could only work this confusion out by talking it through with him. And yet another part of me was pissed off because tomorrow was supposed to be a *fun* day out. Fun? *You don't deserve fun after what you've done to Mr Evans,* I thought. *You don't deserve to ever have fun again.*

In the morning, I realised that I'd re-entered the strange, uncomfortable place that I'd inhabited when I was being terrorised by Neil Braithwaite. I felt as though the world had closed in around me; that I'd been cut off from my stable, ordinary life once more. My family seemed to rub my 'otherness' in by being their usual Saturday morning selves – cheerful, lazy, *simple*. And yet... and yet – though this is a terrible thing to admit, and something that I am not proud of – I also felt a kind of despicable superiority to them. At least something *important* was happening in my life,

something with *scale*. I shuddered with disgust at myself for thinking like this, but I couldn't completely banish the feeling.

Later, after lunch, dad offered to give me a lift over to Kit's on
his way to do a small carpentry job in Leek.

"No thanks, dad," I said. "I'll bike it. I'd rather get the exercise."

He smiled and nodded, and as he left I realised that this was the
sort of job that, in the past, I would have volunteered to do. I
realised, too, that dad had never uttered a word of complaint
about the way in which I'd suddenly lost interest in carpentry, but
had offered, instead, to go miles out of his way to deliver me to a
friend. *He wouldn't be so pleased to help,* I thought, *if he knew the
truth about me.* And I suddenly felt a huge, yearning love for him
that I knew I could never fully express.

Fighting waves of self-pity, I cycled over to Kit, dreading the
conversation that I knew we must have. I was getting fitter and fitter and, though the action of cycling over the moor to Kit's house
flushed my body with vitality, the rest of me felt sluggish where
before it would have felt scoured.

The weather belied my inner mood. A thrush was singing in
the beech trees by the gate as I turned into the courtyard, and even
the shade of the dark pines at the back of the house looked cheerful. Kit was already out on the front step, looking ridiculously
composed and well-groomed, in black jeans and a dark, thick,
well-tailored shirt.

"Hi," he said. "Give me your bike, and I'll put it in the hall.
And then we can go."

It seemed incredible that Manchester was only thirty miles
away. I felt as if I was going abroad. I couldn't feel any enthusiasm
for the gay side of the trip, given the events of the day before, but
I recognised that in a way it was something that had to be done,
to be got over – like losing one's virginity – so that subsequent visits would have the comfort of familiarity. Even though I'd known
I was gay for years, I had still never been to a gay establishment –

a gay shop or café, let alone a gay bar. It was time, too, that I famil-
iarised myself with the city. Although I was brought up in London,
I left when I was twelve and so there had been no sense of adult
attraction about the place. Now, Manchester seemed like The
Metropolis in many ways, not just gay.

I'd told my parents that we were having dinner up there with
a relative of Kit's, and I wasn't expected back until midnight. So we
had plenty of time for talk. Even so, I felt I had to get on with it
straight away.

"I felt so bad last night, I hardly slept at all," I told Kit as we set
off. "I kept doing visualisations to try and help Mr Evans."

"I didn't go to bed at all," said Kit. "I was working on a very
specific visualisation for the same reason. What was yours?"

I described it – the golden light and the angular, surgically
sharp silver light, and Kit smiled.

"Well done," he said. "To have done that spontaneously, without being encouraged to do so, means that you won't be scarred
by this. I'm pleased."

I looked across at him as he concentrated on the road and I
could see from the shadows round his eyes that he was exhausted.

"Look," I said, "maybe we should call this trip off. Put it off
until a better time."

"I *have* to go," Kit said wearily. "But if you want me to take you
back, I will."

"No," I said, "if you're going, I'll come with you."

"Thanks," he said and smiled again, and I felt easier than I had
done since all the ghastliness blew up.

Easier, but not *at* ease. I watched the passing countryside for a
while.

"Tell me," I said. "What should I do now? What do I need to
know?"

"I've been thinking about that," said Kit. "It's difficult."

"What is?"

"When I first saw you," he said, "I noticed that you had a – for want of a better word – *quality* about you that I recognised as a potential that needed to be brought out. Nurtured, if you like. Usually it's quite clear, but in you there was something muddled, unfocussed. It's difficult to put into words, but normally I can tell quite clearly... it's not something obvious, like a facial characteristic or a mannerism—"

"You mean it's a bit like telling when someone is gay?"

Kit glanced across at me and laughed.

"Well, yes," he replied. "Actually, I think it's probably very like that. With gay people there are those who are obvious because they're stereotypes, or archetypes, and then there are those who conform to none of the standard clichés, but whom, even though you don't know why, you still recognise as gay. This is similarly intuitive."

I nodded. "Right. I get the gist of what you mean. But what *is* this quality?"

"I..." Kit paused and seemed to sidetrack my question by concentrating on his driving. Eventually, he glanced back at me with a sort of yearning look.

"I can't tell you, Greg," he said. "I'm sorry."

"You can't tell me?" I said, confused and frustrated. "Do you mean you don't *want* to tell me, or that you don't know?"

"Neither," he sighed. "But under the circumstances, I'm going to have to explain up to a point. Although I'm not quite sure where to start."

When he looked at me again I raised my eyebrows as if to say, 'Well, get on with it, then.' He nodded and gathered his thoughts.

"You know I mentioned meditation to you?"

"Yes."

"Meditation is a useful analogy for what I want to describe," he said. "There's a transformation that comes with the practice of meditation. You achieve an internal stillness, and an inner peace.

But that only comes with a lot of practice. Meditation brings immediate rewards in terms of stress relief, but further than that, progress can be slow. You have to keep on practicing, even though you might seem to get little or no extra reward. What must keep a person going is their faith that in time they will get much greater benefits. The same is true of this energy that you have. You have to learn to focus it – a learning process that isn't easy, or even linear in a one-rung-of-a-ladder-at-a-time way. I mean, that stunt you pulled with Mr Evans is an advanced thing to have done, which is why it took me so much by surprise. But, and this is a *huge* but – to know any more about your own energy is to largely defuse it. I can't tell you more because it will stop you in your tracks. The whole crux of the process of moving forward is that you must have a sense of mystery about what's going on."

"How can I fail to have a sense of mystery?" I asked. "I don't *know* anything."

"It is within that sense of mystery that your power lies," Kit told me. "I know it must be frustrating, and difficult to follow because I'm being so oblique. Maybe another analogy would help." He thought for a moment, and tapped the steering wheel with his pale fingers. "Okay. You know the feeling of suspense you get when you're watching a particularly engrossing film – one with a twist to it, like *The Usual Suspects*?"

"Yes."

"It's like that. The mystery only works because you don't know the ending. If someone told you the final twist just as you sat down to watch it, then there would be no suspense. Whilst it might still work in other ways, a part of it would have been ruined."

"I suppose so," I said, unconvinced.

"So, I can give you one or two exercises to stop you spraying out that kind of uncontrolled energy in future, but you have to trust me – have faith, if you like – that the rest of your journey needs to be, in many ways, a solitary a journey of self-discovery. Friends can help point you in the right direction, but they can't tell you where, or how, to move forward."

I thought about that for a while and, as we slowed into the stop-start traffic edging its way into Stockport, I felt a great sadness descend on me, as well as some of the worry that Anne had expressed to me the day before.

"But there is so much that can go wrong," I said. "It's too uncertain. I don't want to fuck myself up, and I don't want to fuck others up with me, like I did with Mr Evans."

"You're right to be worried," Kit told me, "and it's a legitimate worry. All I can say is that you have no choice. You can go home and pretend that you're just a normal schoolboy, getting on with a normal schoolboy's life, but you're not, and you know it. And sooner or later you'll have to confront these things about yourself. They will come to fruition whether you want them to or not. If you walk away from it now, you might have no one who can help you when the time comes."

I pondered that for a moment.

"And what is your role in all this?" I asked. "Are you my teacher, my *guru*, or what?"

"No," he smiled. "I can't really be that, though in other circumstances I might have made an attempt to take on that role."

"Why can't you?"

"Because..." he said hesitantly, braking for some traffic lights, "...because I find you too attractive."

Of all the things I might have expected him to say, I hadn't expected *that*.

"Oh," I said.

He faced directly ahead and said, "I'm afraid that when it comes to you, Greg, I'm not capable of impartiality. Which is what is required."

He looked at his watch. It was just coming up to three o'clock.

"Look," he said, "I know it's probably impossible, but try to put this business with Mr Evans out of your mind. I know how guilty you feel, but you're not going to help him by feeling bad. You made your apologies, indirectly but I'm sure extremely effectively, last night, and now you need to put it out of your mind or the rest of the day will be pointless."

We remained silent after that, each taken up with our own thoughts. There were brooding clouds gathering that threatened rain and soon the windscreen became spotted with drizzle. I watched the intermittent wipers streaking the moisture across the glass, and found myself holding my breath in the long gaps between sweeps.

We parked the car on a derelict piece of land that was being used as a temporary car park and walked across the cinders and broken bricks to an ornate, crumbling stone archway which gave onto the back of Piccadilly station. Part of me felt that I should be elated by what Kit had said about finding me attractive, but my emotions seemed to have collided head-on, somehow, and cancelled themselves out, so that I was beset by a strangely settled sense of calm. Kit looked calm, too, and far too adult and no-nonsense to be interested in someone like me.

The city centre was busy with cars, buses, and the slick new trams. And people – lots of people. I was pleased to be anonymous like this amongst all the bustle. We began by going to a second hand bookshop, walking down past Chorlton Street bus station, skirting the top of the gay village, and then on past the museum. We stopped at a rather grand building, and Kit explained that the bookshop he needed was in the basement; one of those places that smell of dust and old leather and where a lot of the books are locked behind glass. Kit was obviously expected because there was a small package there for him, ready-wrapped in brown paper as though awaiting postage. I browsed whilst he chatted to the man for a while, and then he came over to join me and we stood together, silently looking at all those titles. Before we left, he took two books from the paperback section and bought them, then handed them to me as we left.

"A present," he said.

I looked in the bag: two novels by Hermann Hesse.

"Food for thought," he said.

We headed over to HMV and then up to a second hand music shop where we idly bought ourselves some CDs from the bargain bins. After that we had a coffee in Café Pop and talked a bit about getting fit together out on our bikes. And then we went to buy me some cycling gear before the shops closed. I'd saved some money for this, and bought myself some Lycra shorts, a top, fingerless gloves, some shoes and a pair of cool sunglasses. By the time we got back to the car to drop our goods off, it was after six o'clock, and Kit suggested that we grab an early meal and then head into the village – a motion that I seconded with alacrity.

We went to one of those eat-as-much-as-you-like Indian places and sampled virtually everything. It felt as though I was out on a date with Kit, or something approximating that, and I kept looking at him, wondering if he was expecting to *do* something about the fact that he found me attractive. I was certainly not going to go home without finding out, and hoped that the ambience of the gay village would allow me to make a pass at him, or at least declare my intentions.

Even though we'd lingered as long as possible in the restaurant, and walked slowly over to the village, it wasn't even eight o'clock when we got there. The drizzle from earlier in the day had passed and a fresh, cool breeze was blowing along Canal Street. The lights reflecting from the black water of the canal seemed unbearably romantic to me, despite the clots of sodden rubbish and bobbing upturned bottles that lingered along the edges like warts. Canal Street was already getting busy and I thought to myself, *This is Life with a capital L.* Within as little as two or three years, I was to become healthily cynical about the gay scene and its so-called promise, but that night I felt acutely the tremulous thrill of my introduction to it, and it remains one of the most affirming moments of my life. I felt young, intelligent and *accepted*; I felt sexy, too, and desired. I took Kit's hand in mine as we wandered over the cobbles and into a vibrant bar for our first drink.

Sitting, surrounded by smiling, laughing gay people made me smile and laugh spontaneously, too. Kit caught some of my enthusiasm and laughed along with me about nothing in particular. He was softened here, more approachable. A little like the time we'd gone out with the bikes to Shutlingsloe. Something in the atmosphere, in the way we were separated from our ordinary environment, made him lose that air of unassailable maturity that so many people at school took for arrogance or aloofness.

We went from bar to bar. I bought half a pint in each, though after the first two, Kit drank orange juice because he was driving. I was wearing a tight-fitting tee-shirt and jeans and, cliché though I might have been, I felt wonderful, and lapped up the covert and not-so-covert looks that I got. Kit seemed oblivious to it all, but given that the only attention I'd ever got before, regarding my sexuality, had been quiet acceptance from the girls or sneers from the boys, to me it was a marvellous revelation.

By the time we reached Via Fossa, I was halfway drunk. The interior of the bar was all pulpits, pews and fancy panelling, and the sacramental feel to the place, the loud music and the buzz of bright conversation made me feel an exhilaration that I could barely contain. I exaggerated my drunkenness and used it to lean against Kit as we sat together on a wooden bench. I rested my head on his shoulder and he stroked my arm, letting his fingers trail down my forearm in a way that raised the hairs there as they passed.

I was going to kiss him at some point, and I was nearly drunk enough to do so, but as I finished the last of my beer, he beat me to it. It wasn't a lingering kiss and, though I opened my mouth hopefully, we barely touched tongues before we parted. But I felt the *frisson* of that kiss right the way though my body. Kit smiled a hooded smile and patted my hand and turned and said, "Maybe we should go."

I looked at my watch. It was just after eleven. I couldn't believe it. Three hours had passed in moments.

I nodded and we got up to leave. Outside it was more busy than ever. The evening was absolutely still now, which made it feel warmer than it actually was, and we meandered up past the chip shop by the depressing, grey concrete bays of Chorlton Street bus station, now busy with club-going men who smiled and jostled with each other, and called out, seemingly to no one in particular. And for the first time in my life I was drunk in a public place. And for the first time in my life I was with someone that I was falling in love with, and who I thought was so indescribably beautiful that it made me want to cry.

And then we were out of the gay village and, having crossed over a definite but invisible boundary, we found ourselves walking along just another dark, dirty, empty inner city street. A taxi ambled past us as though unsure of where it was going and I felt suddenly cold for the first time that evening, and shrugged my jacket more closely round my shoulders. I heard a noise of people behind us, but didn't register it any more than I registered the general city noises of traffic that echoed around us from the tall buildings amongst which we were passing. It was only when Kit grabbed my elbow that I realised they were angry voices, and when I turned, I could see that there were five or six young men approaching us, dressed in smartly pressed grey or black trousers and those baggy, pleated 'designer' leather jackets. Townies.

"Oi!" one of them shouted, breaking into a run. "Oi, you fuckin' benders, you've had it!"

"Run!" Kit shouted, and we sprinted off, an action which

caused inchoate yells behind us and the sound of a raucous, dishevelled chase. We hadn't gone more than a hundred metres when Kit yelled, "Down here!" and side-stepped into a narrow alley. It seemed madness to head away from the public arena of the main road ahead, but Kit had already done it and so I followed him, trusting that he knew where we were going. As soon as he'd rounded the corner – into a blind alley – he stopped. I bumped into him, nearly sending us both sprawling, and he grabbed my arm to stabilise us. We had only been a few metres ahead of our would-be attackers, and I felt a nightmarish lurch of panic at their approach.

The next two or three seconds seemed to happen in slow motion. Kit pulled me back against the wall and closed his eyes. The look of concentration that came over him was extraordinary, a sort of suspension of expression that, even in that frantic moment, I registered as bizarrely instantaneous. The effect on me was equally bizarre considering that my overwhelming instinct was to flee.

I froze.

The youths came piling into the mouth of the alley and stopped, only feet away from us, in confusion.

"Shit," said the first, "where the fuck did they go?"

The second one ran a few metres further along and tried the handle of a thick metal door, painted black but pitted with lighter patches of rust.

"They must have ducked into one of these doorways," he called, and kicked the door brutally as though he imagined it was one of us. He tried the next, too, even though it had a huge pad-lock and chain.

And, with that, the thrill of the chase left them. It was almost as if they were deflating, belittled by a confusion that left them physically smaller than they had been before they'd come after us. I stood, plainly in view, breath held. The lad who had kicked the door came back past me, a look of bewilderment on his face.

"Weird shit," he whispered to himself and joined his friends. There was some murmuring and scuffing of feet, and then they turned and sauntered off back down towards the bus station.

Kit opened his eyes and turned to me. He smiled a slightly lop-sided smile and his knees buckled as he reached out to steady himself. I jumped forward and caught him round the waist and he sagged against me for a moment before finding his balance. I still held on to him and he rested his head on my shoulder, and I kissed his forehead which had a patina of dampness on it that tasted of brine. He remained silent, breathing deeply for a while before pulling his head away and bracing his shoulders.

"Okay," he said, "let's get back to the car."

As we walked away, I looked across at him. He looked deflated too, like our thwarted muggers.

"That's the second time you've saved me from having the crap beaten out of me," I told him.

He smiled back at me.

"Glad to be of service."

He didn't say any more as we came out into the light and bustle of Piccadilly, and we wandered up to the car park in silence. There, the archway through which we walked looked antiquated in the street lighting, Roman almost, redolent of faded imperialism, and the dark puddles beyond reflected the glimmer of moonlight.

Getting out of Manchester at this time of night was far easier than getting in had been and I realised that I would have to speak now or else we'd be home before I had my chance.

"So," I said as we passed along the A6, down Buxton Road, "how did you do that? Or is it another one of those things you can't tell me about?"

Kit didn't answer for a while. I could see his look of concentration as he drove, and his long, straight eyelashes, motionless as he stared unblinkingly ahead. Then he closed his eyes for a moment before glancing across at me.

"It's another concentration exercise," he said. "It's a question of focussing your energy outside yourself and *towards* your objective. I concentrated on those boys not seeing us... and they didn't. Normally you get the energy for that kind of thing by meditating on it, *building up* to it. When you do it off-the-cuff like that it's so intense that it drains you completely. I'll definitely sleep well tonight."

I looked at the road ahead and chose my words carefully as I spoke.

"I'm incredibly grateful for what you did this evening," I told him, "but I have to be truthful and tell you that you've scared the shit out of me by doing it. It's so... *weird*. I just want to have an ordinary relationship with you, but you're not ordinary, are you?"

"And neither are you," he said.

"Well, I *feel* ordinary," I said. "This evening – going for a curry and then on to the gay village... it was wonderful. I managed to forget about Mr Evans, and all the strange rumours about you, and I managed to forget about your mind-reading a couple of years ago, too, and what you did to Neil Braithwaite..."

I looked across at Kit. His expression was neutral.

"What *did* you do to Neil Braithwaite, anyway?" I asked. "There was a rumour that he had a nervous breakdown. Did you do that – wish a breakdown on him like I wished harm on Mr Evans?"

"No, not at all," he said. "I did something very similar to that positive visualisation I taught you to do a couple of days ago – sending him up into a golden sun. There's no way that that would have caused him to have a nervous breakdown."

"But it doesn't explain the way he looked at me after you'd spoken to him," I said. "He was *afraid*, Kit. Doing a visualisation to send him off into the sunset wouldn't have made him afraid."

Kit pursed his lips slightly and tapped the steering wheel.

"When I spoke to him," he said, "I simply explained that if he continued to victimise you, it was in my power to make life a lot more difficult for him than he was making it for you. It was a threat of unpleasantness, I know, but one that I assumed would be unnecessary to carry out. And fortunately I was right."

"So how did you make him believe you?"

"I can't say."

"You mean, by telling me, you would ruin the mystery of this *process* I'm supposed to be going through?"

"Yes," he said.

This wasn't putting my mind at rest. Anne's warning against socialising with Kit, let alone trying to emulate him, kept ringing in my head. Perhaps I wasn't strong enough. Perhaps Kit's purposes were malign? What *had* happened to Neil Braithwaite? I couldn't shake the conviction that it was something like the horrible accident I'd wished on Mr Evans, even though Kit said it wasn't.

"I'm not sure that I can trust you," I said, realising that I was growing ever more wary. "I know you saved us both from being mugged this evening, and I'm grateful to you for that, but everything else that has happened seems to have a dark side to it, where someone, somewhere along the line, gets hurt. And I also feel," I added, picking my words carefully, "that if I go any further down this road, the person who gets hurt is going to be me."

Kit frowned as I said this and looked at me with a pleading expression. "No, that's not how it is at all, Greg," he replied. "The problem is that things blew up in our face with Mr Evans. If it hadn't been for that, you'd have a much more positive feeling about what's been happening."

"Would I?"

Kit didn't reply. I looked out at the profound darkness of the passing countryside and studied the dim reflection of my face in the glass of the window. The rest of the journey passed in silence. I was thinking hard but reaching no conclusions. All this weird shit, as the boy back in Manchester had so aptly put it, was disturbing me more and more by the minute. The Kit I had kissed in Via Fossa and the Kit who had pulled that invisibility stunt later on were two different people. One was a schoolboy, like me, and the other was... well, what? Elemental? Ageless? *Dangerous?* If there was anything guaranteed to dampen my ardour it was this. I had to feel that Kit and I were on an even footing, somehow, for me to go any further with him.

When we got back to Horton he stopped the car outside my house and turned the engine off. I didn't know quite what to do – whether to kiss him or not. His face, with its angled cheekbones and firm, wide mouth invited me to, but I had become so uncertain about what Kit was, what he represented, that I stopped myself.

"Look," said Kit with a touch of disappointment, "I think you need few days to work out how you feel, and it's clear that seeing me would only make that more difficult. Next Saturday is the first day of the holidays, so why don't we meet again then? We could go off for the whole day on our bikes – take a packed lunch."

I nodded, suddenly unable to speak.

"I'm sorry you've been upset, Greg," he said. "That's the last thing I wanted to happen."

I smiled a wan smile, and groped around on the back seat for the gaudy carrier bags that contained my shopping of the afternoon.

"See you next week, then," I said as I got out.

"See you."

Nine

Despite my decision to distance myself from Kit, the next day I found I couldn't stay away. I was like a satellite trapped in orbit. The day before had been *huge* in so many ways, and had promised so much, that now I couldn't relax, couldn't lie on my bed and listen to music, and couldn't concentrate. It was all very well for Kit to suggest that we didn't see one another for a week. A week! How could I possibly hold out for a week when every hour saw me endlessly seething with questions. I also felt a strong, yet conflicted, lust for him; conflicted in as much as I yearned to touch him, yet also strove to recoil. Kit was far too complicated for me. In the end, I decided to go out on my bike. After lunch, I would cycle over to Kit's and see if he was there. If he wasn't, then it would have been good exercise anyway. If he was, then we'd see what happened...

It was great to be out on the bike again, and once again the physical exertion operated as a release for my pent-up energies. My pleasure was enhanced because I loved my new cycling gear and I knew that I looked good in it. I'd even gelled my hair and spiked it before leaving, fully aware of the effect it would have on Kit. I wasn't sure if I liked the knowledge that I was acting like a flirt.

Kit's house was near the top of a slope, so I could see the roof and chimneys from a good mile away, and experienced an increasing sense of anticipation as I approached. When I got there I rode into the courtyard at speed and bounced over the uneven cobbles, which, in the mood I was in, delivered a curiously erotic sensation. I saw Kit straight away, in conversation with someone over by the garage. I had a strangely exhilarating sense of spontaneously reading the situation in its entirety, and before I'd even stopped, or properly looked at her, I knew that this girl was profoundly in love with him. She had her arm round his waist, and there was something telling in the way she appeared to adhere to him, almost, rather than merely lean against him. She was tall, only an inch or two shorter than Kit, and had long, fair hair pulled back into a pony tail, and high arched eyebrows, beneath which brooded a pair of intense, pale eyes. Kit and the girl were turned towards the partly opened doors of the garage, and looked secretive and intent, as if they were conducting a ritual; as if they had just been worshipping at a shrine concealed within the garage.

And they looked like the perfect couple. Although Kit was only eighteen, he could easily have passed for the owner of this house, standing there with his young bride. I've already mentioned that he had an androgynous look, and this was especially true now. But whereas at school it had led to accusations of gayness, here, in the context of his loose embrace with the girl, he gave the impression of the dashing young heterosexual lover – lean, sensual, confident and controlled.

The girl, or young woman as I should more correctly describe her, looked at me with only the mildest of curiosity, and then glanced at Kit, who seemed, for the first and only time since I'd known him, genuinely surprised. I reacted unexpectedly, too. I laughed. It was a sudden, ringing, shouting laugh that cleared my mind and made me realise that at least I no longer had to worry about whether or not I should try to seduce – or allow myself to be seduced by – him. But immediately behind that thought was a crushing feeling of betrayal and, swiftly after that, disappointment and anger of an almost literally blinding intensity that lasted maybe two seconds, and which then burnt out in an incandescent flurry. Within moments, I had run a gamut of emotion so varied and intense that the abject emptiness that finally settled on me seemed, for the first few seconds, to be an absence of any emotion at all.

"Greg," Kit said, and waved his hand vaguely, in an unreadable gesture. After his initial surprise, he now seemed calm and unfazed, and in a curious, impossible way, more beautiful than ever.

But I couldn't act unfazed in return and, though I managed a half-hearted smile, I said, "No," and somehow put all the emotion I'd just felt into that one word – with an added dash of hysteria. Then I turned my bike and pedalled out of the courtyard so fast that Kit's raised voice hardly reached me.

As I rode, I tried to recall what he'd said to me when I'd asked him if he was gay. What were the precise words? *In some ways.* I'd found the remark ambiguous enough at the time, but now it seemed to taunt me with its lack of precise meaning. Did he mean that he was bisexual? I presumed now that he must. But what did *bisexual* mean – apart from the obvious? Would it mean, for example, that even if he had a sexual relationship with me, he would always be longing for the embrace of a woman? And vice versa?

I'd only just had my first taste of the gay scene, in Manchester, and had still to lose my virginity. I was completely out of my depth when it came to pondering the hidden dimensions and complexity of Kit's sexuality.

In the end, I decided, the gender of the person he'd been with was irrelevant. I realised that I felt betrayed by him because I'd imagined that some sort of basic rules applied to the whole business of flirtation and seduction; that Kit, as a decent friend, would only focus on one person at a time.

I also felt a sense of irritation with myself, because it was *me* who had pushed intimacy away the previous night, after Kit had saved us from harm. I steadied my thoughts and asked myself some basic questions: I had been wondering all along whether it was right to have *any* kind of relationship with someone who scared me as much as Kit did, so why did I smart inside so badly at what I had chosen to regard as a rebuttal? And why did I now long for his embrace with a redoubled fervour that made me feel almost physically sick? Simple jealousy? But jealousy of this kind is never simple – it is so intensely complicated that maybe it's not worth even trying to unravel it.

Perhaps the most startling emotion was my sense of loss. Not that I actually had anything tangible to lose, as such, but I'd always regarded Kit as being friendless – had assumed that because he was isolated at school, the same would be true of the rest of his life. I'd imagined that I was his only friend, and that he would somehow have a sense of gratitude, at least, and maybe a feeling of loyalty to me because of this. I'd always imagined that he was exclusively mine – not that I'd ever articulated it to myself like this – in a way that went beyond the idea of simply being his lover, and the thought of sharing him with another person made me feel weak, trembly, and vaguely tearful.

Enough, I said to myself. What right did I have to expect *anything* of Kit, who was, after all, a boy who had gone cycling with me a few times and kissed me once? It was absurd. The best thing I could do would be to go home, have a long, relaxing bath and forget all about it.

The next day at school I had a taste of what Kit must have experienced throughout his entire school life – being completely alone in a crowd. In the simplistic way of things at school, my public association with Kit had contaminated me, which meant that I, too, was now being ostracised – and to judge from a snippet of overheard conversation, this was because it was believed that I had somehow caused Mr Evans' accident. Clearly, the phones had been buzzing over the weekend, and a consensus reached declaiming that I was a pariah. Anne refused to come near me, and Richard Murray, whom I met in the corridor, pretended not to see me.

Mr Evans, it seemed, was still in hospital but recovering well. His hand, which had originally been thought to be crushed beyond redemption, was nowhere near as badly damaged as first feared. I wondered if the positive visualisation that Kit had done, and the one I had invented, had had any effect, but realised that there was no way of telling. Instead, I concentrated on my school-work and tried not to think about Kit.

In the lunch break I wandered off to the basketball court, wondering if Kit would follow me out. I was not sure if I wanted him to, but felt that perhaps he should be allowed the chance if he wanted to take it. In the end, he did come. He was quiet, with a subdued grace to his movements, and wore an earnest expression of solicitude.

"Greg," he said, "about yesterday..."

"Yes?"

"The person you saw me with. She's my cousin. Well, second cousin, really. We've known each other since childhood."

"Look, you don't have to explain," I told him.

"Yes, I do," he said. "I want you to know how things are. I want you to understand."

I looked at him expectantly and waited for him to talk, which he did after a considerable pause.

"It's a complicated sort of relationship," he said. "Mary knows quite a lot about my... difference. I used to talk to her about it when we were kids, and she understands me more than anyone else I know. There is a sexual element to our friendship, or there was. There isn't so much now, it's more just being close. But the thing is, Greg, it doesn't make any difference to how I feel about you."

"Okay," I said, "but what about whether it makes a difference to how I feel about you?"

He looked at me with such intensity that I flinched.

"Oh," he said. "And how do you feel about me?"

"I'm not sure."

Actually, I knew quite well what I thought, but I also knew that my fury of jealousy was immature and I didn't want to admit to it. Kit looked away, as though I'd given him the wrong answer. His shoulders tightened and I could see the tendons bulging in his neck. But when he spoke, he spoke with a quiet calmness.

"You dreamt about me last night, Greg. I want you to think of that dream, and know that it was meaningful."

This was so absurd that I let out an involuntary yelp of derisory laughter. Kit's remark, which a few days before would have seemed deliciously romantic, now sounded like the worst kind of hubris. It fuelled my burgeoning antagonism, which was focussed on him as a person, but was also meant for his hints that I was linked to him; that I had the same powers... that we could know each other's dreams.

"Oh, fuck *off* Kit! Of course I didn't dream of you last night. You may have some weird power, or energy, or whatever you want to call it, but this is ridiculous. And arrogant. I've become an outcast at school because of you. In some ways I wouldn't mind. I wouldn't mind, for instance, if we were shunned because we were lovers. That's something I could stand up and admit to with pride; it would be worth enduring ostracism for that. But we're not lovers. I'm being avoided because people are assuming that I have the same dark powers as you. Well, apart from Mr Evans' accident – and the more I think about it, the more I think it's just a coincidence – there hasn't been any manifestation of *my* energies. And before I get embroiled in a dangerous, elitist charade, I want to get out. I thought I was falling in love with you, Kit, but I want Kit the schoolboy, not Kit the black magician. If I do have embryonic *powers*, I want them to stay that way."

Kit looked at me as I spoke, and a great sadness seemed to come over him. "Are you giving me the brush off?" he said. "Don't you want to come out on the bikes next weekend?"

"I don't know," I replied, "I really don't know."

The mention of bikes seemed to put our friendship back onto a boys-together footing, but I knew that it could never be how it was. Even if we never became lovers and just remained friends, I wouldn't be able to forget what Kit was capable of, and the fact that he was hoping to impart his knowledge to me, to groom me for some dark future that I wanted no part of. Would I be able to have an ordinary friendship with someone like that, or to spend time with him without yearning to make love? Probably not. Much better to stand back, to step away. I didn't want to lose my Idyll of normality for a third – and possibly final – time over something as ambivalent as a friendship with someone as impenetrable Kit.

But as it happened, the matter was resolved for me. The next day, Kit didn't come in to school. Nor the next. On Thursday I went to the school office to ask about him and was told that he'd had to leave, quite suddenly, and would be finishing the preparation for his 'A' levels elsewhere. I experienced a powerful sense of *déjà vu* when I learned this, and when I cycled over to his house on Saturday, it was with a sense of the inevitable that I regarded the obviously abandoned building. The downstairs windows were shuttered, and the curtainless upstairs windows looked down like blank, staring eyes.

I sat in the courtyard on my bicycle and looked at the bereft scene. *Kit must have known,* I thought. He must have known, when he'd suggested that we go out on our bikes for the day, that he would already have gone. Unless... Unless my rejection of him had precipitated some kind of accident. My feeling of *déjà vu* increased as the similarity between Kit's removal and the sudden disappearance of Neil Braithwaite hit me. I began to panic. Had my jealousy and anger inflicted something awful on Kit?

And then the panic subsided as a new thought fought its way into my consciousness: The reason why the *déjà vu* was so strong was because I *had* seen it before. I'd dreamt it. Kit had been absolutely right – I *had* dreamt about him. How could I have forgotten? I'd had the dream on the night we got back from Manchester. In my dream, I'd sat right here, on my bicycle, in this cobbled courtyard, looking up at the empty house. The difference was that in my dream Kit was waiting beside the Volkswagen estate in which he'd driven us up to Manchester. The car was crammed full of boxes, bags and cases. His bike was strapped to a special bicycle rack on the roof, and as I looked at him, he'd smiled.

"Would you like to come with me?" he'd asked.

In that dream-state way, I didn't have to answer him aloud, and he took my bike from me and hoisted it up onto the roof rack and strapped it in beside his. Then he went round and opened the car door for me, and I smiled at him and he kissed me as I lowered my head to get in, and I thought, *We're going away together. We're going to go away and start a new life. Together.*

And that was all I remembered.

Kit had known, when we last spoke, that I'd dreamt this dream; a dream in which he'd invited me away with him, to share – I presumed – his 'special' life of strangeness and power. And I had refused, or rather, the part of me that had suppressed the memory of the dream had refused for me. And now the time for acceptance had passed, and I'd lost Kit.

How could life ever be bearable again?

It turned out that Kit had been right in a number of ways. I couldn't go back to my 'ordinary' home life. I felt stifled amongst my family. I tried to tell myself that it was because I was gay and wanted to get away from parochial village life, but I knew it was more than that. I finally recognised that my sisters were terminally nice and that I would never have anything in common with them.

I got back into more of a routine with my father, helping him on Saturdays and maybe on an occasional weekday evening in the little workshop that he'd built onto the side of the garage. But although I put in many more hours than I had done of late, we both knew that my heart was no longer in it and he gradually stopped talking of the possibility of my taking up carpentry as a profession. It seemed that I had lost my Idyll after all – and I had also lost the alternative that Kit had offered. Instead, I found myself in an uncomfortable limbo state which strained my nerves almost to breaking point.

The following term I threw myself into my studies, in an attempt to forget about it, and as a result, did far better in my GCSEs than I might otherwise have done. In Kit's absence, life at school returned to an approximation of normality. But there was something missing. Although Anne was talking to me again, we no longer engaged in the intimate lets-go-to-the-pub conversations that we had previously enjoyed. And Richard Murray still avoided me. My homosexuality, however, became less of a big deal without Kit there to accentuate it, and people left me alone. There was no animosity, but no friendliness either, and so I settled down to a continuing life of isolation.

Mr Evans never came back to school. He was hospitalised for several weeks with his fractured skull, and then had a period of convalescence. I returned to the choir in the summer term, but without the enthusiasm I'd once had. The assistant music teacher who took Mr Evans' place wasn't anywhere near as talented, and there was something rather dismal about choir rehearsals after that. But I still went, because I had to fill my life with *something*. Which was fortunate – or perhaps unfortunate – as Mr Rawnsley shed some further light on Kit's mysterious powers.

"As you may know," he told us at the end of the summer term, "Mr Evans has made a full recovery from his accident at Easter. But he will not be returning here. During his convalescence he took the opportunity to do some job hunting and has been taken on at Sandbach School. The doctors say that his arm and hand will fully recover in time, and that he will soon be able to teach piano again. So in the end, there was no lasting harm done after what seemed at the time to be a career-ruining disaster. Which just goes to show..."

Once again, I battled with conflicting thoughts about Kit. He *had* managed to put things right for Mr Evans through the power of visualisation. I tried not to dwell on this now that Kit was gone. But at the back of my mind, I couldn't rid myself of the thought that Kit had invited me away with him, and I had refused because I didn't trust him.

I'm sorry Kit, I thought. *I should have had faith in you.* I knew now, absolutely, that if he were ever to make the offer to me in the flesh rather than in a dream, I'd accept it without a second thought. But, as with so many things in life, it appeared that one chance was all I'd been offered.

When I got home, I took out my camera for the first time in weeks and clicked off the last three exposures indiscriminately so that I could have the rest of the pictures developed, the ones I'd taken the day we cycled to Shutlingsloe.

There Kit was, bright, smiling, eager on his bicycle and staring straight at me with a candid, simple expression. I put the pictures away. It was far too painful to look at them at the moment. *Far* too painful.

If life can be compared to an evening of television viewing, then the summer holidays after my GCSEs were the commercial break at the nine o'clock watershed. I felt as though one phase of my life had ended and another was yet to begin: the light entertainment of my childhood was over and the pithy drama of adulthood was ahead of me. But as is so often the case, I felt an overwhelming sense of nostalgia for what had passed, and harboured a conviction that I would never again feel as whole as I had done – however briefly – in Kit's company.

I worked for my father for two full days a week, but spent the rest of my time out on the bike. Whenever I passed Kit's old house, a pang would pass through me along with a feeling of desperate hope – like someone phoning through to find out the lottery numbers. A hope that, against all odds, I might find Kit in residence once more, having returned as suddenly as he'd left. As soon as I saw the place, still empty, I would realise how absurd, yet how inevitable, my hope had been.

Through all the cycling I did – sometimes as far as Shining Tor and the Cuckoo Rocks – I became extremely fit and, physically, more assured. And it was during this period that I lost my virginity. I finally mustered the nerve to cycle down to the large area of waste ground beyond Hanley, down by Fenton and the clay pits, where it was rumoured that, at dusk, it was possible to have what I referred to as a 'tryst'. Having revolved the knotty problem of my sexual inexperience in my mind for some time, this was my preferred solution, not because I enjoyed the idea of al fresco sex, but for more prosaic reasons: I was far too shy to go into a gay bar on my own and try to pass myself off as eighteen, and wild horses wouldn't have dragged me into a public toilet.

So I visited the clay pits, on several occasions – maybe five or six times over the course of the summer – though the fact that I can't remember the precise number is testament to the sameness of what went on. The first time I went I had to wait for nearly ninety minutes before I saw someone that I could imagine approaching. The silhouettes under the trees had all looked too portly, or too old, or too unlike the kind of gay man that I'd seen on my one foray into Manchester's gay village, for me to approach them. But eventually, a baggy-trousered 'lad' had turned up and without any fuss or time-wasting, had said "Over here," and within a further minute he had both our trousers round our ankles and was wanking us off at undue, but effective, speed. I left the scene with a feeling of relief that I'd 'got it over with', but also an inevitable sense of anticlimax – in far more than the biological sense. My other visits were less perfunctory when it came to the 'act', but all, in one way or another, were equally anticlimactic. I would sometimes wonder why, and the answer that most often came to mind was that it was because none of the young men bore any resemblance to Kit.

And all through those long, languorous days, I dreaded my return to school. Before I'd met Kit I'd been surrounded by people who were friendly, but without really being *friends*. Now, I knew that I could never return to that casual interaction with my peers, and furthermore, I had no desire to. From now on it would have to be all or nothing. I quickly realised that in the light of past events it would be the latter. Thus, the prospect of two further years of friendlessness was like a great, grey incline stretching before me, up which I would have to toil for seemingly no reward.

And then I met Philippe.

PART TWO

Ten

I met Philippe on my third day back at school after the summer holidays. I'd set out for home at the end of the day, only to find that I had a slow puncture (I habitually cycled now). I always took a puncture repair kit out with me when I went into the hills, but had yet to learn to do so when cycling into school, so I was walking the bike to a cycle shop that was a couple of miles away, towards Hanley. I was hurrying because I was keen to get there before the shop closed, so I didn't notice, at first, that a boy of about my age had drawn alongside me on his bike. When I looked up, he smiled.

"Puncture?" he asked.

"Yes."

"You'll never make it to Garforths in time," he said in a soft French accent, looking at his watch.

I looked at my own watch.

"You're right," I said, and stopped.

I wasn't sure what was the best thing to do, and looked around as though someone – my father driving past on his way back from a job, perhaps – might come to my rescue. The boy spoke again.

"I have a repair kit at home," he said. "It's not far. Come back with me and we'll make a repair for you."

I had never been subjected to this kind of casual friendliness, and was surprised by it. It reminded me of Kit's forwardness the first time I'd met him.

"If you're sure," I said, embarrassed by the boy's easy intimacy, and by the exotic sensuality of his demeanour. Everything about him reeked of *double entendre*.

"I'm Philippe, by the way," he said in a lilting accent that spoke of raw sex. He smiled and reached out to shake my hand, then got off his bike and walked beside me.

"Greg," I said.

"So," he said, "I haven't seen you around. Where do you come from?"

"You mean where do I live, or where do I go to school?"

"Well, obviously you go to school *back there*," he said with a derisive jerk of his head.

"I live in Horton-in-the-Moors," I told him.

Philippe shrugged in that French 'this means nothing to me' way, and I laughed, and he laughed back. He was about my height, but with a fairer complexion. He was thinner than me, but I could see that he possessed that deceptive, wiry strength common to those who are both very slim and very fit.

"Are you a keen cyclist?" I asked.

"Yes," he said, pausing to look me up and down. "And you too, I presume. Even in that uniform I can see you have very strong legs."

It turned out that he was a year older than me, studying for his 'A' levels at a sixth form college near Kidsgrove. There was a wantonness about him – a stark, sexualised aspect that was unequivocal, and to which I could respond much more fully than I'd ever been capable of with the ambiguous Kit.

I'd like to say that Philippe took me home and ravished me, which is more or less how I think of that first tryst between us. But the truth is that we fell into each other's arms as soon as his bedroom door was closed.

"We won't be disturbed," he said, noticing some hesitation and concern in me. "I'm always alone here at this time of day. We have plenty of time."

And with that, we tore our clothes off and fell onto Philippe's bed and did various, all-important things that I'd been unable to do whilst standing up in the dark on the waste ground outside Hanley – namely to look at Philippe as I kissed him, and to see the expression on his face as he responded to my touch. It was a revelation to me how much more there was to this form of sexual contact, and how great it was to lie there in each other's arms, gently breathing and silent, without there being any hurry for me to say goodbye and scuttle away.

As we lay together, I noticed that although we both had dark hair, we were very different. He was aristocratically slender, with perfect pale skin, and the hairs of his arms and legs seemed etched there by an artist. He looked like one of those young counts who populate late-nineteenth century decadent fiction: tubercular, wirily but muscularly thin, an excellent swordsman who bathes in icy water every morning before breakfast, but who will ultimately be consumed by dark and lustful diseases.

I, on the other hand, was slightly shorter than he, but broader. We fitted together well, I thought, and it never occurred to me that we wouldn't see each other again, that we wouldn't continue on from that initial physical exploration into the realms of the emotions and the intellect.

When we'd mended my puncture and I'd cycled off with a promise to drop by the following evening, I found that my whole being felt light and vibrant. Of course, it was impossible to say that I was falling in love with Philippe, because I'd only met him ninety minutes earlier and I didn't think in those terms, but I was without a doubt, most definitely, *in lust* with him. My entire body was already yearning for the following day and what I imagined we would do to each other.

Later that evening, when I was in bed and after I'd relived our rendezvous of the afternoon, I wondered for the first time about the impression I'd had when I first saw him, that he was similar to Kit. I mean, they *looked* completely different – Kit was blond and definite, where Philippe was dark and slyly graceful. Kit was androgynous where Philippe was smoulderingly masculine. And the attraction itself felt different. With Kit it had been a slow-burning, gentle feeling whereas with Philippe it was uncontrollable. My only thought was to get him on his own the following day and rip the clothes off him. It was curious. The rules of attraction are never straightforward, I know, but I still felt it was odd that I could be so attracted to two such demonstrably different people. I thought about that for a while, then slowly realised that the similarity between them was not the fact that I'd been attracted to them both. It was something quite different.

With a jolt that made me sit up in bed, I realised what it was. Philippe had the same *energy* as Kit.

Part of me felt a fiery thrill at the thought, whilst another part of me quailed at the prospect of being sucked into that mysterious and dangerous world once more. Hadn't I rejected Kit precisely because he possessed this energy? Why should Philippe be any different?

But I had lived to regret letting Kit slip from my grasp. I would not make the same mistake twice.

The following day, my mother mentioned that I looked dreamy, and I smiled at her and said nothing. As I left the house, I told her that I was likely to be late home again that evening and she laughed and said, "Enjoy yourself." For once, the school day didn't loom ahead of me like a great blighting shadow. Lessons passed without effort or boredom, and the fact that no one particularly spoke to me made no difference to my mood, which was one of scintillating anticipation.

When I rode off to Philippe's I felt pleasantly nervous. He was there when I arrived at his place – a detached Victorian house on the near side of Hanley – and as soon as he opened the door, he grabbed my tie and pulled me in, kicking the door shut behind me and locking me into a ferocious kiss that lasted all the way upstairs to his room, as he walked slowly backwards, pulling me with him, his tongue searching my mouth all the while. His room was decorated a dark blue, with rich, red velvet curtains. There was a smell of incense and, beneath that, something heady that I presumed to be cannabis of some sort, which gave the place the feel of a voluptuous drug den.

Of course, I did what I'd been imagining for the last twenty-four hours – I began to tug off his sweater, and then his tie, and he did the same for me, and soon we were sprawled naked on his bed once more, desperate to get at each other. Philippe traced the line of my ear with his tongue, his hand rhythmically stroking my dick, and whispered, "I want to fuck you." I wasn't quite ready for this and recoiled. He laughed quietly, murmuring, "But there's no hurry," then leaned down and took me in his mouth, and I lost all coherent thought for a while.

Later, Philippe rolled a joint and I smoked a little of it, sitting naked on the bed. It was my first experience of grass and I got light-headed and giggly, then slowed down and became strangely serious. I was mesmerised by the small gold pendant, on a simple chain, which hung in the hollow of Philippe's neck, and stared at it for a long time. It seemed fantastically significant, and strange. Ancient.

"I've got a question to ask," I said in a slow voice. "Ignore it if it doesn't mean anything to you."

"Okay," he said.

I looked out of the window at the gently swaying branches of the ash tree outside, then into his cool, dark eyes, and said, "Do you ever practice magic?"

Philippe looked intensely surprised at this. I had startled him. And then he leaned back and laughed. The sound was deeply unnerving, but I couldn't help joining in – perhaps because of the grass. He lay on the bed and looked up at the ceiling, smiling to himself, then raised his hands in a gesture that I couldn't interpret. And then he laughed again.

"I wondered," he managed after a while, "I wondered whether I ought to broach the subject with you. I never thought that *you* would mention it to *me*."

He sat up and draped his arm over my shoulder.

"How did you know?" he asked.

"You know how I know," I told him. "I could see it in you."

He stroked my shoulder and kissed the side of my neck.

"So," he whispered, "you've been *initiated* by someone else?"

"No," I said. "I... met someone else, who told me... a little. That's all. He's gone now."

Philippe nodded.

"I see. We'll talk about this later, Greg. Another time. Don't worry. We need to get to know each other better first."

He pulled me back down on the bed and pressed his burgeoning erection against my thigh. I felt myself responding in turn, and turned to kiss him.

"One thing," Philippe murmured. "Be aware of the power in what is happening right now. Don't question it, or try to direct it – but know that it is there. And this time," he added with a slight grin, "perhaps you would like to fuck *me*."

He passed me his joint, which I accepted, and then, after I handed it back, he dropped it into a small glass ashtray and turned his attention to me.

That evening, the evening that I first fucked Philippe, was not rendered weighty by mystic ideas the way my time with Kit had always been. Instead the magic was inherent, implied. Somehow, there was a flow of magic in what we were doing. In a superficial sense, I was fucking something out of myself when I had sex with Philippe, but it felt as if I was fucking something even more important *into* myself at the same time. When I went home that night, I remained unperturbed by the thought of Philippe's magic, because this sexual energy between us had nothing dark about it – it was light, and joyful, and it was impossible to imagine harm coming from it.

I am tempted to say those late summer weeks were 'magical', though I mean the word in its secular sense. Suffice to say, I was totally engrossed in my relationship with Philippe. I was in a constant haze of erotic desire that seemed sometimes to border on madness. If I was forced by circumstances to go for a few days without seeing him, for example, my agitation was so intense that I couldn't do *anything* except pace about or go for long, punishing bike rides. Everyone at home knew I was in love, and so I came out to the family, which was a formality anyway. Mum immediately wanted to meet the boy who had so completely captured my heart, but Philippe was curiously reticent about the idea of meeting my family, and even more reticent about me meeting his. In fact, after my first few visits to his room, he didn't allow me to come back to his place any more. But he made up for it in other ways. His dad (I presumed it was his dad, though Philippe was so secretive I couldn't be sure of anything) was an estate agent, and Philippe would meet me outside school with a set of keys and we would cycle off to some empty house and make love in the large, cool, empty rooms. I enjoyed this as it made me feel that I was having an 'unusual' affair, especially one occasion when we went to a large, deserted factory that was full of detritus and long-disused machinery, and made love amongst the wires and pipes, where gentle flurries of dust furred our tangy lips.

When we first began to have sex in these strange, empty properties, Philippe told me that sexual energy was a gift, a sacrament, and that in order to preserve that energy you should channel it, like a gift, towards something that you regarded as sacramental. Of course, I channelled it towards him, which was something that I didn't even have to think about – it just happened, and whether or not it had any power I didn't know and didn't care, because I wasn't having sex with Philippe to create energies. I was having sex with him because I was utterly infatuated with him.

Weeks later, when the whole subject of SexMagic came up more definitely, Philippe explained it to me more fully.

"Because we're gay, we don't experience the distraction that heterosexuals feel regarding fertility: the conviction that biological reproduction is the fundamental force behind SexMagic. It most definitely is not. The fact is that sexual feelings – and especially the moments before and during orgasm – are amongst the most intense emotions that a person can have. And there are a number of ways to intensify them even further, if you want to travel that path. Intensity is like a quotient, it is like the stretched elastic of a catapult that will throw your thought forward with real power. Most people throw out thoughts with no intention behind them, but if you do so with a purpose and a set intention, then the power of an orgasm will turbo-charge that intention. The only power stronger than sex is hate. But that's another subject altogether. Love is powerful as well, but it tends to be too fuzzy round the edges."

People at school noticed the change in me. I became completely self-contained and assured. I didn't study well, however, as I was too distracted, and I didn't bother to socialise for more or less the same reason. People must have known that Philippe was the reason for this. He was a most conspicuous person, after all. On the days when he was already outside the school waiting for me, he would smile a great, ravishing smile and drape his arm round my shoulder and walk over to the bike enclosure with me, a defiant this-is-my-boyfriend-and-what-are-*you*-going-to-do-about-it? look on his face. And of course, nobody did do anything about it. Philippe's brashness gave me a confidence so blatant that no one ever tried to tease me about it, either. Quite the contrary, in fact. I noticed a hint of jealousy in the eyes of many of the girls at the sight of someone as refined and immaculate as Philippe – an envy that was hugely magnified one day in mid November, when Philippe arrived driving one of those dinky Mercedes two-seater roadsters. It was silver and he had the top down. He looked devastatingly handsome as he flashed his great, carnivorous smile in the watery autumn sunshine and opened the passenger door for me to get in.

"Is this yours?" I asked, impressed.

"Yes," he said.

I got in beside him and we roared off, and I laughed at the amazed expressions of my schoolfellows.

"But where..." I asked him, as we he set off towards Biddulph, "where did the money come from?"

He looked over at me possessively, gloatingly, and definitely lustfully, and I felt a shiver pass up my spine.

"Do you remember that factory we went to at the beginning of last month?"

"Yes," I replied, "of course."

"I sold it."

"You sold it?"

"I organised the sale," he said. "I saw how it should best be sold, and had a go at it myself. Not only have I managed to sell the building, I've also managed to shift the machinery that was inside it. The commission to me personally is worth, well... a lot more than the price of this car."

"But you're only a schoolboy, Philippe," I said.

"I may only be seventeen," he said, "but I know more about buying and selling property than most people who have been in the business for years. Why shouldn't I use my knowledge to my own advantage when I see the opportunity?"

"No reason," I said. "I'm just surprised, that's all."

I felt oddly crushed. Previously, I'd been pleased – or even smug – to know that I'd learned a professional skill that I could use to make some good pocket money when I needed it, but in comparison to Philippe, my carpentry seemed piddling, insignificant.

"Where are we going?" I asked.

"You'll see," he said. "There's someone I want you to meet."

He took out his mobile and punched out a number and said, "We're on our way."

We drove part of the way up Mow Cop, the hill with the folly that looks like an old ruin on top, then down the other side, over the railway, and then along by the canal. When Philippe turned left onto an old drive, I thought for a moment we were going to another one of his empty houses. The gates through which we drove were tall and rusted, one of them hanging askew from its hinges, and the short gravel drive was choked with grass. There was a peeling sign just inside the gates that read 'Gillow Manor Farm'. The main house had a huge porch of crumbling stucco over ancient brick which peered through the building's skin like ancient sores. But it was inhabited. There was a car parked outside and, to one side of the house, in some huge, open outbuildings, I could see a tractor and other farm machinery. Philippe parked on the large turning circle and we got out and went up to the door, which was opened on our approach by a boy who looked a little older than us – perhaps nineteen or twenty – and who smiled shyly at Philippe, then held his hand out to me.

"I'm Mark," he said.

He was pale and blond and was almost pathologically reticent. There was something in the droop of his shoulders, and the expression of his slightly puffy face, that made me think of deep, deep disappointment. He was a strangely ugly boy, too, and although I was annoyed with myself for having this response, I couldn't help feeling sorry for him because of it.

"I'm Greg," I said, and he stood back to let us past.

The interior of the house was in less of a state. The hall was long and wide, with a sweeping staircase at the end. Although the carpet was threadbare in places, the huge, ancient pieces of furniture were magnificent – a hallrobe; a dark, oak dresser; a Tudor chest; a long pew-like seat, heavily carved and ornamented...

"Amazing stuff," I said, running my fingers over the polished wood.

"Greg's a budding carpenter," Philippe told Mark, who nodded sagely and smiled in his sad way.

"Go on up to my room," he said. "I'll get us some beers."

As we wandered towards the stairs, a door opened at the end of the hall, and a middle-aged woman looked out.

"Oh, hello, Philippe," she called, "I thought I heard something."

"Hello, Mrs Daniels," he called back, "how are you?"

"Fine," she replied, "fine. Go on up, now, don't mind me."

"See you in a moment," Mark whispered.

A cupola above us lit the stairwell, revealing that the staircase was worn and had shallow, wide steps. It was well dusted at ground level, but higher up it grew tatty and the paint was peeling. Philippe took me up to a broad landing off which were four huge, dark wooden doors and a corridor to the right. Philippe opened the first door on the left and we went into an oddly contemporary room. It was wide and airy and tall. There was a huge oak desk with a computer and playstation on it; a neat, black stereo with tall speakers and a large tv in the corner. The marble fireplace had pale ashes in it from a recent fire. There was an old bed with a rucked duvet on it, and two desperately sagging sofas. Philippe dropped into one of them and motioned me to do the same.

"Who is this guy?" I asked. "He looks a bit weird."

"He's okay," Philippe said. "And there is one enormous advantage to knowing him, which you'll discover later."

He kissed me then, grabbing the back of my head for emphasis, and placed his hand on the front of my trousers and rubbed, so that my arousal was almost instantaneous, then broke away and laughed at my expression as Mark came into the room carrying a six pack of Budweiser.

He handed me one and I murmured my thanks and opened it, taking a gulp and waiting for either Philippe or Mark to start the conversation. Philippe drank half his can in one long gulp, then wiped his mouth with the back of his hand and grinned at Mark, who grinned back.

"Mark, here," said Philippe, "knows some of the basic principles of what you might call magic. Don't you?"

"Only the basics," he muttered, looking at the floor.

"We were talking about it a week or two ago," said Philippe, "and I thought maybe we could continue where we left off. We were saying that one of the basic principles is the need to follow your own nature – to be true to yourself. Isn't that right?"

"Yes," said Mark.

"*Whatever* that nature is."

I looked over at Philippe, curious that he was staring at me so intensely.

"*Whatever* your nature?" I asked.

"Yes," said Philippe.

"Even if it's in your nature to murder someone?"

"Yes," he said, and drank some more of his beer. "Though I don't suppose it's in many people's *nature* to murder anyone. That's generally a circumstantial thing, not a question of nature. Which leads to the question – and this must surely be the fundamental principle of all occult practice – what *is* my nature? *That's* the point, isn't it? That's the great question posed by all true religions. Who am I? How can I ever be true to myself unless I know who I *really* am?"

"Who are *you*, Greg?" Mark asked earnestly, and I felt a strange thrill race through my body as he spoke.

I pondered his question and drank some of my beer, but came up with nothing apart from some basic impersonal description.

"I'm just *me*," I said. "I've never thought of it further than that."

"But," said Mark, "when you think about what you want from life, how can you make a good, informed decision if you don't know what your true self wants? I mean, we all want things – like computers, cars, sex, money, and respect... but how do we know whether it's our inner selves that want these things, or if we're just succumbing to our base instinct to grab, grab, grab?"

Philippe finished his can and reached for another one.

"Quite," he said, getting up. "Now, let's go. I want to show Greg this house's little secret."

Mark nodded and stood up. He'd also finished his first can and, in taking another for himself, handed me one. I drank down the last half of my first one quickly and smiled my thanks as I took and opened the next.

"You take Greg down," he said, "and I'll get some more beer."

Philippe took my elbow and steered me out of the room behind Mark and led me along the corridor, whilst Mark went downstairs. The corridor had a couple of doors on one side and two windows about ten feet apart on the other, that looked out across the canal and the farmland beyond the house. The back courtyard was a mess: old farm machinery rusting to pieces; an ancient Ford Escort with broken windows skirted by tall, dead nettles; a mildewed, dented caravan, askew on perished tyres...

"I'm going to own this place one day," said Philippe.

"It'll need a lot of work," I said, without wondering how Philippe expected to get hold of it.

"Yes. But you've worked with your dad, haven't you? You've seen what places like this can be turned into."

I thought of that great, airy hall, the stucco frontage and the curving drive. It could be spectacular.

"Of course," I told him, "if you ever need a carpenter..."

Philippe laughed and kissed the side of my neck, growling into my ear.

"Oh, no," he said, "I've got *much* better plans for you than that."

The conviction with which he said this electrified me. With Philippe, anything might be possible; anything at all.

At the end of the corridor there was a narrower, cobwebby staircase that descended in a curve down to a back hallway that led into the rear courtyard on one side, and through the back doorway on the other. The door was open and I could see the edge of the turning circle at the front. Straight ahead, over some grey flagstones that looked as though they might have been slate, was a set of double doors that were even more ornate than any of the others. They were taller, too, and Philippe looked like some eager dignitary as he leaned his weight against one of them and swung it open.

Inside, there was a small chapel. There were four pews on each side. In front of them was an altar and a side lectern and, behind it, an arched stained glass window split into a triptych – angels at the top with Jesus and Mary facing each other, below. There were two embrasures facing each other at either side that had presumably once held statues but were now empty. For a chapel it was tiny, though I suppose it could have held twenty people comfortably and thirty at a push. All around the walls there were small marble plaques commemorating the memory of various members of the Daniels family. The whole place was under layers of dust, and had clearly been unused for years. Philippe looked at me with a smile and gestured around.

"Not bad, huh? Mark's family are Catholic. Lapsed now, as you can see, but they were really quite devout a hundred-and-fifty years ago. I suppose if you looked at the dates on all these foul memorial slabs, you'd be able to work out more or less when they gave up on God. It could do with a good clean, but even like this it's got a *feeling*, hasn't it?"

"Of sanctity," I said.

"Yes," he agreed. "You know what I'd most like to do in here?"

"What?"

"Fuck you on the altar."

I laughed, but stopped once I noticed his expression.

"You're being serious?"

"Never more so."

Philippe hadn't fucked me at that point. He'd done everything but that. I looked at the plain, flat stone altar. It was almost big enough to service as a – most uncomfortable – bed.

"What about Mark?" I asked.

Philippe didn't have time to reply because Mark came in at that moment and handed us each another can of beer. There was no way that I could drink this quickly, and so I put my third can on one of the pews. The light was fading fast, now, and shadows seemed to be creeping down from the vaulted ceiling of the chapel. Mark sat down on the right hand front pew, and I went to join him. I could see that this pew was dustless, as was the altar, I noticed, now that I was near enough to look at it more closely.

"I come in here to think," said Mark. "To sit amongst the shadows of my ancestors. My parents are so superstitious about the place they would never set foot in it, so I'm assured of privacy. I used to come in here to wank when I was twelve, before I was allowed to lock my bedroom door. Do I shock you?"

"No," I said. "At home I used to lock myself in the toilet, but I'd have preferred to do it somewhere like this."

"I used to keep gay porn mags under the pews, but one day they all disappeared so I guess one of the farm workers found them."

Philippe, who had been looking up at the darkening stained glass, turned round and sat on the altar, looking down at us as if in benediction.

"I want to do some kind of ritual in here," he said. "I haven't thought of something absolutely appropriate yet. But on an auspicious date and at an auspicious time, we should use this place. Is it still technically consecrated?"

"Yes," said Mark.

"All the better." He laughed and lay back on the altar and raised his can of beer.

"To the future!" he shouted, "which is brighter than words can describe!"

"To the future," murmured Mark, and slugged back more beer.

Philippe looked at me.

"Are you drunk, yet?"

"Not really."

"Never mind," he said. "Look, Mark, we have to go. I'll give you a ring when I've worked something out."

He stood up on the altar and jumped down to where Mark sat, and patted him on the shoulder. Mark looked down at the spot where Philippe's hand had just touched him.

"Come on, Greg," Philippe said, tugging my arm and dragging me to the door. "Bye Mark, thanks for the beer."

And then we were outside in the gloom of deep dusk, Philippe laughing. He went to the car and got in, pausing whilst the hood clicked into place. I got in more slowly beside him.

"You felt uncomfortable in there, didn't you?" said Philippe, "at the thought of being fucked on a consecrated altar."

"I'm more concerned about being driven home by someone who's clearly well over the limit," I replied.

"Loosen up," he said and started the engine, revving hard before skidding off down the drive. "And," he added, "you haven't answered my question."

"Yes," I told him. "I can see that if I'm going to be fucked for the first time, then being ravished on an alter would be... well, appropriate in some ways. But, yes, it does make me feel a little uncomfortable."

"Good, because when I do it, you'll get that extra *frisson* – the thrill of forbidden pleasure. I can't wait."

For the first time in ages, he drove me back to his place. It was dark, empty and cold inside. We went up to his room, where he put the gas fire on full and we huddled under the bedclothes for a while, and then I fucked him and he yelled out with an exhilaration that enthralled me. When he drove me home afterwards, he kept stroking my leg and humming and smiling. But then, I wasn't surprised. If I'd bought myself a Mercedes at the age of seventeen, I'd probably have been pleased with myself, too.

He stopped the car round the corner from the house and let me out. He was still adamant that he didn't want to meet my parents, which I thought was odd, considering how extrovert he was in all other respects.

Eleven

When one is collected from school by a handsome young man in a Mercedes sports car two or three times a week, one's *cachet* increases considerably. And whilst it's true that I made no new friends out of it, I was now regarded as sophisticated and rarefied rather than a pariah. I loved it – was enchanted that, by the standards of my peers, my life had become Glamorous and Interesting – although I was fully aware of the superficiality of it all.

Philippe had declared a moratorium on visiting empty properties for sex, because the weather had turned cold, but he managed to acquire a bolt-hole for us instead. It was a studio flat in Hanley that was nominally on the market but whose owners were either abroad, disinterested, or perhaps – as sometimes happens with individuals or companies that own a lot of property – unaware that the place existed. Philippe installed a bed and a sofa and one of those electric convection heaters with a thermostat and a timer, so that when we arrived there after school the room was already warm for us.

For my seventeenth birthday my parents bought me a course of driving lessons, at my request, and sometimes Philippe let me drive the Mercedes, even though I wasn't insured to do so. This would happen out of town, when he was driving me back home.

"You won't crash the car," he said when I voiced concern over it, "and if you did, I'd just say that it was me who was driving."

One day, there was a particularly large glut of students from my year spewing out of the school gates when he pulled up to collect me. He grinned at me as I waved, and levered himself into the passenger's seat. I laughed, and jumped behind the steering wheel, waving at Anne, then put the car into gear and raced off up the road, showing off, exhilarated. *Oh, to be young and in love!* I thought.

That winter passed so quickly and joyfully. My one disappointment was that Philippe refused to let me photograph him. I thought he was fantastically handsome and I kept telling him it was a sin that he would not let me record it, but he laughed and told me to live for the present moment, and not to try to capture it in any way. The upshot of this was that I completely dropped photography for that period, except for one occasion when I took my camera into school and took a single, surreptitious shot of him with my telephoto lens. But the result wasn't what I'd hoped for – it was too grainy and too much of a hurried snap-shot to be impressive – so I never tried again, although I was pleased to have something to look at to remind me of him. I also dropped cycling at that time. There was no point in biking it into school if, as likely as not, Philippe was going to be collecting me in his car, then driving me home later.

Occasionally, he would take me to some grand, unusual property where we'd make love as we had before, in curious cellars, in great panelled drawing rooms, or (once) in a room in a tower. After six heady months I was still as infatuated with him as ever. And apart from that one, brief meeting with the tragic Mark, our friendship remained enclosed, protected from the outside world, which I found neither strange nor undesirable. He was mine, and mine alone. The thought of sharing his company was unthinkable.

Alcohol soon became an intrinsic part of our time together. Philippe always had a bottle or two of good French red wine with him in the car. Occasionally he'd have champagne, but he thought it a little tacky, or obvious, and besides it was difficult to keep it cold enough. He always had a couple of fine, heavy antique glasses to drink out of, too – different ones each time. I supposed he was collecting them. And, gradually, it came to seem that wine was an anointment of some kind for our passion. I found getting drunk with Philippe an exquisite pleasure, because it made me wallow in his presence, and feel cherished and *alive*. Of course, we never got *drunk*-drunk. The wine we consumed was sacramental, and to overdo it would have changed that.

In the earliest days of spring, Philippe finally said to me, "Can you spend both Saturday and Sunday with me this week?"

"Of course," I said, pleased. "You want me to spend the night with you?"

"Yes."

I had waited for this for months, had wondered many times why he'd never asked me before. My parents certainly wouldn't have minded. Yet Philippe always drove me home at the end of the evening, so we'd never actually *slept* together. Being asked to spend the weekend with him boded well, I thought.

Although I still did quite a lot of work for my dad, he'd given up going out on jobs at the weekend. He was earning good money and didn't need to work the extra hours. What I did now was perform simple renovation or clean-up jobs on old furniture that he'd picked up here and there. Dad would help me with the more difficult or fiddly work, but the rest I could do largely on my own in the workshop. I was learning all the time, and, in that pendulum-swinging sort of way, was beginning to fall in love with wood again. I was no longer so sure that I didn't want to make it my profession, after all.

Another reason why I spent so much time working was because I needed money. Philippe was so well turned-out that I wanted to be as well dressed as he was, and that was expensive. I bought a sharp suit and a flashy jacket, expensive shoes, scents, jeans, tops... and Philippe complimented me and said what a perfect pair we were, and how much we matched.

I felt good, and exuded a confidence that fed upon itself. Seeing me as confident, everyone treated me with respect. Everyone except my teachers, that is. I was now being taught English by Mr Blandford, who called me in one day and said, "Mrs Hodson tells me how diligent you were in the fifth year, Greg, and I know how well you did in your GCSEs, but now you seem to have gone completely off the boil. It's not that you don't have plenty of natural ability, but what's happened to your concentration?"

He looked at me earnestly, took off his glasses and rubbed his watery eyes.

"No," he said, "don't bother to answer that. We've all seen you being collected after school by your supermodel boyfriend. I can quite see why that sort of thing would be a preoccupation, but you'll have plenty of time for fun and games later, Greg. Right now you are building the foundations, the springboard if you like, from which to launch the rest of your life. Don't waste your potential. I know it sounds as if I'm trying to spoil your fun, but I'm not, really I'm not. But I have to warn you, if you don't get some work done soon, you'll regret it later."

His words, though wise and true, had no power over me. I was so caught up in Philippe that I had no space for anything else.

That Saturday, Philippe collected me from home immediately after lunch. As usual, I gave my parents the impression that I was going to get the bus, and met him round the corner. He was unusually quiet as we drove off, although he did smile briefly when I leaned over and kissed his neck and asked him where we were going. In reply, he pulled out a road atlas from beside him and handed it to me.

"It hasn't got a name," he said, "but it's on the far side of Oswestry, in Wales. I've marked it on the map with an X."

"Oh, yes," I said after scanning the relevant page, "I've got it."

"I can take us through Oswestry," he told me, "but you will have to map-read me from there."

The nearest place to our destination that actually had a name on the map was Llanrhaedr-ym-Mochnant, and for a while we had a rather hilarious time trying to work out how to pronounce it. Most of our attempts included hacking or puking sounds. Puerile, I know, but amusing.

"What's there?" I asked Philippe, "why are we going?"

"To see a person that I want you to meet," he said. "And don't worry, you'll like him. He's a person of... stature."

I was disappointed at this. I'd hoped we were going to be alone. Still, we had the journey together, which was brilliant. Although it was only ninety miles, it took us nearly three hours because of the traffic. The scenery was magnificent, especially over the last few miles, when the hills reared up in front of us, bleak but magnificent, the last streaks of winter snow still visible on the tops. They were quiet and powerful.

"There's a slip of paper at the back of the atlas which will give you the final directions," Philippe told me.

We came to a long, rutted lane that we took with care in the Mercedes. But we arrived without mishap outside an old farm building, obviously renovated to its original condition, which engendered an odd feeling of stepping back in time. The upper windows were tiny, and above them the roof angled steeply in a plane of mossy rough stone tiles. The low outhouses that flanked the house were also immaculate – whitewashed, well-guttered, newly glazed. The courtyard was cobbled with stones that resembled well-worn pebbles from a beach.

Philippe parked, and as he got out a man opened the front door. He was about sixty, taller than either of us, with steely grey hair and intense dark eyes which peered from a lined, intelligent face. He was wearing dark jeans and a baggy canvas shirt and looked like a painter, I thought, who had just been called away from his easel.

"Ian!" Philippe called, and they both burst into delighted laughter. Philippe crossed to where Ian stood on the wide, stone doorstep and they embraced. I followed more shyly, but Ian broke away from Philippe and reached out to shake my hand.

"Come in, come in. Welcome," Ian said, and placed his free hand on my shoulder. His grip was firm, masculine.

We were ushered into the house, and as I followed them down the hall, I realised who this person was. Ian was Philippe's mentor. As soon as I saw him, I knew that Ian possessed *whatever it was*, that energy that I had yet to put a name to. He exuded it, much more strongly than either Kit or Philippe. And there was a powerful connecting energy between the two of them. He was an attractive man – strong, craggy, muscular – and something in the way they touched made it clear to me that they'd had a sexual relationship in the past. It made me wonder whether sexual connection was an important part of exploring this energy.

We were shown into a large, low-ceilinged room with a blazing fire. The floor was of bare wood with dark rugs on it, and the wide sofas were covered in a deep blue canvas-like material which looked black from some angles. Philippe sat in one and pulled me down beside him and held my hand as we talked.

"I'm not surprised by the car that you're driving," Ian laughed. "Though it's a somewhat *gaudy* bauble, I would have thought. You know what they say about possessions…"

"Beware, or they'll end up possessing you," Philippe smiled. "But we both know that to enjoy them is not necessarily the same thing as to be controlled by them. It's only if I found I couldn't give them up that I would be in danger."

Ian nodded briefly.

"Well, I always had more simple tastes than you," he said. "I can't blame you for being who you are."

He turned to me.

"And you are?"

"Greg," I said.

"Well," he said, "for what it's worth, I approve of you. I don't mean that in a derogatory, superficial way. It's clear that you're in love with Philippe, and he's needed someone *on his own level*, so to speak, for some time."

"Greg and I haven't really discussed any of that, yet," Philippe said quickly.

"Oh?" Ian said.

"We will, though," Philippe assured him. "When the time comes."

"I would have thought," said Ian, "that there is no better time than now. Today."

"That's what I meant when I said 'When the time comes'," Philippe added hurriedly, with an unreadable glance in my direction. "I meant later today."

"Okay," Ian nodded.

He stood up and went to the window, then turned and leaned against the wide windowsill, facing us. Silhouetted against the glass like that, the cool pale blue of the late-afternoon sky behind him, he looked elemental, ageless. Powerful. I felt a tingle of something that might have been fear, but with Philippe there, holding my hand, I was comforted and forced myself to relax.

There came a knock on the door and, after a moment or two, a man of about forty came in carrying a tea tray. He was dressed casually in cords and a plain white shirt.

"Ah, Bernard," said Ian, "well done."

"The butler," Philippe mouthed to me as Bernard carried the tray to the table in front of us, then left, wordlessly, without acknowledging the presence of anyone in the room; as though it had been empty. I don't know why it came as such a surprise that Ian had a butler. The rustic look of the farm house from the outside, perhaps?

It had none of the grandeur of the places that Philippe admired.

I looked around the room once more, to see if there were any signs of 'magical' practice, but there were none, unless you were to take a dark landscape and a set of three (Roman?) pots on the windowsill as vague circumstantial evidence.

"You pour," said Ian, and Philippe reached for the teapot with a grin.

"I thought perhaps you'd greet us with something stronger than tea," he said.

"I might have if you'd arrived half an hour later," he replied.

It felt strange drinking tea and eating home-baked cake like this. The atmosphere in the room had a kind of ultra formality about it, masquerading as ease. I felt that Ian was looking at me all the time, trying to size me up, to mark me perhaps, as though I were an exam paper that Philippe had submitted to him.

Conversation was desultory and neutral, but the atmosphere was pregnant with things that remained to be said. I was intrigued that Philippe had promised Ian that he would tell me certain things 'later today', 'when the time was right', because he'd never intimated as much to me. And did that mean he'd tell me *here*? With Ian, or in private? I was getting nervy, and could half-imagine myself jumping up from the sofa and running away in terror, but then I remembered that I'd stepped back from this threshold before, with Kit, and I'd regretted it. So I steeled myself for what might come.

I'd always known that Philippe had access to the same kind of energy as Kit, and as I drank my tea, I wondered why I had never asked him about it after that first time. Perhaps it was because, once the sexual momentum had begun, I hadn't wanted anything to spoil it. The connection between myself and Kit had proved so frail that the possibility of losing Philippe at more or less the same point – and for the same reason – may have given me the subconscious jitters.

Now that I felt a certain stability between us, I was more ready to go on to the next step, whatever that was. Kit had been right when he'd said that, after having a glimpse of what might be possible, I wouldn't be able to go back to ordinary life. Now, here I was with Philippe and this charismatic man, and I knew I was about to take that next step...

Twelve

We ate in a dining room that was long, narrow and low, the dark beams above us illuminated by flickering candlelight from the table. The angles were softened and the shadows deep.

"This was the main room of the old farmhouse," Ian told me. "It goes back to the time of Cromwell. Not as old as I might have liked, but – it has the *right* history, if you know what I mean."

I nodded, but was not sure if he meant that it was imbued with an atmosphere, or whether other – occultists? – had lived here in the past.

We drank a dark spicy red wine with our food, though Ian refused to let Philippe have more than one glass because he was driving, so I deduced that we wouldn't be staying the night – which was a relief. I waited patiently for one of them to start talking about occult things, but they didn't. I chatted a little about school and life at home, which seemed so prosaic that I might have been embarrassed by it a year before. But, inspired by Philippe, and, I suppose, by Kit before him, my confidence was growing and I thought, *I'm seventeen, I'm a schoolboy, what kind of life am I supposed to be living?* But on the other hand, Philippe was a schoolboy, too, and one could hardly describe *his* life as prosaic.

After we'd finished eating, Ian got up from the table and said, "Let's have our... liqueur... in my study, shall we?"

Philippe nodded. We left the room and walked back along the short, stone-flagged corridor towards the sitting room, but before we got there Ian opened a plain, dark door in the wall and ushered us through it. We found ourselves in a small room fitted out with a desk and a student lamp, a room that conformed very much to what I might have expected of our host. There were shelves and shelves of books, some old – ancient, in fact – some absolutely contemporary. There was a lap-top computer sitting incongruously on the great, leather-topped desk, flanked on one side by a large, completely spherical stone, and on the other by a tiny skeleton of what may have been one of those miniature breeds of monkey, perhaps a foot high, held up by a brass rod.

"I can tell from your demeanour, Greg, that Philippe hasn't told you anything about our... connection," Ian said as Philippe and I sank down into a small sofa, holding hands. Ian perched on the chair by the desk, and gave Philippe a deep, searching look. "I can't think why. But seeing as he brought you with him tonight, he must have intended you to be present now, so I'd better give a few words of explanation."

I raised my hand, to stop him going on.

"Let me make a guess at a little of it, first," I said.

Ian laughed and nodded.

"Okay."

"It's clear to me," I said, "that you were Philippe's teacher. I mean, that you taught him about these *energies*. From the way you interact with each other, I also presume that you taught him about sexual energy and how to use it. From what you said earlier about there being no better time than today for Philippe to tell me certain things, I would guess that today has a particular significance – some kind of anniversary for you both?"

Ian was impressed.

"Good," he said. "I could see from the start that you're intuitive, but that's really rather good. And you're right, of course, with most of it. But the anniversary is not an anniversary of something that happened between Philippe and myself. It is a much older anniversary than that. I shall let Philippe tell you about it at another time, but make sure you pester him until he does. His secrecy is absurd, when you are patently so ready to learn."

He turned to a small cabinet and opened the richly lustred wooden door. Inside was a small silver-trimmed jug-like decanter that contained a green liquid and which he brought out along with three simple, conical liqueur glasses, which resembled miniature cocktail glasses. Handing one to me, he poured a measure of the liqueur.

"What is it?" I asked, staring.

"Absinthe," he told me. "Czechoslovakian, not the fake muck that you get nowadays."

"I've heard of it, but I don't know what it is, exactly," I said.

"It is a spirit that has been used for centuries to unlock the dream centres of the mind. Artists and writers have used it over the years – to great effect, I might add. But occultists have used it, too, and though I must admit to a certain bias, I would say that we have used it to *greater* effect."

I looked at my glass, at the light refracting through the liquid.

"Don't worry," Ian told me as he poured some for himself and Philippe, "although it is strong, one little glass like this won't have a powerful effect."

He added a small quantity of water to our glasses and the liquid flushed a cloudy yellow, then he tipped his own glass, gently, until a few drops fell on the carpet.

"This *libation*," he said, "is symbolic more than anything. And now," he added, "you must follow me and drink it down in one."

He raised his glass in a toast and, tipping his head back, gulped it down. There was only a small mouthful in each glass, but I could see from the contraction around his mouth that it was strongly flavoured. I knocked mine back unceremoniously and felt a searing fire as it went down my throat, which made me choke. Philippe, who had drained his glass neatly and without any fuss, laughed and said, "The neat liqueur is 80% alcohol, Greg, so it's hardly surprising that it made you cough."

"Now," said Ian, "there is to be a little ceremony. But not a ritualistic one. Philippe and I are going to exchange our amulets."

He reached into the front of his shirt and loosed a chain, which he pulled over his head, and deposited the amulet in his palm. It was identical to the one that Philippe wore: a gold coin set in a plain silver mounting with an eye at the top for the chain. Philippe took his off and exchanged it with Ian. They kissed, briefly and formally, then slipped the new pendants back over their heads. It was simple, but clearly highly symbolic. For a moment I was reminded of the first time I'd seen the amulet, the afternoon I'd first had sex with Philippe. Once again, I had a powerful yet abstruse sense that great significance was attached to them.

Ian turned to me.

"It would be a shame," he told me, "if you couldn't somehow participate in this."

He went to his desk and, opening the central drawer, took out an identical, but unmounted, coin. This he handed to me. It was obviously extremely old and had the sovereign's face on one side with the words *Rex Carolus* across the top, and a complicated shield or coat of arms on the other.

"Guard this coin," he told me. "It is precious beyond words. There were a small number of these minted in the mid-seventeenth century. They are exactly like the crowns of the day – minted for King Charles between 1642 and 1649. But if you look closely, there are two extra and specific marks on these ones, one on each side of the king's head. On the right is a cup, representing the chalice of spiritual knowledge, which on the proper coins would be a letter X, and is not dissimilar at a glance; and on the left there is a figure of eight on its side – a lemniscate, the symbol of eternity, amongst other things; again, not something that you would particularly notice unless you looked at it closely. Especially on a coin like this, which is slightly worn. At that time, when it was considered heretical to follow any kind of occult practice, it might have cost someone like yourself his life if he were ever discovered. So in the same way that the Masons developed their secret handshake for identification, we used this – and have used other coins, also, over time. They are so discreet that someone who doesn't know anything about the special markings would never recognise such a coin as different from other coins of its type. And yet, if you were looking out for it, it would be unmistakable. You could openly handle such a coin in public without fear – that was its great advantage."

I didn't know what to say to such a precious gift, so I just said, "Thank you," and for an instant I discerned a powerful smell of incense, which vanished as quickly as it had arisen.

"You're welcome," said Ian with a smile.

And that was the end of the ceremonials. We left the farmhouse soon afterwards, but before we did so, I asked Ian a question that had been growing within me for some time.

"Is it a gay thing?" I asked him. "First I met Kit, then Philippe, and now you... Is everyone who has this *energy* gay?"

Ian laughed.

"No, no, of course not. You've met gay people because like attracts like. When you've settled down you will meet others."

On the journey back, there was nothing to look at in the dark and so we absorbed ourselves with conversation.

"Why haven't you told me more about these powers, and about people like Ian?" I asked Philippe.

"You didn't want me to," he said.

"How do you know that?"

He became uncharacteristically defensive. "Because you could have asked me about it *at any time* – and you didn't. I would have been happy to tell you most of what I know if you'd ever expressed an interest. Sure, you raised the subject when we first met, but you never mentioned it again. I presumed that you were wary, or perhaps a little bit scared, and so I decided to wait for you to request information. Foisting things on people before they're ready can be extremely counter-productive. And I could sense, as well, that you had been freaked-out by the person you met before me." He paused. "Am I right?"

I thought about this for a couple of minutes.

"I suppose so," I agreed with a nod.

"It's easy for Ian to say that I should have told you more, but he's forgotten that you have to be ready to accept information, or you'll end up rejecting it."

"That's what the boy I knew before told me," I said. "But I feel that I *am* ready now, and Ian obviously thinks so, too. So what do we do?"

He smiled at me and reached over to stroke the side of my face.

"I'll tell you whatever you want to know. But there's one thing I'd ask," he said.

"What?"

"Don't ask me now. This evening. I'll tell you what you want to know, but formulate your questions first. Come up with a list, if you like, and I'll do my best to answer them. But tonight is special; it's an important day, and I want it to have a certain... mystery to it."

I remembered Kit saying the same thing – that the mystery was intrinsic to being able to get something out of an experience. I had been too stressed-out at that time to let myself go with the flow, but I was determined to make more of an effort this time.

"Do I take it, from what you've just said, that we're not just going straight back somewhere to bed – that there's some more... ritual... to come?"

"Mmm," Philippe nodded.

"In that case," I said, "I leave myself in your hands. I trust you absolutely, Philippe. But remember, I'll ask you *all* about it later."

"Fine," he laughed.

As we approached Stoke, Philippe turned off the main road, making for Kidsgrove, and I looked questioningly at him.

"Don't ask," he said. "You'll see."

We skirted the railway and the canal and, in a flash, I knew where we were heading. We were going to the crumbling farmhouse with the private chapel, where I'd met Mark. Following swiftly after that realisation, I also understood that Philippe was intending to make love to me there. Although the idea of it was bizarre, it was also intensely erotic. I closed my eyes and thought, *Let this happen. Go with it.* And I found myself smiling with anticipation.

"What about Mark?" I asked. "Will he be there?"

"No," Philippe replied. "He's away for the weekend, with his parents. The house is locked up, but no one ever locks the chapel. There's nothing in there to steal."

"It could be vandalised," I pointed out.

Philippe nodded but said nothing.

"Does Mark know about this?" I asked.

"No."

"Oh."

"There was no reason to tell him," Philippe said. "He would only be upset that he hadn't been asked to join in, and what we're going to do this evening is private."

"Aren't there other people around? You know, farm workers, who might see or hear us."

"No, none that live close enough," Philippe assured me. "Don't worry, I've checked."

"I'm not worried," I said, truthfully.

Philippe pulled off the road beside the rusted gates to the drive and switched the headlights off. He took a small torch from the glove compartment, and got out. We held hands and walked along the short drive, with ash trees whispering above us in the dark as we followed the pale silvery beam of Philippe's torch. With my free hand I felt in my pocket and touched the coin that Ian had given me. So... I was part of some hidden lineage that went back, at the very least, for centuries. The thought made me shiver in the cold, still air, and for the first time, I felt positively towards my difference.

At the far end of the house, the door leading into the back courtyard stood ajar, as it had before. It was in too poor condition to be closed, I guessed. It resembled an ancient barn door, with its great, long, bolted hinges, and seemed incongruous, impossible, as part of a house. The flagstones of the floor in front of the chapel looked black in the light of Philippe's torch, and when he turned the handle of the door and pulled it slowly open, the shadows inside looked even blacker. I was surprised by a touch of warm air against my cheek as we stepped inside. It was almost as if the chapel were a living thing.

Philippe had set two large, pale candles on the altar, which he proceeded to light once he'd closed the door behind us. He had also brought the electric convection heater from the little studio flat that we had been using as our bolt-hole, I noticed, which explained the warm air. I could see the flex, plugged in to an electrical extension, snaking out under the door.

"When did you set this up?" I asked.

"I came over here before I collected you at lunch time. At first, I didn't think I'd be able to find somewhere to plug the heater in, but there is an accessible point in that disused store room by the back door."

In between the candles there was a brass dish with a perforated cover. Philippe took the top off this and picked up a small black disk from inside.

"Charcoal," he said, and proceeded to play the flame of his lighter beneath one edge of it. This went on for some time with no discernable result, but after a while a thin stream of pale smoke rose from the disk, and the lower side of the charcoal began to glow. Philippe dropped the disk back into the censer and then turned to me.

"It'll take another ten minutes to properly get going," he said. "Come here."

Our first kiss was slow and searching, and Philippe was careful, gentle, as if I were fragile and might break. He pulled my bomber jacket off, then unbuttoned my shirt, running his cool fingers over my ribs, which made me shiver, but not with cold. I reached out to undo his shirt, but he stopped me.

"Not yet," he said, pulling the shirt off my shoulders and letting it fall to the floor.

There is something thrilling about being exposed and naked when one's partner remains fully clothed, because all the attention is being directed one way. And so it was now. Clearly my role was not to reciprocate, but to accept Philippe's homage to my body, which I did. Philippe unbuckled my belt and eased down my jeans, then my boxer shorts, which was indescribably erotic in the warm, sepulchral darkness. I removed my watch and dropped it on the pew beside me, idly noticing that it was 11.40 p.m. Philippe kneeled in front of me to unlace my shoes, then, once I'd stepped out of them, he pulled my socks off one by one, thus rendering me completely naked. When he stood up, he stepped towards me and leaned in, so that the only part of us that was touching was our lips. His kisses moved from my lips to my ears, and then down my neck to my chest, and nipples, which he attended to with a flurry of nibbles. Then he traced his tongue further down, pausing briefly at my navel, before making a definitive contact with my straining erection.

Philippe sensed that I was dangerously close to orgasm and ceased his ministrations. He stopped and stood up with a mischievous grin. Without a word – and I knew by now not to interrupt this ritual in any way – he moved me to one side and pressed me down, so that I was sitting on the inner edge of the first pew. He left me there and went to the alter, where he picked up the candles and placed them in the embrasures on the wall above. Then he went to the door, behind which I noticed he had piled three flattish, square cushions and a holdall. He lifted two small jars from the bag and, opening one of them, took a pinch of material that looked like wood shavings, though as he passed, I saw that there were semi-luminous crystals mixed in with it, too. He dropped the mixture onto the now-grey charcoal disk in the censer, and tendrils of fragrant smoke sprang up immediately. He replaced the perforated top of the censer and positioned it on the floor immediately in front of the altar, then went back for the cushions. These he placed on the top of the altar, thus transforming it into a raised mattress.

He turned to me and, standing with one foot on either side of the censer, took the top off it and added a further, generous pinch of incense. Then, standing straight again, he started to remove his clothes. As he took each item off, he folded it carefully and put it on one of the cushions behind him. It was almost impossible to sit there and watch his extraordinary physique being exposed without running forward to catch hold of it. With candlelight to either side of him, and smoke wafting up from below, he looked wild and mysterious. This side-lighting delineated the musculature of his chest with such precision that I wished I'd brought my camera with me. When he'd peeled everything else off, he also removed his pendant – for the first time since I'd met him – and stepped forward to hook it over the end of the pew on which I was sitting.

Unsmiling now, he took his neat pile of clothes and placed it on the other side of me. He looked completely calm, and, were it not for his achingly firm erection, I wouldn't have thought of him as being aroused in any way. He closed his eyes for a moment, muttered something that I couldn't quite catch, and then came over to me. He took me by the shoulders, pulled me to my feet and led me over to the altar. What was happening was so surreal that I almost laughed, but that was the last time mirth came into it, because, once I'd been helped up onto the altar, the dark dreaminess of it overwhelmed me, like the smoke that wreathed the air around us.

Lying on my back, silently, was strange because it made me feel intensely passive – something that I had never previously experienced with Philippe. It was powerfully erotic, and I wondered whether being fucked was going to hurt. I closed my eyes to still that anxiety and felt Philippe's hands stroking my chest. He'd taken position at the end of the altar and, leaning down to put yet more incense onto the burner, he picked up the second small jar – of lubricant, I presumed. I did not raise my head, but looked to one side at the candlelight. As he pushed my knees up, I was surprised by the coolness, in that warm space, of the lubricant he applied to me.

He heaved himself up and leant over me, and I wondered for a moment how bizarre this must look, but then I didn't care any longer. Philippe's face was hovering above mine like a shadow, his full, dark eyebrows knitted and his nostrils flared. I instinctively curled my lower spine to raise myself for him, as he had done on so many occasions for me, then closed my eyes at the pressure of him. I willed myself to relax, but Philippe halted there, poised, for some time. Slowly, my breathing – which I hadn't realised had become ragged – returned to normal and he pushed forward a little, then stopped again. This went on for some minutes, Philippe pushing himself into me so slowly that I had time to get used to it and relax further before he would continue. By the time he had fully entered me, I'd felt no pain – only a minor discomfort that was irrelevant. We lay like that for a minute or so, me feeling *attached* to him, and filled by him, which was an amazing sensation in itself. But when he began to move inside me with slow, gentle thrusts, holding me firmly by the waist, I felt that a totally new sensation was building up. It was a path to orgasm, of course, but different in an all-important way from anything I'd known before – as if I was coming to it from an oblique angle. Although the end result would be the same, I knew that the journey there would be completely different. I reasoned that this was the difference between fucking and being fucked – or perhaps it was the spectacularly different setting and ambience in which it was happening. Whatever it was, I was so totally transported that Philippe's breathing seemed to come from a long way off. Then he cried a triumphant "Yes!" and I responded with a groan, reaching out to pull his buttocks towards me, to keep him moving inside me just a little bit longer, and a few seconds later I came myself with a juddering finality.

Philippe lowered himself onto me, and held me in a tight, sweaty clasp, kissing the side of my neck, then ran his fingers up my sides until I squirmed. Then he clambered off me and, taking me by the hand, pulled me into a sitting position. He put his fingers to my lips to keep me quiet, and indicated my clothes.

We both dressed casually, without hurry. I caught his eye once, and we smiled at each other, secretively. Once we were dressed, Philippe took me by the elbow and indicated the door.

"What about all this stuff?" I whispered.

"I'll come and get it tomorrow," he whispered back.

We walked to the car, hand in hand once more, and Philippe drove me back to Horton without speaking. I was happy with this silence, which was replete in so many ways that words were superfluous. A part of me was disappointed that I wasn't going to be spending the night with him as he'd inferred, but on the other hand, I felt that I had transcended the need for it. Ordinary modes of behaviour no longer applied to us. We were free and dangerous.

When he dropped me off at home, he looked at his watch. "One-thirty a.m.," he said. "It's my birthday today. I'm eighteen."

Thirteen

I slept late the following morning and rose feeling rested and content. I ate a lazy breakfast in the kitchen where my mother was doing some preliminary preparation for lunch. We chatted about nothing in particular, and then, after a second cup of coffee, I went out for my first weekend cycle ride in weeks. I went up past Kit's old place and, for the first time, I didn't feel a pang of loss as I cycled under those two great beech trees that guarded the gates. Kit seemed such ancient history now, when in fact it was only a year since I'd last seen him. It seemed like a lifetime.

After lunch I worked for a while on a Victorian bowed chest of drawers that had been painted (badly) with white gloss and had sustained damage on one of the rear corners, and I found that I was still glowing inside from Philippe's attentions of the night before. At the end of the afternoon I even sat and watched tv with my sisters – something that I hardly ever did. When the local news came on, I didn't notice the coverage of the accident at first because there was nothing unusual about it, but when they showed a photograph of Mark Daniels, I jolted upright.

"I *know* him," I said.

Or rather, I knew him. He was dead. Along with his parents, in a head-on collision with an articulated lorry on the M6 near the junction 14 turn off to Stafford. The lorry driver had been unharmed, but when they showed pictures of the car, it had been mashed so completely that it was impossible to tell what make it was, and was barely bigger than a fridge. I stared in horror as the announcer told us that the accident had happened in the early hours of that morning.

"Was he a close friend?" my older sister asked quietly.

"No, not at all," I said. "I only met him once, but..."

My voice petered out. It wasn't that I knew him, but that I knew, without any doubt whatsoever, that the 'accident' had been no accident at all. I was suddenly desperate to talk to Philippe. I jumped up and said, "I've got to go," and ran out of the house to get my bike as my sisters stared after me in surprise.

I cycled the five miles to Philippe's house so fast that when I arrived the sweat was dripping agonizingly into my eyes. All those months without cycling had taken their toll. I banged on the door but there was no answer. Desperately frustrated, I went on to the studio flat, but that was empty too. Then I realised where he would be. The chapel.

It was about ten miles to Gillow Manor Farm and I was already tired, but I got there in just over half an hour, as dusk was giving way to full darkness. My legs were so tired I could hardly stand up. I went straight into the chapel, but found it as we'd left it the previous night, with all the accoutrements of our SexMagic strewn on and around the altar: the cushions, the candles, the censer... even the little jars of incense and lubricant. But all the beauty and excitement had gone from it now. Mark was dead, and we had been trespassing. I sat down on the front pew and put my head in my hands, my breath still coming in gasps.

What could I do? I *had* to speak to Philippe. I wanted to be reassured that what had happened was not anything to do with what we'd done here. But as I sat there in the rapidly gathering gloom, I knew absolutely that I was clutching at the most tenuous of straws.

I waited in the chapel for some time but he didn't come, which I found mildly suspicious, because Philippe had told me he would come back to clear up all the mess. When I finally limped home on the bike, hours later, I went straight off to my room without eating, which was allowed to pass without comment by my parents, who must have been warned of my strange behaviour by my sisters.

The next day at school I ached all over from my desperate cycling of the day before. Time passed so slowly that when lunch time finally arrived, I was more exhausted than I had been on arrival at 8.45. The afternoon crawled by even more slowly, something that I wouldn't have thought possible. When the bell finally rang at the end of the afternoon, I made my way warily to the gates, wondering if Philippe would come to get me. When I saw his car coming round the corner, I was so relieved that I felt tears prick my eyelids. An odd reaction, in retrospect, because the meeting was not to be an easy one. It stands as proof, if any more were needed, of how infatuated, how *narrow* I had become, that all I could think about was how it would effect my relationship. What I don't understand is why I wanted to see him at all. Why didn't I turn and walk in the other direction? I already *knew* that Philippe had 'caused' Mark's accident. Why did I feel the need to hear it from the horse's mouth? A sudden disappearance on my part, Kit-like and mysterious, would have worked so much better. And it might have averted what was to come later.

Philippe opened the passenger door and I got in. He studied my expression.

"I see that you've heard," he said.

"Yes."

"Let's go to a bar. We both need a good strong drink."

We didn't talk any further until we were in a café bar on the Hanley road. Philippe ordered a bottle of Bordeaux and leaned back in his chair, apparently unperturbed.

"Okay," I said, as he poured us both a glass of wine. "Yesterday, you said that I should formulate some questions for you."

He nodded and raised his glass to me, then sipped.

"And I want to remind you that you also told me that you would do your best to answer them."

"Mmm," he said.

"Right. Question one. Did you have anything to do with the accident in which Mark and his parents died?"

Philippe looked at me with his I-want-to-ravish-you expression and said, "It was a car accident, Greg. I was nowhere near it."

"Don't be evasive. You know what I mean. Did you... *influence* events in any way?"

"You mean did I cast a spell on them?"

"Yes."

"No."

I sipped my own wine and thought how to put the next question.

"Okay. Question two. Do you benefit either directly or indirectly from what happened?"

An extraordinary, hooded look came over Philippe and he looked away.

"Well?" I asked.

He drew a long breath and sighed.

"Gillow Manor Farm is now mine," he said.

"How do you mean?"

"Mark made a will," he said, "and left me everything. He was an only child, so what would have come to him via his parents, now comes to me."

I felt a thump in my chest, like a blow.

"But Mark was just a kid. Why would he have made a will?"

"Mark was nineteen. His parents made him draw up a will on his eighteenth birthday. There were feuding factions in the family and his parents wanted him to make a will that prevented certain relatives ever getting their hands on the house and farm."

"What did they say when Mark left everything to you?"

"They didn't know. He did that later."

I stared at Philippe, at his super-calm face.

"How did you get Mark to do that for you? Did you force him?"

"No," said Philippe, "of course not. He did it of his own accord."

"I see," I said, realising. "Mark was in love with you, wasn't he? I can see it now, though I didn't notice at the time. And did you have sex with him?"

Philippe looked away.

"So, you coolly made him fall in love with you," I said, "for your own ends."

"We made one or two attempts at SexMagic," Philippe told me. "That was all."

"But you *killed* him," I hissed. "You killed Mark and his parents to get your hands on their property."

Philippe leaned forward earnestly. He spoke quietly, but with a fierce intensity.

"Alright, I *did* bend my will towards the ultimate goal of possessing Gillow Manor Farm, that's true, but as far as 'causing' anything goes, that's not how these things work. What happens is that you wish for something, and then fortune, luck, *coincidence* – call it what you like – begins to work in your favour. You don't *make* anything happen, it just *does* happen, of its own accord."

"Sounds an impossibly fine distinction to me," I said.

I stared down at my hands and focused my thoughts.

"So tell me," I said, "how did you get the money to buy your Mercedes? And what about the factory you managed to sell off... Did you *bend your will* towards that as well?"

Philippe shrugged.

"I can't believe this. You've done these... these *evil* things, and you don't seem to care."

"Care?" he scoffed. "Care? Why should I *care*? I haven't done anything to be ashamed of. I haven't caused a war, or mass starvation, or done anything to make this world a worse place. Precisely the opposite, in fact. What good were Mark and his parents? We're talking about three inbred, indolent, *incompetent* dregs of a once interesting aristocratic family. Why should I give a shit that they're dead? Now that they're gone, I can make something of that place. I can sell off all the land on the far side of the canal to people who have the ability to *use* it, rather than let it fall into dereliction. And I'll use the money that I raise to renovate the house. I'll be generating employment, Greg. *That's* what I call useful."

"And it's come to you on your eighteenth birthday," I said. "How neat."

Philippe's attitude was so repulsive that it killed my feelings for him abruptly. So complete was the change – as swift, efficient and unequivocal as the flicking of a switch – that, as I regarded his perfect physical beauty, I wondered how I had ever seen any inner beauty in him. He had never cared for me, he had simply wanted to have sex with me – and I'd been so grateful for that that I'd never looked for anything more.

And then another thought struck me.

"All this sex," I gasped. "You've been *using* it, haven't you? You told me once that SexMagic was extremely powerful, but you never talked about it again, except to say I should channel my sexual energy into something or someone that I felt sacramental about. And I felt sacramental about you, so I gave you my energy. I *gave* it to you, and you combined it with your own, and you *used* it."

I looked at him with loathing, now.

"You used Mark and then discarded him. How long was it going to be before you did the same to me? Or is that what you're doing now?"

"There's no comparison between you and Mark," Philippe said.

"For a start, Mark had no intrinsic power, like you do. And it's difficult to get a resonance going with someone you don't fancy."

"Christ, you're so... *calculating*," I spat as the whole ghastly truth revealed itself to me. "It was all for you, wasn't it? All those so-called erotic trysting places. You had sex with me in that factory, and then you somehow managed to sell the factory. You had sex with me in the chapel at Gillow Manor Farm, and now it's become yours... How many other times did you use me for generating personal gain? How many times have you twisted what I gave to you with love into something that you wielded with hate?"

Philippe didn't answer, and seemed to be waiting for me to peter out, which I did. I'd said my piece and now I'd had enough. I rose to leave, but he grabbed my arm and forced me back into my chair. I was going to punch his arm away, but I was curious to see what he had to say.

"I knew that you'd find out what I was doing," he said. "It was inevitable. I also knew that you would react in this way, and I can understand why you feel the way you do. You think what I'm doing is evil, but it's not. It is morally neutral. Amoral, if you like. Now that you know, Greg, you could come in with me and help me with this 'magic'. If you came in with me, willingly, you would gain at least as much as I would. Just think what you could do with the money. You could give it away, make a difference, do *good*."

I stood up once more.

"Fuck off, Philippe," I said. "If you think murdering people – because that's what it amounts to, and you know it – is morally neutral, then there's nothing left to say except, please, never try to contact me again. This is over."

I walked out of the bar, but Philippe followed me and grabbed me by the shoulder.

"You think you can get away from me that easily?" he asked with what amounted to a sneer. "We're attached, Greg. We've got bonds that you can never break. Remember that."

I saw that he was smiling as he said this, and, in a reflex motion, I punched that perfect face as hard as I could. Philippe staggered back and crashed against the door of the café, where he fell to the ground and lay immobile. I looked down at him for a moment.

"No, Philippe, you're wrong," I informed his recumbent body. "I'm stronger than you think."

And then I turned and ran.

PART THREE

Fourteen

After I punched Philippe and ran away, I suffered acute anxiety for several weeks. Firstly, I thought I might have killed him, and then, when there was no sign of it in the papers, I thought he might attempt some kind of retribution. Also, it suddenly occurred to me, about a week after I'd last seen him, that we'd been indulging in the most unsafe sex imaginable. If he'd been having sex with Mark before me, then how many others had he slept with? And, of course, given the carnivorous sexual rapacity that he possessed, who knows what he'd got up to with them, especially given that he had a preference for the passive role? So during the summer, I summoned up the nerve and secretly trekked to Manchester for an HIV test. Which came back negative. As for the retribution, nothing happened, and as time passed I calmed down and focused on my school work, and the upcoming 'A' levels.

During that period of hard work, I often wondered about the feeble justification Philippe had offered for his acts – that with the rewards one reaped, one could do good. It was laughably reductive, and patently wrong. But it was a long time before I realised that maybe Kit had said the same thing, in so many words, when he'd argued that Judas' 'bad' deeds could ultimately be recuperated as 'good'. In the end I decided, somewhat reluctantly, that Mr Evans had got it absolutely right: to argue that good coming of bad proves that bad is really good is just playing into the hands of the Devil. Not that I believed in the Devil, of course. In their own way, Kit and Philippe were as bad as each other, I decided. One was genuinely evil, the other a naive fool. But it didn't matter now. I had consigned both of them to the past and intended to keep them there. I decided that if I ever came across another person with that *energy*, I would turn and walk away before a word was spoken.

That summer, I was pleasantly surprised to get into Oxford. I'd like to say that I found it easy, but I didn't. With all the disruption of Philippe in the lower sixth, it's a wonder I managed it at all. But, after he'd gone, I had nothing left to do but slave to get the necessary grades. Mr Blandford had spurred me to apply to Oxford because he'd been there himself, and one or two of the professors who'd taught him were still there. I had had more of a leaning towards UCL or Cambridge, largely because Kit had been headed for Oxford and I was determined to have nothing further to do with that side of life. But Oxford it turned out to be. And that, as I was beginning to learn, was clearly no 'coincidence'.

So there I was, an undergraduate, just beginning my first year. I had no past. No one on my course was aware of the rumours that had abounded at school. Whilst Richard Murray was at Oxford, too – at another of the colleges, studying maths – our worlds were so separate now that there was no cross-pollination of gossip. On the odd occasion that we saw each other, we didn't speak, or even acknowledge each other's presence – as sometimes happens when two people have mutually outgrown a situation-specific friendship.

I had imagined that we'd all been behaving like young adults at school, in the upper sixth, but when I got to university I realised that we'd still been children. Here, no one whispered about my homosexuality. It was completely open, accepted and acceptable in a way that I found almost shocking. I was taking my studies (English) moderately unseriously; I had money in my pocket from working for dad and not spending what I'd earned; and I had a bunch of new friends to go out drinking and dancing with. My life was brash, loud and exhilarating. I slept around a bit, drank a lot, and took more drugs than perhaps I should have, and generally had a fantastic time. I even managed to get enough academic work done to neither fail nor shine. It was perfect.

At the beginning of my second year, I had the opportunity to move out of halls of residence and into a house in town, which I shared with four others – two women and two men, one of whom was gay. Whilst most people imagine those cool, silent college rooms, with their mullioned windows and thick stone walls, to be the apotheosis of the Oxbridge experience, I found them stultifying. To me they reeked of outmoded privilege, archaic – almost medieval – ceremony, and pretension. And the rules of conduct were absurd. Contrastingly, the atmosphere in the house was cool. There were occasional bitching sessions, occasional arguments, and regular periods of frenetic, panicky, amphetamine-fuelled studying. But it all worked well, especially in comparison to some of the other student houses, which quickly degenerated into nightmarish hells of personality clashes and domestic problems. We all liked to play our music loud and come in at seven o'clock in the morning, but we also respected each other's need for peace in the approach to important deadlines.

Considering the scale of what had gone on between myself and Philippe, it was amazing to find that, in time, it took on such an air of unreality that I began to wonder if the whole thing couldn't be perfectly explained in ordinary, unmagical terms. As far as my experience with Kit went, that was so unextreme that I could easily cast it as a cross between simple trickery on his part and youthful gullibility on mine. Philippe was more difficult to dismiss. I kept imagining him living at Gillow Manor Farm. It was probably in fantastic condition now – and he was only twenty. But then, what had actually happened? What had he *done* to get it? He'd sold some property, and then a boy and his parents had died. Did that *prove* anything? The more time passed, the more it seemed absurd that he had exerted power of any sort over anything but my imagination. I thought of trying to tell the others in the house about it, and knew they would laugh derisively at the thought that Philippe had used our sexual relationship to generate energy that he could direct for his own purposes. Put like that, it *did* sound ridiculous, and childish, too.

And then, one afternoon in early November, after a seminar on Hogg, it all started happening again...

It was one of those utterly still afternoons when the sun still has a vestige of warmth to it, and people were sitting out on the grass by the River Cherwell. I was walking along the banks of the river in Magdalen College's deer park, more or less aimlessly, but with half a mind to end up in the library at some point. The other half of me was looking for distraction: a coffee, or perhaps a beer. I wasn't much of an afternoon drinker, but – so long as I only did it occasionally – there was something excellent about giving up on studies and retiring to the riverside with a few cans, to while away the rest of the day with laughter and conversation. That day was the twentieth birthday of Janine, one of the women in our house, so I knew the day was going to slip away from me at some point, anyway, as the whole house was being given over to a major party.

As I smiled in happy anticipation, I felt an odd tingling in my gut, like nerves before a concert. This was accompanied by an unusual alertness, and I looked around, wondering if perhaps someone had called out my name. There was no one around that I recognised, however, so I continued. The feeling built rapidly until I wondered if it was something I'd eaten, and then, just as it was becoming genuinely uncomfortable, I saw Kit, sitting under the tree that I was passing.

He'd been on the far side of the trunk so I didn't see him until the last moment, when we were only a few metres apart. Along with the jolt of recognition came an absolute conviction that it was Kit's (unseen) presence that had caused the flutter of nerves in my stomach. Had I known that he was going to be there – had I seen him up ahead, for example – I might have tried to avoid him. But, instead, I stopped dead, and looked down.

He was sitting cross-legged with his eyes closed, seemingly in a deep meditative state. His hair was slightly longer, but otherwise he looked exactly the same. Time had evened us out, somehow, and I no longer had the feeling that he was so much older than me. He looked like just another undergraduate, where before, at school, he'd looked so much more adult than everyone else. But then, I thought, when you're fifteen or sixteen, two years makes so much more difference than it does when you're nearly twenty.

On one hand, I wanted to rouse him so that I could talk to him, and on the other hand, I felt an irresistible urge to run, or creep away. The curious influx of nervous energy I'd felt as I approached the tree was enough to give me a sinking feeling of, 'Oh no, here we go again'; but then there were questions I found I was still burning to ask him. For example, why he had so suddenly disappeared, almost exactly three years before?

Kit didn't stir. A tremor passed over his eyelids for a moment, but he remained inert. The stillness of his face made me remember the photograph of him that I still kept somewhere in one of my files. He retained that high-cheekboned, angular-jawed look, and had clearly kept up with the cycling because he was wearing shorts and I could see the muscle definition in his thighs and calves, and the golden hairs catching the glinting sun. Now I'd been looking at him for a while, I thought perhaps his shoulders were a little broader than they had been. And then it struck me how strange it was that I hadn't seen him before, if he'd been studying here all this time.

He opened his eyes and looked up at me, but otherwise didn't move at all.

"Hello, Greg," he said calmly, making me jump. "I wondered when I'd see you."

"Jeez, you gave me a fright," I said.

Kit stretched out his legs. Now that I was in his company, it was hard to see Kit as a possible threat to my equilibrium. There was something comforting about him, where Philippe had always been so... hard-edged. As if on cue, as I thought his name, a cloud passed over the sun and the temperature suddenly dropped. I shivered.

"Do you want to go for a coffee somewhere?" Kit asked, heaving himself up.

"Fine," I said. "Or perhaps you'd like to go for a beer?"

He looked carefully at me, then shrugged.

"Whatever."

We went to The Eagle and Child, whose atmosphere was dim and sober, and I bought us both a pint before finding a seat beside the inglenook.

"You're looking very well," he told me as I raised my glass to him.

"So are you," I said. "Still cycling?"

"Yes, and you?"

"Only in and out for seminars."

"We should go out somewhere together. It's not as wild round here, but there are other compensations."

I laughed and said, "The first time we met you invited me out for a bike ride."

Kit smiled, too.

"Yes," he said, "I did, didn't I?"

He looked out of the window and I noticed how beautiful he still was. There was something easy and comfortable about the way we were sitting together like this, but there were unspoken things hanging between us, too. I wondered how long we could keep up this odd semblance of casualness. I decided that Kit might be waiting for me to raise the subject of the past, in which case I might as well get on with it.

"What happened?" I asked him suddenly. "How come you disappeared like that? One day you were saying you'd see me next week, then the next day you'd gone and your house was empty."

He looked at me directly, as though assessing my ability to hear what he had to say.

"I could see you were closing down... against me," he said. "There was no point in trying to coerce you, so I... left."

"You don't leave school, and get your family to move house, just because you're not getting on with a fellow pupil..."

"Is that all you think it was?"

"I..." I hesitated. "I don't know. That's how it came to seem."

Kit looked down into his beer and traced his finger through the condensation on the side of his glass.

"Well, you must have got on alright," he said, "otherwise you wouldn't be here." He made an expansive gesture which encompassed the whole of Oxford.

I felt a flash of anger.

"Oh, academically things were alright," I said. "Or at least, *salvageable*."

"You sound bitter."

"Oh, really? How astonishing. I was falling in love for first time in my life, and you abandoned me. What else do you expect me to feel?"

I hadn't meant to say that. I hadn't really known, until then, that that was how I *did* feel.

Kit nodded. "I'm sorry if you feel it was like that," he said.

I had forgotten how sincere he always sounded and, without particularly wanting to, I found myself relenting.

"It's ancient history," I sighed. "But I have to tell you, I had a ghastly relationship on the rebound. I got fucked over. Literally."

Kit's eyes narrowed and he stared at me, then shook his head.

We sat in silence for a few moments.

"But don't worry about me," I told him. "As I said, it's ancient history."

He nodded and drank down the last of his pint and went to get us another one. He looked as assured as ever as he stood at the bar, laughing, briefly, with the barmaid and tapping the bar with his long, fine fingers.

"And how are your studies going?" he asked when he came back.

I shrugged.

"Okay," I said. "I found it odd at first, not having any lectures or classes. You know, just going off and doing all the reading on my own, then coming back for one intensely intellectual seminar. I spent the whole of last year wondering why nobody was teaching me anything."

Kit laughed.

"But now it's much easier. There's too much else to do to find enough time for studying."

"Such as?"

"For a start, sitting in bars *talking*, like we're doing now," I told him. "And there's a big birthday party for one of the girls at my digs tonight. Do you want to come along?"

"I don't think I can, but thanks."

"Well, let me give you the address anyway, just in case," I said, taking out my pen and pulling a receipt from my pocket on which to write it down, along with the phone number. I included Janine's mobile number for good measure. "It's just off Woodstock Road."

Kit nodded and took the paper from me, putting it absently into his shirt pocket. Conversation became more general after that and, when I offered to buy us both another beer, Kit refused, saying he had to go.

"Where are *you* staying?" I asked him as he got up.

"Oh," he said, vaguely, "between the Isis and the canal, not far from the ice rink."

"Well," I told him, "even if you can't make it tonight, give me a ring and come over some other time."

Kit nodded.

"Thanks."

I watched him leaving and he seemed, unequivocally, like just any other ordinary young man. I found it amazing that I'd ever thought of him as having superhuman powers.

The party was great, and very busy. The house was absolutely rammed by eleven-thirty. There was dance music in the sitting room, which was a chaotic fury of arms and legs, and Janine had cleared the main bedroom, where there was chill-out stuff playing – a gentle, ambient thumping which encouraged late night philosophic chat. The corridors were thick with faces both familiar and strange, and people hung out of every available window. I'd hidden a private stash of cans in the garden, so I didn't have to worry if there was enough drink in the kitchen – where the table was piled with cans, cartons of juice, bottles of wine and platters of food, all surrounding the conspicuous centre-piece of a bottle of tequila that no one felt they quite had the right to open – yet.

Janine cornered me at about midnight and dragged me off to my bedroom to snort a couple of lines of cocaine – a birthday gift to her from her brother – where we found a girl talking to her – boyfriend? – about Jean Paul Sartre and the fluidity of Time. I'd only had cocaine once before, and snorted this offering off the top of the bedside table with alacrity, along with a few gulps of the tequila that she was now carrying with her to pour down the throat of anyone who crossed her path.

"You know what Sartre says?" Janine informed the girl as she passed over her bottle. "Everything is an instant of now. And it looks as if your 'now' happens to be this tequila."

The girl coughed when she took a gulp, the boy laughed and

refused, and we left. As we descended the stairs, I somehow managed to appropriate the bottle. Later, I ended up snogging a friend of Alan's, the other gay guy in the house – a boy who purported to be straight but who was either lying or being extremely politically correct and liberal.

By half-past-midnight the cocaine was buzzing to the max and I was utterly mashed. I shimmied into the kitchen, grinning and waving the now three quarters empty bottle of tequila above my head, and came face to face with Kit. I can't say that it sobered me up – no one who'd consumed as much as I had could sober up as easily as that – but that's how it felt.

"Um..." I said, lowering my frantic arm and trying to look vaguely normal, "...tequila?"

Kit smiled and raised a clear plastic glass.

"I have some red wine," he told me. "But thanks."

I was at a loss as to what to say, but eventually managed to mumble, "Come through and sit down."

He followed me through the crowded hall and into the sitting room, where we managed to find enough floor space to sit with our backs to the far end of a large sofa. Legs were flying, only inches from our faces; music was crashing around us; and the babble of yelled conversation washed around us like a tide. I took a swig of tequila and smiled at Kit.

"It goes well in red wine," I said.

"What does?"

"Tequila."

"I'll take your word for it."

I leaned my head back on the arm of the sofa and closed my eyes for a moment.

"You're so drunk," Kit said, with no inflection in his voice either of approval or censure.

"It's a party," I said. "What do you expect?"

He put his hand on mine and then took it away.

"It's fun to get drunk sometimes, I know," he said. "But it can be distracting."

"I believe that's the point of it," I told him, taking another swig.

Kit shook his head and looked away. I leaned towards him to say something, but lost my balance during the process and found that I couldn't stop myself, and I slumped gently onto him and passed out in his lap.

The following day I had less of a hangover than I'd expected, and certainly less than I deserved, probably due to the cocaine or perhaps the cleanness of the tequila. On the other hand, it was only just after nine when I made a start on the clearing up, and I was probably still drunk. I had no recollection of getting to bed, nor of Kit leaving. In fact, at first, I wasn't absolutely sure that he'd been there at all. But then I remembered, with a wince of embarrassment, meeting him in the kitchen.

It's odd that, having thought of him on and off for so long, and being so equivocal about what I would do if I saw him, I should have blown my first real chance of getting to know him again – at exactly the moment that I realised I *did* want to re-establish our friendship. Of course, he hadn't left me his address or phone number. And having passed out on him – literally – he'd probably been well and truly put off dropping by or phoning.

Although I wasn't apologetic for being off my face in front of him, his comment about distraction smarted. But then, I was genuinely enjoying my time at university – something I felt I deserved after my intense experiences at school – and I wanted him to know that many of those boozy conversations held in pubs were *intellectual* discussions, not the superficial bawdiness he'd implied. It made me want to get in touch with him even more, to show him that the party animal side of me wasn't all there was. I don't know why I felt so defensive about it.

Having more or less cleared and cleaned the kitchen, I left the appalling mess of the sitting room for the others (none of whom had yet appeared) and set out into in the unwelcome glare of late morning sunshine. I dropped into the Registrar's office to find out where I might find Kit's pigeonhole, so that I could leave him a note to get in touch with me. I realised that, as he was two years ahead of me, he must have graduated the summer before and now be doing postgraduate studies of some kind. But there was no sign of him on the register of students. It seemed he was not at the university, and, when I asked about it, was told that he had never been a student here at all.

I had simply assumed that Kit was studying here, but now that I replayed what I remembered of our conversation, I realised he had never actually mentioned his own studies. I considered this new information and wondered what he was doing in Oxford if he'd never been a student here. For a moment, I had an eerie presentiment that he had appeared simply in order to show me that my life had become a form of dissipation. But then I remembered that he'd told me he was living down near the ice rink. But where? Where...

Out on the High Street, with the rather absurd pillared spire of St Anne's rearing above me, I felt bereft, suddenly. I didn't know what to do with myself; I was still feeling too fragile to face academic work of any kind. In the end, I wandered down towards the river. I knew that the chances of bumping into Kit were negligible, but I comforted myself with the logic that it was not statistically *impossible*. I found the whole now-you-see-him-now-you-don't aspect of what had happened infuriating. It so reminded me of the way he'd slipped away from me before.

"Well, fuck you, Kit," I said aloud to the impersonal, modern building in front of me. With that, I decided to abandon my half-hearted search and set off back to St Aldgate's and the encrusted, hallowed architecture of the universities.

Back in the house, Janine and Maggie were sitting in the kitchen drinking coffee along with a pale, hungover-looking young man with whom, I took it, one of them had slept. In the sitting room, Alan was lying back on the sofa whilst Steve (the straight one) was blearily regarding an unopened can of Pils.

"Does hair of the dog actually work?" he asked me as I came in. "I've never tried it. I feel like even a sip of alcohol would make me puke. But, on the other hand, I feel like *anything* would make me puke."

"Stick to water," I told him. "I'll get some for you."

I went out to the kitchen. Janine was saying goodbye to the young man in the hall, and, when I'd got some water for Steve, I followed her into the sitting room.

"So, a birthday boy for the birthday girl," I said.

She touched her hand to her forehead, then massaged her temples. Maggie came in with her coffee and sat down beside me.

"He was alright," she said. "Are you going to see him again?"

Janine shook, or perhaps nodded, her head in an ambiguous gesture of uncertainty.

"Hey," I said, feeling a sudden flash of inspiration, "don't anyone move."

I ran upstairs to my room and got my camera out. It was months since I'd used it, but couldn't resist the scene downstairs. When I came back, Maggie groaned.

"No, Greg, you can't do this to us."

"It'll be a record of a major event," I said. "The entire household strewn amongst the debris. What better testament to a party than that."

"But you won't be in them," Steve pointed out.

"There's a timer," I said.

The next half hour turned out to be rather hilarious, as we posed as corpses amongst the bottles, papers, pizza boxes, empty cigarette packets, juice cartons and brimming ash trays. In spite of my fragile stomach, I felt that I was *doing* something, and began to feel better – even if only by virtue of the fact that everyone else was clearly feeling so much worse.

"Who was that bloke you collapsed onto last night?" Maggie asked once I'd finished with my camera. "You looked quite smitten by him."

"Oh," I said, "an old flame."

Janine laughed.

"You sound so tragic, Greg. Were you in love with him?"

"Yes. Unrequitedly, too."

"And he put you to bed so considerately," Alan said. "I thought *he* was the one who was in love."

I closed my eyes tightly. Maggie reached over and squeezed my hand.

Fifteen

Inevitably, the third year arrived, along with the dark promise of Finals. We all grew tense and serious, and I was ruefully amused because it seemed that I had learned nothing from my experience at 'A' level, where I'd done exactly the same thing: early dissipation followed by manic damage limitation.

It was during this period that I felt that strange flutter in my stomach for a second time, so subtle that I wouldn't have noticed it at all if I hadn't already experienced it. I was studying in the library one morning when it crept into my gut like a whisper of anticipation. Without thinking, I jumped up from my seat, causing those on either side of me to look up, startled. I raced out of the library and onto the quad, but couldn't see Kit anywhere. There were a group of foreign students to my left, a gaggle of third years ahead and... on my right, leaning against the wall, a young man staring directly at me. As I noticed him, he raised his right arm in greeting.

I walked over to him. He was about my height, but thin to the point of emaciation and with a nervous edge to his movements that communicated itself to me. His pinched face held an intense expression, and his large hazel eyes were narrowed in concentration. But he smiled as I walked over to him.

"Who are you?" I asked.

"William," he said, holding out his hand. "And you're Greg Chaley. I'm pleased to meet you."

"How did you do that to me back there?"

"What?"

"You know, make me *feel* that you were there."

He raised his chin in a tiny, triumphant movement.

"It's something I've been practising," he said.

"And how do you know my name?"

"I was in the same halls as you last year, though I don't suppose you remember me."

"No, I'm afraid I don't," I said. "I'm sorry."

"I recognised you," he said, "because I could see that you were *elect*."

There was something absurd in the grand way he said it.

"Elect?" I scoffed.

"Yes."

I took a deep breath.

"I'm sorry," I said. "I do know a little of what you're talking about, but it's always caused much more trouble than it's worth, so, please, leave me alone. I'm not interested."

I went back into the library to collect my books, but he came after me.

"Look," he said. "You don't choose it. It chooses you. You can't do anything about it."

I stopped and turned to him. He was looking at me intently, as if he wanted me to clap my arm round his shoulder, drag him off to a stone circle and enact some arcane initiation rite with him.

"It's been more than three years since anything... odd... happened to me," I said, "barring a brief meeting with an old friend, about six months ago. And I seem to be doing perfectly well since I chose to have nothing whatever to do with this *unnamed* energy."

"Don't you know it's name?" he asked.

"No."

"Oh, I thought... I thought you were supposed to..." He petered out and looked away, embarrassed. "I thought," he murmured, "you might be prepared to be my... guide."

I laughed.

"No," I told him. "I expect you know more about it than I do."

"But you are gay?"

"Yes."

"So am I," he said. "I've been working on this on my own, but I can't get any further without help. I've seen you about, and knew that you had a power about you, and I thought you would be able to show me how to get on to the... next stage."

"I'm sorry. You've got the wrong man," I said.

"But you did feel me when I exerted myself towards you," he said, "so we must have a connection. If we worked together, we'd really get somewhere."

"That may be true," I said, "if I *wanted* to. But I don't. And I'm afraid my only advice for you is to stop meddling in it yourself before it destroys you."

"Those who are elect," he said, "have a duty to follow their calling. It is their destiny. And their duty to seek further."

I smiled. I could see that this boy was exhilarated by the thought of strange powers; but he was exhilarated by the unexamined concept, like someone who'd been watching too many *Star Wars* movies, or who'd read too many nineteenth century gothic novels. There was clearly no sense of actual reality. It might have been endearing if it wasn't also highly dangerous.

"That's bollocks," I told him. "I don't have any *duty*. You should look out for someone else who does."

"It's you or nobody," he mumbled. "Please..."

The realisation that he was attracted to me might have been more flattering if I'd thought it was *me* he was fancying, rather than the idea of my mystical powers. He himself was a perfectly presentable young man, in a thin sort of way, but I didn't fancy him in the least, and the thought of having to cope with that agenda as well as everything else led me to be firm now.

"Look," I said, "I'd be grateful if you'd leave me alone and not try any of your 'exertions' towards me in future. It's distracting, and I'm trying to prepare for Finals. I'm not prepared to join you in any of your activities, so you're wasting your time."

William looked crushed and stared at his shoes.

"I don't mean to be unpleasant, but that's how it is," I added.

Over the next few months I seemed to see William everywhere. I didn't find that disturbing of itself, but the fact that I could always *tell* when he was in the vicinity was unsettling. It wasn't materially too much of a problem, but I hated what it represented. Each time I felt William's presence and then had it corroborated, it proved to me that what I'd been managing to discount from my past as either imagined or conjured, had in fact been – at least partly – real.

One day, in early February, when I was in a café in town with Alan, I felt that now-familiar feeling, and looked over to see William coming in, on his own as usual, casting a large-eyed stare towards me. He looked even thinner these days, I thought.

"Your little acolyte," Alan smirked. "You know, I've seen him hanging around outside the house once or twice."

"Have you? I hadn't noticed."

"Well, he has. Perhaps you should shag him and then he might leave you alone."

"It might make him even worse."

"Not if you made sure you were crap enough."

I laughed.

"I don't know why I'm laughing," I said. "It's so creepy. It's got to stop."

I took a deep breath and stood up.

"I'll be back in a moment," I told him.

I walked over to William. He looked up at me and flinched, as though I might be on my way over to hit him. I sat down opposite him.

"William," I said, "will you *please* stop following me around. People are beginning to notice. I feel like a psychic homing device and it's getting well beyond freaky."

"It's okay, Greg," he said. "I'm not trying to get anything from you. I just want to be close to you. Physically. It kind of charges my batteries. I won't try to get any closer."

He was so patently sincere that I didn't know what to say. I looked at him for a moment, at the open longing in his expression. It wasn't a lustful look. It seemed more like a cry for help, and I felt a whisper of sadness.

"If you're somehow... I don't know how to express this... *feeding* off me," I said, "then please stop it. It happened to me once before and people *died* as a result of it."

"Then the person who was doing it must have been doing it with hate," William said. "Whereas I *love* you."

I felt a pang in my stomach.

"Oh, William," I said. "This is hopeless. Please, stop."

He made no answer and I stood up.

"Look," I told him, "just as it seems that you are able to tell where I am, I can also tell where you are. I don't want to do it, but if this stalking continues, then I'll have to take evasive action. Whenever I feel you approaching, I shall leave. It'll be tiresome for me, but ultimately rather humiliating for you. And I suspect I'll be the one with more stamina for it."

He looked down at the empty coffee cup in front of him. I went back to Alan.

"Well?" he asked.

I sat down and shrugged.

"He loves me."

"That's news?"

"I feel so sorry him," I said.

"Fucking freak. You should report him to the Dean."

"I resorted to threats of another kind," I said, "so hopefully it won't come to that."

Alan threw me an odd look and I shrugged.

Things did quieten down after that, which was just as well because Finals were looming imminently on the horizon. I felt stricken by remorse at the amount of time I'd spent *not* working over the previous two years and focused on my need to redeem myself, however slightly. At the beginning of my third year it had been made clear that if I didn't do anything about it I was heading for a low Two-Two, and now my intention was to scrape a Two-One. (A First was – and always had been – out of the question.) It would be hard work, but not impossible.

The house that I shared had turned, over the summer, into a third year residence; from a party place into a tension-filled sepulchre to academe, an atmosphere which deepened into barely restrained panic as the year progressed. Not having William hanging around me improved my mind-set considerably. I did see him about, but never with the accompaniment of that internal flutter. I could see that his previous state of obsession had been replaced by an anger at my rejection of him, and I was pleased that he was angry with me because at least it would make him both leave me alone, and move on. Once, I saw him in town with a much older man who looked hard, somehow, and sexually dangerous, and I wondered if he was getting into a situation similar to my experience with Philippe. But, ultimately, William wasn't my responsibility and I didn't have any extra emotional energy to deal with what may or may not have been happening to him.

That was why, when I was sitting in the library one day in mid-March, and I felt that dreaded flutter in my stomach again, I felt a spurt of anger at him for disturbing me when I was, finally, working so well. I was copying a quote from a book and I put my head down and concentrated on what I was doing. The flutter grew and grew until I could see, peripherally, someone standing at my side. I turned my head away and kept on writing, but the flutter continued. Eventually, I stopped writing and addressed my notes.

"Just fuck off and leave me alone," I hissed, furious.

There was no reaction.

"That's not a very polite way to greet an old friend," said a voice at my side.

Sixteen

Of course, I recognised the accent immediately and looked up to see Philippe standing there with a cool grin on his face. To say that I had a sinking feeling is an understatement of epic proportions. I closed my eyes.

"Aren't you going to say hello?"

"Philippe," I said. "I don't *need* this."

"But I *need* you," he told me.

"How did you find me?" I asked. "No, don't bother to answer that."

He smiled and I saw that he had matured, physically, in the years since I'd last seen him. He was powerfully built, instead of lean, as though he'd been working out in the gym ever since I'd last encountered him. Although, in his way, he was even more attractive than he had been – in that mature-man porn-film/escort sort of way – he looked so preened, so immaculately groomed that I felt repelled by him and his tanned, ultra-clean-shaven cheeks. Of course, I had other reasons to feel repelled by him, too.

"Is there anywhere we can go to talk?" he said.

I looked at my watch. It was five-thirty. I decided to hear what he had to say, because who knew what he might be capable of if I refused.

"There's a bar round the corner," I said. "Or we could try the

café at the Museum Of Modern Art if you want a bottle of wine...
if you're still into that sort of pretension."

"Good, good," he said, failing to rise to my remark. Or perhaps
he was so self-absorbed that he hadn't noticed my sarcastic tone.
"Let's go and get a good bottle of something French."

I handed my books in at the desk, and we left. Philippe loped
along beside me with his super-confident gait and smiled to himself now and again. I remained steadfastly silent, but recalled, once
we were ensconced in the tastefully converted warehouse with the
wine, that it was in almost identical circumstances that we'd last
spoken.

"I see that you're remembering our last meeting," Philippe said
with a smile, touching his face with an absent-minded movement
of his hand. "You broke my nose then, you know. I had to have it
reset. Mind you, I had the lump at the top removed whilst I was at
it, so in some ways I should thank you for giving me the motiva-
tion for an improvement I wouldn't otherwise have made."

He poured us both a glass of wine, and suddenly it was as
though no time had passed. I was back at school, confronting the
horror that I knew Philippe had perpetrated with my unwitting
help.

"Okay," I said, "what do you want from me?"

He pouted at me as I said this, a peculiarly unattractive expression, especially from him.

"Aren't you going to ask me how I've been?" he asked.

"I don't care how you've been," I told him. "I presume you've
continued to aggrandise yourself at other people's expense ever
since I last saw you."

Philippe visibly bridled at this.

"That is not exactly true, as it happens," he said. "I admit I did
manage one or two spectacular feats with you, but I haven't managed anything on that scale since."

"Not that you needed to, seeing as you became a man of

property on your eighteenth birthday. And with a fair bit of capital at your disposal, judging by the car you chose to drive."

"I drive a Jaguar convertible these days."

"Oh," I said, "you're *so* impressive."

Philippe drank some wine, savouring the taste before he swallowed.

"You've become cynical, Greg," he said. "I'm disappointed in you."

"I'm only cynical regarding you, Philippe," I said. "Give me one good reason why I shouldn't be cynical about you appearing like this and pretending to be friendly."

"I'm not pretending," he told me. "I *am* being friendly."

"Just get on with it," I said. "What do you want?"

He nodded, realising that this pretence of charm was fooling nobody.

"There's an important date coming up," he said. "In fact, it'll be the fourth anniversary of the day I fucked you on the altar at Gillow Manor Farm. I've had the whole chapel renovated, by the way, so it's far more impressive. It's still consecrated, too, as it happens, which is useful. I want you and me to do a repeat performance."

I laughed.

"You must be joking," I said.

"Believe me, Greg, if there was anyone else I could use, I would. I know how you feel about me. But I have no choice. You're the only person with the requisite energies."

"No way," I told him. "Apart from anything else, I wouldn't be stupid enough to indulge in unsafe sex like that again. How many more people have you been fucked by in the last four years? And how many of them wore condoms? I don't suppose condoms figure very prominently in your rituals, do they? And don't say something like 'people like me are immune to HIV' because, even if it were true, what makes you think I would take your word for *anything*?"

Philippe didn't reply. He regarded his well-manicured hands.

"If that's all you've got to ask me, then I might as well leave," I said. "The answer is no."

Philippe looked up at me, then, and I could see a deep-set anger behind his eyes.

"Oh, but you have no choice in the end, Greg," he said. "If you refuse, I have subtle ways in which I can make you do as I please."

"Is that a threat?"

"A statement of fact."

"I suppose it would be stupid to underestimate what you can do," I said, "seeing as you killed Mark Daniels and his parents. But if my choice is to collude with you or take the consequences, then I'll take the consequences every time."

"You might end up regretting that," said Philippe, taking a slip of paper from his wallet and writing an address and telephone number on it. He held it out to me.

"Here, take this," he said, "in case you change your mind."

"I won't," I told him, ignoring the piece of paper and standing up, my wine untouched. I had vaguely remembered some super-stition from childhood conversations about ghosts and so on, which said that to take a gift from an evil person was to give them power over you, and I was taking no chances. I stared at Philippe across the table.

"And if you thought for a *minute* that I might want to have sex with you again, after the way in which you abused my trust, then you're mad," I said.

As I left, Philippe leaned forward and pushed the slip of paper into the back pocket of my jeans. I ignored it, and didn't look back. There was a crisp chill to the air outside, but it wasn't that that made me feel cold to the very core of my being. I dreaded what Philippe might try to do to me. I knew he was a man who would not take kindly to being thwarted.

I went home and cooked myself some food, then went to my

room and tried to do a little more work. But it was no use. Philippe had unsettled me too much. I kept yearning to see Kit again. He would know what to do. I tried to think of what Kit might say to me, and, quite suddenly, I remembered the visualisation he had given me all those years ago to protect me from being bullied at school. I remembered that he'd told me to envisage an icy blue light coming down from above, like a beam, encircling me with a protective force. It seemed almost too simple, now, too childish, but I closed my eyes as I sat at my desk and I concentrated hard on activating the visualisation. After I'd finished I decided that, rather than sit there doing nothing and fretting about it, I'd be better off going out for a walk to clear my head.

Of course, I found myself wandering down past the ice rink. Although I knew I wouldn't find Kit like this – just by wandering the streets hoping to bump into him – I couldn't help it. I ended up on the path by the River Isis (the maiden name of the Thames before she reaches the Big City). The moon was only a couple of days off full so that the trees cast crisp black shadows on the grass beside me as I slid beneath them in the darkness.

It was strange. I felt that I was being completely aimless, but when the path divided, I found myself decisively taking the branch that wound away from the river and climbed gently uphill. Very quickly, I could look back over the shimmering lights of Oxford and out at the clear horizon around me. It was beautiful. I'd seen this hill many times before, but had never thought to climb it. And especially not at night.

Part way up I could see the loom of trees to my right and heard the susurration of the gentle breeze in the branches. Instead of skirting the wood, I found that I had a compulsion to enter it. At the back of my mind I wondered if this was a trick on Philippe's part, to get me on my own out here. But I felt light and almost happy, so I doubted it. Nevertheless, I stopped and did the blue light visualisation once more before walking under the branches of the first trees.

After carefully picking my way for fifty metres or so, I found that it was more or less pitch black. The going was slow and difficult and there didn't seem any point in going on. Looking behind me, I could see the eaves of the wood and the moonlit field beyond that, and I decided to go back. But, just as I turned, I heard a clicking noise a short distance away. I turned and saw a light that flared up, briefly, before simmering to a steady, gentle glow. It was a further fifty metres into the wood, and it took me a few moments to realise that what I was looking at was the flame of a distant candle.

I waited, listening intently, and heard a rustling sound. As quietly as I could, I began to creep forward towards the light. I found that the wood wasn't as dense here as I'd first thought, and there was the masking sound of the breeze above to cover any noise that I made, so all I had to do was wave my hands vaguely in front of me to make sure I didn't walk into any low branches in order to proceed relatively quickly and quietly. I didn't know why I wanted to be silent, or why I felt the need to approach the candle, but simply obeyed my instinct to do so.

When I was within a few metres of the light, I stopped again. There was a shadowy figure, kneeling on the ground with his or her back to me. They were setting something out on the ground. A few items, perhaps, for a ritual. Fascinated, I wanted to get closer to have a better look, but knew that if I did so I would be heard.

The preparations took what seemed a long time, though it was probably only three or four minutes. When, finally, the figure started to murmur some sort of chant, the sound made the hairs on my forearms and neck prickle. There was something cracked, almost inhuman in the voice. Something broken and desperate. It took me a while to recognise who it was, and when I did so, I found myself involuntarily surging forward.

"William," I called out, no longer worried about the noise I made. The figure lurched up with a cry and made as if to run, but

I was up to him in three or four strides and grabbed him by the shoulder. He let out a gasp and dropped something to the ground. Then, looking at me in the flicker of candlelight, he cried, "Greg! What are you doing here?"

I felt suddenly calm and knelt down to pick up the item that had just fallen. It was a knife.

"What are *you* doing here is more to the point," I said.

He was wearing a dark coat, underneath which I could see a thick shirt, pulled open to reveal his pale chest.

"Were you going to kill yourself?" I asked, suddenly aware of what a stupid question I'd just asked. Of course he'd been about to kill himself. I suddenly felt overwhelmingly sorry for him. William seemed to droop as I watched him and, in moments, he was sobbing. I pulled him to me and he cried against my shoulder, the most disconsolate sound I had ever heard.

"I've been so lonely," he choked, "and I've done some terrible things. Terrible."

He sighed and stopped crying but still clung to me.

"I've seen you with someone," I said. "Older, a bit dangerous-looking."

"Yes," William groaned. "He made me do all sorts of things. And I knew I shouldn't, Greg, I *knew* I shouldn't, but I did them anyway... and for that I deserve to die."

I shook him gently.

"No," I told him.

"Yes," he said with an intensity and vehemence that shocked me.

"No," I said gently. "Look, why do you think I'm here? If you were meant to die, why were you stopped at the last minute?"

"Is that why you came, then?" he asked.

"I didn't know why I was coming up here," I told him. "I just felt compelled. Now, of course, I can see why it was important."

William started to sob again, but more gently this time.

"Thank you," he managed, "thank you."

I let him be for a time, until he had cried himself out, then said, "Don't thank me. Thank whatever it was that guided me here."

He pulled away from me and stood upright. I smiled at him, but he was between me and the candlelight so he probably didn't see.

"You see," he said, "you *see*. You *are* elect, whether you want to be or not."

I took a deep breath and shook my head.

"I've got my Finals in two months," I told him. "I don't want this hassle. I don't want to be wandering around in the night at the behest of who knows what. I want to *get on with my studies*."

I turned and yelled out at the trees, "I don't *want* to be elect!"

But the trees only whispered among themselves.

We ended up back in the sitting room at my digs, drinking coffee. William wouldn't be specific about the 'dreadful' things that this man had 'made' him do, but after my previous experience with Philippe, I had an inkling of the direction they might have taken.

"Look," I said. "Whatever it is you've done, once you've decided definitively not to do it again, you'll begin to grow away from it and outgrow it."

William shook his head.

"You wouldn't understand."

"Oh wouldn't I?" I said, and proceeded to explain, in brief, what had happened between myself and Philippe. William nodded as I spoke, especially when I talked of Mark's death.

"But," he said, when I finished, "Tony made me feel so... electrified. So *desired*. I would do anything for him, *anything*, so long as he didn't ask me to leave."

"Even now?"

He thought for a moment.

"It's irrelevant, now, because Tony's found someone else who's a more... talented participant. He told me to get lost last week."

"Which is a blessing," I told him.

He looked at me and his lips trembled.

"Pathetic, aren't I?"

"No," I told him. "Once you've broken free of him, you'll start getting stronger."

"With your help?"

I felt the burden of responsibility constricting my chest.

"No," I told him.

"But something led you to me. It must be significant that it was you."

"But I have nothing to offer you. I am not a 'seeker', or whatever you might call yourself. I'll admit that I've spent the last few years in denial about the powers that certain people clearly possess, but I still don't see any of it as being genuinely positive."

"You saved my life," he said. "Don't you see that as positive?"

"Yes, of course, but it didn't exist as positive energy on its own – it was a form of damage limitation. It wouldn't have been a positive act without the negative forces that led you to want to commit suicide in the first place."

William thought for a while.

"But," he said, "isn't that almost a definition of what *good* is – an attempt to rectify the negative forces of the world?"

"You make it sound like the forces of good are knights in shining armour."

"Maybe that's what some people are – knights in psychic armour," he told me. "Maybe that's why you've been given the powers that you have, so that you can help people like me to find the right path."

"If that were the case – which I don't think it is," I said, "then I would be unwilling to accept the responsibility."

And that was that. I could go no further with William and eventually asked him to leave, though I couldn't bring myself to refuse to see him at a later date because I worried that he might attempt suicide again. I agreed to meet up with him once a week for a drink or coffee, on a purely social basis. It was an obligation that irritated me, though I was determined to try to help as far as I could without disrupting my studies or giving him hope that anything might happen between us. There was far too much else on my plate to want to take on William as well.

Of course, at the back of my mind I knew it wasn't William I was worrying about, but Philippe. I was wondering when and how he would use the 'subtle ways' he claimed to have at his disposal to make me do what he wanted.

As it happened I didn't have long to wait.

The following evening at about eight-thirty, Alan and I went out for a pint together in order to unwind, frazzled from a day of intense studying. I was finding that if I worked later than eight, there was no way I'd be able to get to sleep without help. I'd given up smoking spliffs for the time being as I found that, although relaxing, they had a tendency to leave me muddle-headed in the morning. The only other effective, and easily available, method of relaxation was alcohol, and so a pint or two after a hard day's studying was more or less essential. If I didn't do this, I would spend the night dreaming about rhetoric, dialectic and aesthetics.

Alan was in the process of being dumped by his boyfriend of two months – not what you want to have happen in the run up to your Finals – but he was taking it reasonably well, and it was actually quite relaxing to have someone unburdening themselves to me like that. It made me forget my own problems for a while. Alan, it turned out, had also decided that he didn't like his course.

"Maths is like religion. Once you've lost enthusiasm for it, it becomes a philosophic nightmare," he told me, becoming maudlin.

Alan did actually ask how things were with me at one point, but there was nothing I could tell him, really. I could hardly say, *You know that boy you described as 'my acolyte'? Well, I saved his life through psychic intervention. Oh, and there's a power hungry magician out there somewhere who has told me he's out to get me.* It made me realise just how far 'being elect', if one chose to take on that mantle, would inevitably set a person apart from 'ordinary' life. It would mean permanent exclusion from the Idyll. Whilst I knew that a lot of people were desperate not to see themselves as ordinary, to me, at that moment, *ordinary* seemed eminently desirable, not to mention the safest option.

When we got home, Janine was in the kitchen and came out into the hall, furious.

"For fuck's sake, Greg," she said, "what right do you think you have to go into my bedroom and take my things. Have you gone mad?"

I stared at her.

"What are you talking about?"

"Don't pretend you don't know," she said. "Maggie and Steve saw you. They saw you going into my room. There was seventy-five quid in my purse, four Es and a quarter of an ounce of Moroccan Black. Now, fucking well give them back to me."

I looked at Alan and shrugged in complete incomprehension.

"I haven't been into your room since the night of your birthday party, Janine."

"You were in there half an hour ago," she said.

"No," I told her, "I've been in the pub with Alan for the last two hours."

"Come off it," she said. "You were caught more or less red-handed. What is this?"

Alan looked confused and walked into the sitting room, saying, "He was with me, Janine. What are you talking about?"

Maggie and Steve were in the sitting room watching television, and they looked up angrily as I followed the others into the room.

"Give Janine her stuff back, Greg," said Steve. "That was a shitty thing to do."

"And how are we going to trust you again, now that we know you're a thief?" said Maggie. "Are we all going to have to put locks on our doors?"

"I *didn't* go into Janine's room," I protested. "I've been with *Alan* – in the *pub*."

"Look, Greg's right, guys," said Alan. "He's been in The Keys since eight-thirty."

I looked at my watch. It was ten-forty-five.

"What, *all* the time?" asked Maggie.

"Yes," he said. "*All the time*. Look, what the hell is this?"

Maggie looked at Alan and said, "Steve and I were on the sofa, right here, at ten o'clock. The door was open, and from here you can see up the stairs to Janine's bedroom. I noticed Greg go in there and shouted up that Janine was in the kitchen if he was look-ing for her, but he didn't come out immediately. When he did, a bit later, he looked so odd, so – you know – suspicious, furtive, that I shouted through to Janine to tell her. Greg didn't come down, and so Janine went up to see what was going on, and discovered that her stuff was missing, and that you had gone."

"Gone? Without anyone seeing me?"

"We assumed you'd slipped out through the back door," said Steve.

"Without being seen, when everyone in the house was obvi-ously looking for me – out to bollock me, in fact?"

"I don't know!" Steve half shouted. "Maybe you jumped out of your bedroom window. But I *saw* you up there, Greg."

Alan spread his arms in a calming gesture.

"Okay, guys, listen. Whoever you saw, it wasn't Greg. Maybe it was someone else."

Steve snorted.

"Who else *could* it have been?"

"I don't know," said Alan. "All I know is that it wasn't Greg because he was with me."

We argued round and round for another hour, but got nowhere. I challenged them to jump out of my bedroom window, which they declined – because it was obvious that anyone who tried it would end up with a broken ankle at the very least – and for their part, they remained convinced that I had stolen the money and drugs and somehow absconded. The argument began to get heated. They started to assume that Alan was an accomplice because he was my alibi, and began turning on him and accusing us both of lying. The evening ended up with Alan and me slamming out of the room.

Sixteen

That was it. The trust was gone. There were now two factions in the house. I was angry about it, but Alan was even more upset because he was a particularly good friend of Maggie's and she stopped being friendly with him, which made him resent me, even though he knew it wasn't my fault.

Philippe's simple plan (for I was sure Philippe was behind this) was incredibly successful. For something so seemingly small, the effect on my life was enormous. The house became a hostile environment and so I had to spend more or less all my time at the library, or shut up in my room. Although it was disruptive, in some ways it helped me focus on my work, because the social life of the house was no longer a distraction. After five or six days, during which I did nothing but work in my room or in the library, attend seminars, and one reasonably encouraging tutorial, I began to feel that, in any case, it was all going to be over soon and that, if I kept my head down and worked hard, I could leave it all behind after my Finals. It was odd that, when I went to have my now habitual weekly coffee with William, it was a normalising experience, when I'd expected it to be otherwise. He lived in a bedsit in a run down house near the old botanical gardens, and however strange I felt about our 'connection', at least he was someone I knew who wasn't to do with my digs.

On the seventh day after the row, just after lunch, I was lying on my bed re-reading *The Double*, when Janine banged on the door.

"Greg," she said in an exhausted voice, "it's the police. They've got a search warrant."

I didn't have a chance to react because the door opened and in came two police officers, one male and one female – who loudly told me that anything I said might be taken down and used in evidence against me. Of course, I asked why they wanted to search my room, and the male officer said, "Drugs, sir. We have a number of witnesses who claim to have seen you dealing outside the Clarendon Centre."

The next five hours were a nightmare. There were four officers in the house. Two searched my room whilst the other two concentrated on the rest of the house. The ones in my room pulled out all my drawers, then searched my papers and bags. I was frisked and asked to empty my pockets. When they found the piece of paper that Philippe had pushed into my back pocket, they questioned me about it. The address on the slip was apparently in the street adjacent to Merton College, which was news to me as I hadn't so much glanced at it. I told them that it was the address of a vague acquaintance of mine and they triumphantly placed it in a plastic bag to take away with them. Downstairs in the kitchen, every container was emptied and searched: coffee, sugar, tomato sauce, curry paste, jams, peanut butter... In the bathroom the soap was cut up, the toothpastes ripped open, the shampoos emptied. Elsewhere carpets were pulled up, the zipped covers on the sofas were removed, the curtain linings examined. The mess was extreme. What was worse, they found two roaches in the ashtray in Alan's room, two (newly purchased) Es in Janine's purse, about a sixteenth of an ounce of Moroccan Black in Steve's room, and a tab of acid in Maggie's bedside cabinet, left there without her knowledge a few months before by an acid-head boyfriend. I was the only one who was clean.

We were all taken down to the police station – the other four to be charged, and me to be questioned. It seemed that four students who had been arrested the previous evening at a local club for possession of ecstasy had told the police that they'd bought their drugs from me. The whole thing was incomprehensible. Of course, I said it must have been a case of mistaken identity, but they were expecting me to say that and ignored me. Still, my ignorance was so complete that they couldn't trick me into giving information that I didn't have. That's not to say the whole business wasn't gruelling and humiliating – but in the end they didn't charge me, though they did warn me to tell them if I was intending to leave the area, no matter for how short a time.

When I got back home, Alan, Maggie, Janine and Steve were in the sitting room waiting for me. Janine stood up to confront me as I came in.

"Well done, Greg," she said. "You've managed to fuck up all our lives, right in the middle of revision for our Finals. I suppose we should be pleased that it looks like we're all going to get off with cautions, but it's going to be *so* helpful, when we go job hunting over the summer, to admit to prospective employers that we have criminal records. Thank you so much. Thank you so much for your thoughtful behaviour. I hope you get done for dealing and get sent down. I'll never forgive you for this."

"I didn't do it, you know," I said. "I've never dealt drugs in my life. This whole thing's a set up."

"You—" said Steve from the sofa. Maggie pulled him back to stop him getting up.

"No," she said, "let Janine finish. We decided it was going to be her that spoke to Greg."

I looked back at Janine.

"We expected you to say something like that, Greg," she told me. "You'd deny anything, wouldn't you? No matter how red-handedly you were caught. Well, we've had enough. We've just had a house meeting and we've decided that we don't want you here any more."

"As of when?" I asked.

"As of right now," she told me. "Alan and Steve will accompany you to your room whilst you get any books and papers that you might need, and then they will escort you from the house. When you want to pick up the rest of your belongings you can ring us and make an appointment to come round when at least two of us are here to supervise you. You can give us your keys now."

"What if I refuse?"

"We'll have the locks changed."

I noticed Janine's hard expression and felt a welling of sorrow at the way in which I was being treated. But I could see why they were so furious with me. And there was no point trying to explain my side of things. Why would they believe me?

"Where am I supposed to go?"

"I don't give a fuck," she said. "If you're at too much of a loss, why don't you try drowning yourself in the river?"

"Also," Alan said, "we've heard *stories* about you."

"What do you mean?"

"About what you got up to at school, before you came here. We've heard that you used to hang around with some bloke who was into black magic."

I groaned.

"Who told you *that*?"

"There's someone on my course – Richard Murray – who was at school with you. I was talking to him a couple of days ago."

Richard. The odd, unpleasant symmetry of what was happening made me feel sick. I turned to leave the room and Steve and Alan followed me out and up the stairs. In my room, the mess was even more depressing now that I knew I was being thrown out.

"Of course," I said to Alan, "you know that I've been set up?"

"I don't know anything anymore," he said, "except that we'll all be better off if you leave."

I filled an overnight case and several plastic bags with books and files, and a few clothes, and let them escort me from the house. What else could I do?

I wondered where to go. There were a number of people on my course with whom I was friendly, and various people that I was on pint-of-beer-in-the-pub terms, but there was no one that I could think of that I felt I could ask to stay with – especially as a lot of the people I knew were also friendly with Janine and the rest.

In the end I went to William. He was surprised to see me, and even more so when I explained what had happened, but he was pleased to let me stay – too pleased, in some ways. His room had a narrow bed, a desk, a chest of drawers, a single wardrobe and hardly any floor space. But it would have to do. He went out to get some beers and when he came back made me tell him the whole story right from the beginning, from when I met Kit.

"It's this Kit guy we need to get hold of," he said after I'd finished. "He'd know what to do. Philippe is clearly out to destroy you, and he doesn't mind how many people he hurts along the way."

"Oh god," I said, "I hadn't thought of that. It might be dangerous for you that I'm here."

"No, no," said William, "that's fine. You saved my life, remember. To say that I owe you a favour is an understatement."

We sat in silence for a while before William spoke.

"So, do you have any idea where Kit might be?"

"No," I said. "It's nearly a year since I last saw him. He said he was staying somewhere down by the ice rink, but that's not exactly helpful."

"No."

We mulled things over, speculating as to how Philippe had managed to get the people in the house to think they'd seen me going into Janine's room. Was it a kind of collective hypnosis, or had there been someone there who genuinely looked like me? And these four students who said that I had supplied them with drugs – were they just lying, or were they sold drugs by this hypothetical lookalike? We could ponder these things as much as we liked, but in the end it didn't lead to any answers.

William was particularly interested in the coin that Ian had given me, and which I showed him now.

"It's clever," he said, looking at the lemniscate and the chalice. "You would never realise there was anything significant about the coin unless it was pointed out to you. You should keep this with you at all times," he added. "You never know what power it might have to protect you."

"Okay," I agreed and slipped into my pocket.

"I've seen something similar to it, somewhere," he said. "I can't remember where. In a book in the library, maybe."

We drank the last of the beer and the conversation petered out. I was exhausted. William offered me the bed, but I declined and made myself as comfortable as I could on the floor, with the help of a pillow, a blanket and a couple of borrowed sweaters. The carpet had some pile to it, but even so, it was an uncomfortable night. I was grateful that William hadn't suggested that I share his bed. I was not equipped to engage in emotional negotiation of any kind.

In the morning, I ached everywhere. We were up by seven-thirty and whiled away the time eating cornflakes and toast, then lingered over several cups of strong coffee. Conversation was desultory and without focus – but it passed the time until ten, when the accommodation office opened. I planned to register as an emergency student. There was no way I could stay with William for another night. If the accommodation office couldn't immediately help, then I'd simply have to enlarge my already spectacular credit card debt and stay in a bed and breakfast somewhere. It also occurred to me to that I could go home. It was only 120 miles to Horton from here. But what would I say when I got there? And how would I study? Would my college even let me sit my exams, or allow me to get my degree, if I was in the process of being investigated for drug dealing? And home was a great deal closer to Gillow Manor Farm, so I would be no safer from Philippe.

When I wandered down to the accommodation office, William's spare key in my pocket, I felt utterly abject, depressed – and furious with Philippe. I arrived at five past ten, but the office was still closed. I stood there looking at the door, wondering what to do, when someone came along the corridor. He was a man of about twenty-five, unshaved, casually dressed and smiling.

"Hi," he said, "you're after the accommodation officer?"

"Yes," I told him.

"You've found him," he said. "I've only just got up, I'm afraid. Had a heavy night last night. Why don't you come down to the snack bar and talk to me while I have some breakfast?"

"Okay," I said.

I'd heard that the college accommodation office was informal, but this was surprising even to me. Still, the man was affable, easy to talk to, and bought me a coffee along with his full English breakfast. I told him what I was after, and stressed how urgent it was, and he was immediately sympathetic.

"Do you have a phone?" he asked.

"Not at the moment," I told him.

He pulled a sheaf of papers from his jacket pocket and leafed through them, stopping to look at one of them.

"Look," he said, "there's a bedsit here, in a decent house on the Banbury Road that you might be interested in. I have to be up that way this afternoon, so why don't we meet there at five, say, and I can show it to you?"

He wrote the address on the bottom of the sheet of paper he was holding, then ripped it off and handed to me. I was insanely grateful.

"And where are you staying at the moment?" he asked me.

I gave him William's address and left the officer to the last of his breakfast. I headed back to William's at once, to see if I could get a little work done whilst he was out.

Fat chance.

My mind was too full of churning questions. And I was seething with resentment that I was in this situation at all. I tried to calm myself down, and practiced the cool blue light visualisation, but it was no good. I had entered that railway-station limbo of waiting. I spent the morning watching the clock, desperate for five o'clock to come. I'd already decided to accept the bedsit the accommodation officer had mentioned, whatever state it was in. And once I'd settled in there, maybe – just maybe – life would settle down enough for me to sit my Finals.

But that illusion was short-lived.

William rushed back at one, breathless with horror.

"Have you heard?" he asked.

"What?"

"There's been a murder down by Merton College. A second year classicist. Under weird circumstances, apparently, though there haven't been any details. People are whispering about Satanic rituals. What do you think? It must be something to do with Philippe, mustn't it?"

I closed my eyes to try and assuage a rising panic.

"I expect so," I said, then had a sudden, awful thought. "The address he slipped into my pocket! The one that the police took away with them. It was somewhere by Merton College."

William stared at me. "Things are getting out of control," he said, "and Philippe's barely *begun*... whatever it is he has planned."

"Yes."

"We've got to stop him," he said.

"It's all very well to say that, but how can we?"

"You're as powerful as Philippe is," William said with conviction. "That's why he wants to use you again. You've got to learn how to focus that power to stop him."

"But there's no time. And I don't know how. We don't even know where he is."

William pulled a loaf of bread and a can of soup from his bag. As he made toast and heated the soup, he wondered aloud – and rather fruitlessly – about what we might do. I couldn't eat anything. My stomach had shrunk to the size of a pea.

"Look," said William, "I've got another seminar at two, but I'll have a think, and then we can talk about it when I get back."

The afternoon continued to drag by. I felt infinitely more stressed than I had in the morning – which, a few hours before, I would have considered impossible. I tried to read, which was a joke, then I tried lying on the bed to rest, but couldn't relax at all. The power of visualization had completely deserted me. It was agony. But incredibly, when William burst in at four o'clock, I felt yet another turn of the screw.

"There's a warrant out for your arrest," he blurted, his face ashen. "The police think you committed the Merton murder."

I gasped and looked at William. "Philippe has murdered someone – just to set me up..."

William sat down heavily beside me.

"No," he said, "Philippe will have murdered someone for his own ends, and then used the body as a conveniently as possible."

I nodded.

"What am I going to do?" I asked. My brain was paralysed.

"Stay here."

"No, I gave the accommodation officer this address. The police will know from Janine and the others that I'm looking for somewhere else to live, and would go straight there. They may already be on their way over here."

Just as I said this, there came a knock at the door.

"Greg," a voice said. "Greg Chaley? Are you in there?"

Seventeen

We froze. I glanced at William, who shrugged at me, then went to the door.

"Focus your power," he hissed. "*Use* it."

He stood by the door but didn't open it.

"Who is it?"

"It's me, Paul Needham, the Student Accommodation Officer."

I sighed with relief.

"It's okay," I said to William, "you can let him in."

William shook his head.

"What do you want with Greg?" he asked.

"I was just passing and thought I'd collect him to go and see this bedsit."

"He doesn't want to see it any more," William said, "so you can go away."

"Greg? Are you in there? What's the matter?"

"Go on, let him in," I said to William.

"No," William whispered, "there's something wrong. How did he get into the building? The front door's always locked."

I looked at William then and it dawned on me, with a creeping sensation, that he was right.

"Look," the voice said, impatiently, "open the door. This is ridiculous."

"Go away," said William.

I felt the hairs on my neck prickle as I realised that this person *wasn't the accommodation officer*. I thought back to the circumstances under which we'd met... He'd come across me in the corridor outside the office, but we hadn't gone *into* the office. We'd gone to the snack bar instead. And I remembered with a lurch that, although I'd given him this address, I hadn't told him my surname.

There came another knocking on the door, harder this time.

"For fuck's sake," the voice said.

I closed my eyes and visualised cool blue protective light descending into the room. For the first time, I could sense some real strength in this action, and for a moment it made me feel safer.

"Go away," I said, and tried to propel my words *through* the blue light, as it were. The man on the other side of the door clearly felt that I was attempting to wield energy against him and I heard him chuckle.

"You'll have to try better than that," he said.

"Who *are* you?" William asked.

"Just let me in," he said, "and maybe you won't have to find out."

There was the muted sound of movement outside and then, without warning, the door crashed open, shouldered in by a brawny young man of around my age. Behind him was the man I'd thought of as the accommodation officer, and another who pushed in past the shattered door jamb and grabbed William. An instant later the brawny youth stepped in over the broken door and punched me so hard between the eyes that I blacked out instantaneously.

When I came to, I found that I was lying on my side in the dark. My hands were tightly bound behind my back with abrasive nylon cord, which dug into my wrists like teeth. My shoulder was numb, as was my hip, from lying on what felt like bare wood, the grain of which I could feel against my cheek. My face felt completely mashed, my head throbbed and I couldn't breathe through my nose, which felt broken. My lips were dry and as I ran my tongue over them to moisten them, I felt how swollen they were. The room was full of an unidentifiable smoke. At first I thought it might be incense, but soon realised that it was something more narcotic than that. I wriggled, to try and get some circulation into my legs, which were also bound, and that helped a little, but not enough to be of comfort. I lay still again and tried to work out where I might be. I could hear a distant hum of traffic, but that was no clue, although it did mean that I was in a town rather than somewhere isolated. I might even still be in Oxford. I took heart from this. But there was nothing I could do now, except wait for the next development.

I don't know how long I was there, but I drifted in and out of consciousness for a while before I noticed that there was some dim light filtering into the room. I glanced up and saw that the door behind me was ajar and that the light was coming from the corridor outside. Now that my eyes were accustomed to the environment, I noticed that there was a censer near my head, letting out a thin stream of smoke. Beyond that I could see a large unfurnished room. Victorian, probably, with hefty skirting boards, an ornate marble fireplace, and, dimly overhead, fancy cornicing. There were thick curtains that were drawn over the deep bay windows. It made me remember the fancy houses that Philippe had taken me to when I'd been with him in Stoke-on-Trent, and I realised that the same thing was happening here, although – obviously – my role had changed.

I didn't need to ask who had just entered.

"Philippe," I said.

"Hello Greg," he said, coming round and into view. He was wearing black jeans, a black roll-neck, and his coin on its chain. "I told you that you had no choice but to comply with what I asked, didn't I?"

I turned away from him and tried to ignore the pain of my bonds.

"You said you had *subtle* ways of doing it," I said through gritted teeth. "I'd hardly call thugs battering a door down subtle."

He laughed – a curiously joyful sound.

"It's good to keep a sense of humour," he said. "I admire that. And it's a great solace in times of adversity."

He sat down on the floor beside me.

"No, don't look away," he said.

He grinned at me. If I'd been able to, and if he'd been a foot or two closer to me, I would have spat at him.

"I suppose," I said, "that after you've done whatever ritual you're planning, this house will become yours."

"Something like that," he said. "It's a wonderful house, too. Much better than Gillow Manor Farm. And much better placed, geographically. I'd love to give you a tour, but sadly, I can't... and the grounds are lovely too. In daylight."

He glanced avariciously round the room, and then, gloatingly, at me.

"What have you done with William?" I asked.

"You mean your little side-kick? He was quite sweet, but I'm surprised at you, Greg. I thought you'd do much better than that."

He thought for a moment or two before continuing.

"We haven't done anything to him – except beat the shit out of him, of course," he laughed. "No, he's going to be very useful. You see, we needed to leave someone behind who could explain to the police what happened to you. This whole thing has been rather brilliantly conceived, actually, though I say so myself."

He stretched his hands in front of him and regarded them.

"When the police investigate the report of your disappearance, this is what they will discover: that your housemates thought you a thief and a liar; that there are witnesses to the fact that you've been drug dealing; that you're suspected of murder, and that you were forcibly dragged off by thugs. They will naturally assume that they're dealing with yet another petty drug-dealer who got in too deep and has now been disposed of. So they're not going to bother to look very hard for you, are they? Why should they? As far as they'll be concerned, you'll be one less criminal for them to worry about."

"So, you're going to kill me?"

He smiled at me, then, with such gentleness that I had to close my eyes.

"Yes," he said. "I'm sorry about that. Genuinely. Apart from anything else, you were the best fuck I've ever had."

I heard him get up and start to wander, aimlessly, round the room. I opened my eyes and watched him.

"There is something extremely aesthetic about this," he said. "Today is four years to the day that I fucked you on the altar at Gillow Manor Farm. That night produced the most powerful magic I have ever created. But it's going to be much more powerful this evening. *Much* more powerful."

He stopped by the door and switched the light on, which dazzled me.

"How many people have you murdered?" I asked.

"'Sacrificed' is a more... appropriate word," he said. "But to answer your question – not many. And no one who has anything like as much *power* as you. You shunned your energies, Greg. And as you so clearly don't want them, I might as well take them for myself."

I sighed, beginning to feel numb emotionally as well as physically.

"And did you repeat your annual pilgrimage to Wales, to gloat with your mentor over what you're going to do this evening?"

He remained by the door.

"No," he said, and I could hear a note of anger in his voice. "I didn't do that. I've been what you might call excommunicated. Ian doesn't approve of what I'm getting up to. He'd try to stop me if he could."

He laughed mirthlessly.

"But he can't, which must irritate him immensely."

He flicked the light off.

"See you later," he said, and left, closing the door and plunging me back into darkness.

I wriggled my hands, but quickly learned that I was not going to be able to work my bonds loose, so I tried to relax as much as possible and lay inert, my head still pounding and my mouth dryer than ever. I tried to think of strategies to get myself out of this situation, but nothing came to mind. I was well and truly stuck.

The most important thing, I realised, was not to succumb to panic. If I did so then I would never be able to make the most of any chances that might arise. I thought of what William had said about using my power to help myself. That was easy to say, but I didn't know how to wield it. I reminded myself that at least I knew it was there. There must be some kind of key to unleash it. Mustn't there?

I curled my legs up so that I was in a foetal position, and found that it offered some relief from the cramps that were beginning to plague me. It also made me aware of the gold coin in the pocket of my jeans. I wondered if I could use it in any way – if I could invoke its protection?

As I was thinking this, the door opened once more, and the light was switched on again. Philippe came in followed by three others: the brawny youth who had broken William's door down, the 'accommodation officer', and the other young man who had stood by whilst I was attacked.

"Take his clothes off," Philippe commanded.

The brawny youth came forward with the 'accommodation officer' and tugged me over onto my front.

"Shall we untie him?" the brawny one asked.

"No. Cut the clothes off."

They were carrying knives, which made the process laborious because, though sharp, they were nowhere near as effective as scissors would have been. I was hauled this way and that as my shirt, tee-shirt and jeans were hacked from me.

"Don't cut him," Philippe warned. "Don't spill *any* blood. Yet."

As my jeans were being cut around the crotch, I heard a chinking sound as my coin fell onto the floor and rolled away. This was either not noticed, or it was assumed to be an ordinary coin, and was ignored. As I was pushed over once more for the final removal of clothing, I could see it lying there, a few inches away from my nose, which was pressed to the floorboards.

In a motion that I tried to make into a kind of stretch, I flexed myself and moved my head so that I was touching the coin with my lips. I pretended to grimace at a particularly hefty hack of the knife and grasped the coin with my teeth, then worked it round with my tongue and managed to get it into my mouth. It tasted of dust. I manoeuvred it further, and tucked it into my cheek, unobserved. The exercise gave me an obscure sense of achievement, although I had no idea how it might prove useful.

After this, I was grabbed by the feet and under the shoulders and carried from the room. I was intensely aware of my nakedness and vulnerability. I was taken across the corridor and into another room. Here there was a wooden chest that had been set up as a makeshift altar. There were tall, carved wooden candlesticks on either side of it which held immense church candles that gave the room's only light, and I was placed face down on the dark red cloth that covered the chest.

"Cut his hands free," Philippe said, "but leave his feet tied, and hold onto his arms."

I remembered Philippe's command to them a few minutes before, not to shed any of my blood, and with an intuitive desire to upset plans as much as possible, I jerked against the knife as it cut my bonds and felt it biting into my flesh. I pushed again, hard, and twisted.

"No!" Philippe yelled, "for fuck's sake, be more careful."

I felt an instant clarity as deep pain intensified my awareness, and I forced myself to relax, so that I could concentrate on what was happening.

"Christ," one of the youths whimpered. "The blood!"

I could feel the warmth of it as it spattered across my back, and I wondered how deeply I'd cut myself.

"No, don't try to bandage it," Philippe said. "Just turn him over and hold him down as I told you before."

He turned to the brawny youth.

"Hold his cut closed, and *hurry*. This means we have much less time."

I was flipped onto my back. Now that my hands had been freed, I realised the purpose of the narcotic smoke from earlier. My body felt rubbery and uncontrolled. Philippe bent down to pick up what I saw as a chalice when he stood up again. From this chalice he poured oil onto me, starting at my chest, which, as I looked down at it, I could see was spattered liberally with blood. I closed my eyes and tried once more to still my feelings of rising panic. The pain in my wrist was intensifying, but at the same time – and presumably due to it – I felt a heightened awareness of what was happening.

The oil was cool, and Philippe poured it down over my navel and groin, pausing to rub it over my genitals and arse. Then, muttering something to himself, he began to unbuckle the belt of his jeans.

"I can't stop the bleeding," the brawny youth whispered. I could feel the pressure of his desperate grip against my wrist and the slipperiness of the blood there. Philippe ignored him and proceeded to pull his jeans off, followed by his top and singlet. When he was naked except for his amulet, he paused. I looked at him, at his gym-defined musculature, and saw that he didn't have an erection. Clearly, this wasn't going as planned. He'd been panicked by the bloodshed. I saw him lower his head in concentration. His face went completely blank for a moment, and then, with a sigh, he pulled his shoulders back, smiled, and opened his eyes. I looked away, but I'd seen the predatory look of power on Philippe's face and knew that he was in control again.

He pushed my legs up and, with a knife of his own, severed the cords holding my legs, which fell numbly, as they were freed. My ankles were grabbed and held by the fourth member of the group. Philippe climbed onto the chest and lowered himself onto me. I could feel his tumescent penis against my buttocks, and opened my eyes.

There was a triumphant look on his face, and he grinned at me – a look that I had once found so alluring. This time, I responded by summoning the deepest breath I could manage, and spat my coin directly into his face. I don't suppose I managed much force, but it distracted him, and the sound of metal on the floor made him look down to see what it was.

I realised that this was my only chance. I yanked my hands free, and in the same movement, kicked out wildly with my feet. I wasn't particularly coordinated, but by lashing out further I managed, in the confusion, to kick one candlestick with my foot and punch the other one with my fist so that we were all plunged into darkness.

"Quick," Philippe shouted. "Matches! And there's a torch by the door."

I staggered a couple of steps forward and bumped into some-one, who tried to grab me, but I was now so slippery with a mix-ture of blood and oil that it was easy to twist out of his grip. I half ran to where I remembered the door to be, and fumbled for the handle. I'd got the door half open before I was grabbed again, by the legs this time, in a kind of rugby tackle. We both went down and again I managed, by kicking out and writhing, to free myself from the grip. The door had swung open and I scrambled out of it, on all fours at first, and then in a low stagger, to where I hoped the front door might be.

"Kill him!" Philippe shouted in fury. "Just kill him!"

I was aware of a tiny amount of light coming from outside but as I ran, I realised to my confusion that it was behind me and that I was running the wrong way – deeper into the house, not out of it. In moments, I could hear footsteps behind me, then saw the beam of a torch lighting the wall in front of me. I was trapped. There was no escape. I desperately tried to visualise some protective blue light, but I had no time. Someone was right behind me. I closed my eyes for a moment, then turned, trying to summon up all my strength, but when I opened them again, the torch beam caught me full in the face like a searchlight. In silhouette behind the light, I saw the brawny youth brandishing his knife aloft with his free hand, ready to plunge it into me, his face a mask of malignancy.

This is it, I thought, and sagged against the wall.

The youth stopped dead and stared.

"Philippe!" he choked, lowering the knife, "I... I thought you were *him*. I nearly... I nearly *killed* you."

It took me a second to realise that he was looking directly at me, yet thinking that I was Philippe. Philippe, I could see, was in the corridor just behind the youth, holding one of the candles, now relit. I held up my uncut arm and pointed to him. The youth turned round and, with a cry of rage on seeing Philippe, lunged forward and plunged his knife up to the hilt into his chest.

Philippe crumpled soundlessly to his knees. As he did so, the front door banged open and I noticed figures rushing into the hall. In a moment the electric light was switched on and we were starkly lit from the bare bulb. I felt myself fall back against the wall and begin to slip down, but could see, in an almost Brechtian tableau, the form of Philippe as he slithered forward onto his front, grasping at the knife still protruding from his chest. Behind him stood William, his face bruised and swollen from his beating, wielding some sort of iron bar, and beside him was Kit.

Then I lost consciousness.

I must only have been out for a few seconds, because when I opened my eyes, Philippe was still lying there on the floor, naked in front of me in a wide pool of blood. William was slapping my cheek. I blearily looked down and saw that Kit was binding my wrist as tightly as possible with some strips of denim from my hacked-off jeans. I was pleased to see them both, but was confused about what had happened. My consciousness was intermittent, and everything was fuzzy, although I was somehow aware of the mess I was in: I was slick with oil and blood and seemed to be sitting in a pool of the stuff, which felt cold and congealed against my buttocks. I saw that Kit was kneeling in the blood to bandage me up. I felt that I ought to be panicking about blood loss, but didn't quite have the energy to summon any emotional response at all.

"Greg," William said urgently, "Greg, keep your eyes open. Try to stay awake. Please."

I could see that he was crying as he looked into my eyes, and so I smiled to reassure him.

"Hello, William," I managed, though it was far harder to speak than I'd thought it would be, and I decided to gather my strength before trying again. I had an overwhelming desire to close my eyes and drift off to sleep, but somewhere at the back of my mind, I knew that I should try not to. Nevertheless, it was so tempting, so deliciously tempting...

We all heard the crunch of tyres on gravel at the same time, and the three of us looked up at the sound of a car door slamming and the rapid thudding of approaching feet. Despite my grogginess, I felt the distinct, and now familiar, flutter in my stomach which signalled the presence of someone of *that* kind, and groaned. When the man came into the hall, William jumped up, ready to defend me.

"Ian!" I managed. Then, to William, "It's okay. I know him."

The surreal quality of my conscious experience now moved to the oblique. Everything became tangential. I heard Kit talking urgently about getting me to casualty, and I remember being hauled out to the car, and Ian passing a coat for me to put on.

I thought Kit was whispering to me.

"It was attempted suicide, Greg. Tell them it was attempted suicide. Do you understand me?"

I nodded, although I didn't understand, but he didn't seem to notice.

Then I lost the sense of myself completely. I couldn't tell if I was a participant or an observer in the proceedings, a bizarre, dislocated feeling that is sometimes reported in dreams.

"Greg, can you hear me?"

"Yes," I said, "yes, of course. It's wonderful to see you, Kit. Did you and William save me?"

I smiled at William, who was leaning into the back from the front seat. He tapped me lightly on the cheek.

"Greg," William said. "Greg, keep your eyes open."

"It's okay," I told him, "I'm fine."

"Try to get him to say something," William said to Kit.

"I *am* saying something," I said.

"I think he's too far gone to be *able* to talk," said Ian.

"Say something to me, Greg," Kit whispered. "Say something."

"I love you, Kit," I said, "I've always loved you."

"He's going," Kit said. "We're losing him."

I could feel my eyelids flutter, but I felt light, and pleased.

"I'm just going to have a little sleep," I told them. "Don't worry about me. I'll be fine."

Eighteen

Looking back on that evening, now that it is several months in the past, it all seems unreal, dreamlike. Of course, that was partly because of the narcotic that I'd been subjected to earlier in the evening, and my terrible loss of blood, but it was also partly because of the way William and Kit turned up so inexplicably. At the time, I didn't question it. I was too far gone for that. But when I woke up, with two drips feeding into my veins – one blood, the other saline – the first questions that came to mind were how William had managed to find Kit, how both of them had managed to find me, and where Ian had come from.

The first face I saw when I came round was that of the doctor, leaning over me.

"Hello," he said, "I think we're getting him back."

I was asked my identity and various simple questions, presumably to test whether I had brain damage or not, and then I was left, briefly, with Kit and William, who looked dreadful – underslept, unshaven, hollow-eyed. I smiled at them and said hello, still feeling weak, but definitely *compos mentis*.

"We've told them William found you in his room, and that you'd tried to commit suicide," Kit told me. "We even went back to get some of your blood to spatter on his carpet, to make it all look authentic."

"Why?" I asked.

"For your own protection," Kit said. "William's told me what's been going on and we've got to extricate you from the web of charges Philippe devised for you. If you tell the truth about last night, the police will think you're making up a story to cover something else. We need a story that they will accept without looking further."

I nodded at the sense of what he was saying. Besides, I thought, it wouldn't be difficult to make a case for serious depression – I'd been thrown out of my digs for something I hadn't done, by people who had been my closest friends; I'd been falsely accused of dealing drugs, and was wanted for questioning for a murder I hadn't committed.

But how *was* I going to extricate myself from all that?

"Oh god," I said, "what a mess."

"Have you any idea," said William, "how close you came to dying?"

A nurse came in then, and that was the last chance I had to talk privately to either Kit or William for a long time. I had a day of grace in bed before being seriously questioned by the police, and then, as it happened – and was this because Philippe was now dead? – the 'mess' seemed to evaporate of its own accord. Firstly, it turned out that there was no case against me for the Merton murder because I had been incontrovertibly in the presence of police officers over the entire period that the murder was known to have been committed, either having my room searched or being questioned down at the station. I explained to the police that the address they'd found in my back pocket had been given to me by Philippe and that he lived at Gillow Manor Farm, and they went off to try and find him – obviously without success. Meanwhile, I got Kit to phone Alan at my old digs and he came in to see me. He'd already heard that I'd tried to commit suicide and was feeling ambivalent about the decision to throw me out.

The drug-dealing investigation was dropped, too, in a way that rather freaked the police out. When the four students in question were routinely shown a photograph of me, they were adamant that it had been someone else altogether who had sold them the drugs. It transpired that the surveillance cameras in the shopping precinct where the deal took place had captured 'me' leaving the scene, and when the students were shown it, they confirmed that it was this other person who was the dealer and not me. The problem, for the police, was that the person was so clearly *not* me. When I was shown the footage, later, I identified the dealer as Philippe – an ID that was corroborated later back up North. The police were mystified. They asked, quite reasonably, how four people could initially mistake two people who looked so different? There was no satisfactory answer to that, but the upshot was that, within a period of forty-eight hours, I was no longer under suspicion by the police for anything.

The most difficult part of my 'alibi' was lying to my parents. They came down on that first day, and my mother cried when she saw me. It was hard keeping up the pretence of attempted suicide with them, but at least I had the comfort of the fact that, as the charges against me evaporated, I could convince them that it had been extraordinary circumstances rather than a general inclination towards depression that had led me into crisis.

"Getting ready for your Finals is bad enough," my father said, "without all the other stuff you've had to deal with."

At the end of the first day, I was disconnected from the blood drip; at the end of the second, from the other one. My father went home at that stage, confident of my physical recovery, but my mother stayed until the third day, when I was released. I was subjected to hours of counselling before I left, which I tried to take seriously, and was referred to a psychiatrist for further help regarding my suicidal tendencies. Meanwhile, Alan had talked to Janine and the others in the house and a general consensus had been reached that 'weird shit' had happened, but that it wasn't my fault and that I should be allowed back. Alan had taken Kit to have a word with them, and, although no one mentioned what Kit had said, he'd managed to swing it for me.

The first thing I did, after I'd seen my mother off at the station, was get back to the house, shut myself in my room with Kit and William, and find out what had happened. It had been so frustrating, not getting them on their own before now.

"Right," I said, as soon as we were alone. "Tell me everything."

I looked at William, whose face, previously puffed up from his beating, was now settling down. There was still a lump on one cheek, (it had required two stitches, put in for him when he brought me into casualty,) and on the other side he sported a fading black eye.

"What happened to you after I was knocked out in your room?" I asked.

"They beat me up," William said, "as you can see."

He rubbed the raised lump.

"Once they'd gone, I had no idea what to do. I sat for a while in a daze and a panic, and then I thought that the only way I could help you would be to find Kit. It was then, when I was pondering the impossibility of doing that, that I realised where I had seen the symbols that are on either side of your coin. There's a house, on the far side of the ice rink, by the river, which has what looks like a coat of arms over the front door, but I'd noticed in the past that, instead of containing rampant lions and that kind of thing, it had something else. I'd stopped and looked at it once or twice but never quite worked it out, because it was so worn. But, having seen your coin, I suddenly clicked that they must have been the lemniscate and chalice that are on your coin, and so I dashed over. I thought that, if Kit wasn't there, maybe there would be someone else who could help me.

"I ran down to the house, and banged on the door and yelled

for help – I was more or less hysterical by this point, I might add. There wasn't any response for a minute or so, and then Kit came out."

Kit smiled.

"It was difficult to get any sense out of him for a while," Kit said, "because he was incoherent. But I pieced it together eventually. And then, we had to locate you."

"You remember how I used to follow you about?" William said. "When you were close, I could always feel it, but even when you weren't I could kind of sense roughly where you were, if I concentrated hard enough. That's the mechanism we used to find you. Kit and I concentrated together on where you and Philippe were and, I suppose, magnified the effect that could be achieved by one person on their own."

"Then we went and got my car," said Kit, " and came after you. We had quite a trek across the fields, which was time consuming and frustrating. But, as you know, we arrived just in time."

William nodded and smiled at me.

"What happened to the others that were with Philippe?" I asked.

"They ran off as soon as they realised he was dead," said William.

I closed my eyes and visualised Philippe, lying there, face down in his own blood, one hand stretched out towards me.

"And Ian? How did he come to turn up?"

"That was as much of a surprise to us as it was to you," said William.

"He knew that Philippe was misusing his abilities," said Kit, "and he also knew it was an auspicious date, and that Philippe was likely to try something grand and hideous. He'd sensed that Philippe was down south, and was heading down this way in his car, but wasn't sure exactly where to go. When William and I started to fully concentrate on you, it helped all three of us to gain our focus, and gave him the direction in which to travel. Without him we'd never have got you to hospital in time to save your life."

"It was so strange," William said, "when he came in and saw you and Philippe lying there. He stopped by Philippe and knelt beside him for a moment, and burst into tears. You could see that he loved Philippe. I mean *really* loved him, and was gutted that Philippe had turned out the way he had."

"He wouldn't come in to casualty," said Kit. "He dropped you and William off at the entrance, and then the two of us went back to the house; me to get some of your blood for William's carpet and him to deal with Philippe's body."

Later, I recounted my side of the adventure, or as much of it as I could remember, in answer to their own questions.

I'd like to say that things returned to the way they had been before Philippe turned up so disastrously. But they didn't. Right from the start there was a different atmosphere in the house, as though I was a fragile object that had to be treated with care. My wrist was heavily bandaged and my cut contained a large cluster of major stitches, so that I abandoned my usual summer wear of tee-shirt and shorts and wore disguising long-sleeved shirts instead, but whether they could see it or not, everyone knew that the bandage was there underneath, a constant reminder of my so-called attempted suicide. Consequently, there was a false air of levity in the house, as if a moment's lack of vigilance on the part of my housemates would plunge me back into my suicidal slough of despond. Of course, the build-up to our Finals would have changed the atmosphere in the house anyway, so as time passed and exams loomed larger, it didn't seem so odd.

I asked about the possibility of a September re-sit. The rules about 'self-inflicted' injury were grey and, in the end, it was decided that I *would* be granted the re-sit, but I'd be treated as if I had failed the sit – which would mean being penalised in my final mark. If that was so, my hopes of doing well were over.

I decided to press on with revision – however compromised it had been. Besides, I wanted to get it over with as quickly as possible now, to put it all behind me.

Although my studies were seriously interrupted, to say the least, I found that, once I was feeling strong again – after about ten days – I had a far more stable perspective on life. Finals didn't seem anything like as important as they had a few weeks earlier and, in that contradictory way in which these things work, the fact that I was more relaxed about them allowed me to work both harder and better on my revision. My tutor called me in and we discussed what I'd been through. He was a kind man and was genuinely aghast that I had fallen foul of misplaced police suspicion. He told me that my upheaval and subsequent hospitalisation would be taken into account when I took my exams – especially in view of the re-sit paradox – which was tantamount to an admission that, so long as I continued to work, I would be given a Two One, whatever happened.

It was strange. I was more busy than I had ever been before in my life, yet I also felt more peaceful than I had ever felt. I thought back to my first cycle ride with Kit, all those years ago, and what he'd said to me at Cleulow Cross, about the fact that we had a purpose – to look for stillness – and I began to have an inkling of what he was talking about. It wasn't a question of active, positive emotion that generated stillness, it was an absence of negative emotion – of worry, anger, fear, restlessness. Contrary to my expectation, I found that, when I thought of Philippe, I didn't feel anger now. I simply felt sad.

I saw a lot of Kit and William. William had somehow blossomed through his experience. I had saved his life, then he had returned the compliment and saved mine – spectacularly. This had given him a self-confidence that was great to see. He had also stopped hoping for something to happen between us. I think this was probably because he'd seen Kit and I together and had realised that we were meant to be with each other.

The first thing Kit did, when we finally had a chance to be alone together, in my room, was take me in his arms and cry.

"I'm so sorry," he wept, "I'm so sorry, Greg. I abandoned you and you nearly died."

"Why *did* you disappear?" I asked. "You did it back at school, and then again after Janine's party?"

"At school I could see that you'd been exposed too soon to some of the things that this power can do – and it was making you hostile. I knew that you needed to be left alone for a while, so that you could come round to it of your own accord."

He let go of me and stood up to look out of the window. As he stood there he looked impossibly young, the way he'd been the first time I met him.

"When I saw you last year," he said, "you were deeply immersed in the hedonistic side of life. It meant that you were still closed off from anything I could offer you. What I had no knowledge of was that you'd had this... relationship... with Philippe. I now realise that you were acting in reaction to that experience. If I'd known that before, I might have behaved very differently."

He turned to me.

"I was always taught that the purpose of these powers is to find peace. They are not meant to be used for show, or to impress others, or to gain possessions – all those things are distractions. We should use our energies to turn inward, and we should do that when we have gained enough experience of life to be able to know what we are turning inward *from*. I was never far from you Greg. I was waiting for you to be ready."

"You sound as though you've been immersed in these teachings for years. But you're only a couple of years older than me," I said.

He came and sat beside me on the bed.

"We are all older than we think," he said. "Some of us come to that realisation much earlier in life than others. Most people never come to that realisation at all. This is not because we are spiritually superior, but because we have been gifted in some way. From my earliest childhood I was surrounded by this kind of energy. There was never a time when I didn't know it to exist."

He took my hand.

"I didn't want to force you to accept any of these things – I wanted you to come to them of your own accord. I know from my own experience that if a person is told 'you must believe this', then the response is an inclination to reject what is being offered. I just didn't know how high the stakes were for you. When I met you by the river last year, and when I came on to the party at your house, I saw you as an ordinary undergraduate who was in the process of growing up. I knew that you were going to have some kind of test at some point, because that's the nature of these energies, but I had no idea how *major* that trial would be for you. I should have realised that it would be something big, because you have a real strength in you, and so it stands to reason that you would have a commensurate test."

He stroked the bandage on my wrist.

"And you learned to wield your power to protect yourself, *without* instruction. You caused yourself to be mistaken for Philippe when you were being chased. That is extremely advanced practice, and *very* impressive, Greg."

He looked into my eyes and frowned.

"I said just now that my understanding has always been that it is a form of vanity to use these powers in the secular world, but perhaps that's not quite right. I now realise that this is true only when they are used to show off, to impress people or for the sake of personal gain, as Philippe did. I used my powers to make those muggers run past us that day in Manchester, and you saved yourself from being killed. *That* is what these powers are for."

"Will you teach me more about them?"

"Of course," he said. "But first there's something I need to do that's far more important."

He leaned forward and kissed me gently on the lips.

"I'm so glad you survived your test," he said.

I returned the kiss and we fell back, gently, on the bed.

Postscript

I started writing this account on the night of my Finals. On and off it's taken me most of the summer. That time has been a healing process, both physically and emotionally. I got the Two One in the end – which I accepted gracefully, and with thanks, given the distractions I had. Not that the summer hasn't been full of other, more pleasant distractions. Kit being the most pleasant of all. But I'm in no hurry to start the rest of my life just yet. I am back at home at the moment, nominally living there and doing some work for my father to tide me over whilst I decide what to do with myself. Kit is back at his old house and we see each other most days, going for long bike rides on the moors and making love in his room. I stay over quite often and he sometimes stays over with me, and my mother makes a fuss of us both, which is fun. He is on his own in the house, but I don't question the mystery of this, or his peculiar lack of apparent family. I know, for example, that he has a cousin, because I saw them together once, all those years ago.

I don't mind that he doesn't want to tell me these things.

He is teaching me stillness. That is all that matters right now. Everything else can come later.

More thrills from GMP

Some Kind of Love
The new Jas Anderson mystery
by Jack Dickson

Is Anderson out of his depth?

Jas is working as a private investigator on a routine case when he finds himself caught up in police corruption, sectarianism and murder in his hometown of Glasgow.

The tough anti-hero of *Freeform* and *Banged Up* will need everything he learned in his days on the force – and behind bars – to solve this mystery, especially when suspicion falls close to home.

Praise for Jack Dickson's other thrillers:

"Intricate plots which combine elements of the hard-boiled and the intensely erotic" *Gay Times*

"A reflection of the darker side of our desires" *Gay Scotland*

"A breath-tightening, rapid-fire style" *The List*

£9.99 ISBN 1-902852-31-1

A Dangerous Thing
The new Adrien English mystery
by Josh Lanyon

Out of harm's way?

In this frightening follow-up to *Fatal Shadows*, Los Angeles book-seller and amateur sleuth Adrien English embarks on a vacation that proves rather less relaxing than he anticipated.

It seems that murder follows him wherever he goes – and as the body count mounts, so does the tension.

Praise for Fatal Shadows:

"This is well written, fast stuff. I'm looking forward to the next one" *G-scene*

£8.99 June 2002 ISBN 1-902852-33-8